EDGE OF NOWHERE

ARROW'S EDGE MC

FREYA BARKER

Freya Barker writes a mean romance, I tell you! A REAL romance, with real characters and real conflict.

I've said it before and I'll say it again and again, Freya Barker is one of the BEST storytellers out there.

God, Freya Barker gets me every time I read one of her books. She's a master at creating a beautiful story you lose yourself in the moment you start reading.

Freya Barker has woven a delicate balance of honest emotions and well-formed characters into a tale as unique as it is gripping.

Such a truly beautiful story! The writing is gorgeous, the scenery is beautiful...

From Dust by Freya Barker is one of those special books. One of those whose plotline and characters remain with you for days after you finished it.

No amount of words could describe how this story made me feel, I think this is one I will remember forever, absolutely freaking awesome is not even close to how I felt about it.

Still Air was insightful, eye-opening, and I paused numerous times to think about my relationships with my own children. Anytime a book can evoke a myriad of emotions while teaching life lessons you'll continue to carry with you, it's a 5-star read.

In my opinion, there is nothing better than a Freya Barker book. With her final installment in her Portland, ME series, Still Air, she does not disappoint. From start to finish I was completely captivated by Pam, Dino, and the entire Portland family.

The one thing you can always be sure of with Freya's writing is that it will pull on ALL of your emotions; it's expressive, meaningful, sarcastic, so very true to life, real, hard-hitting and heartbreaking at times and, as is the case with this series especially, the story is at points raw, painful and occasionally fugly BUT it is also sweet, hopeful, uplifting, humorous and heart-warming.

EDGE OF Nowhere

Copyright © 2023 Freya Barker

This book is a work of fiction and any resemblance to any place, person or persons, living or dead, any event, occurrence, or incident is purely coincidental. The characters, places, and story lines are created and thought up from the author's imagination or are used fictitiously.

ISBN: 9781988733920

Cover Design: Freya Barker
Editing: Karen Hrdlicka
Proofing: Joanne Thompson
Cover Image: JW Photography
Cover Model: Josh Faust

FREYA BARKER

CHAPTER

ONE

LINDSEY

"Thildy!"

She whips her head around, smiling, just as she tosses the bouquet of wildflowers over her shoulder. Beautiful, radiant, and so happy it makes my teeth ache just looking at her. I depress the shutter button, immortalizing this moment along with all the others I've snapped today.

Mathilde Wagner, now Katz, I guess, since she officially became Benjamin's wife about two hours ago.

I met Thildy in college where she'd been my roommate for about two seconds before quickly becoming my best friend. It's hard not to love Thildy, who is probably the sunniest, most effervescent person I know. She's a flower child, an environmentalist, a vegetarian, and believes in the principles of sustainable living. In short, she's a granola, and my absolute opposite. I like my meat, my car, my conveniences, and other than recycling my garbage and buying organic—when I remember to—I'm afraid I don't put enough time or effort into preserving the environment.

Thildy gently tries to correct my disposable habits from time to time, while I occasionally try to lure her to the dark side with a trip to Denver's Cherry Creek Shopping Center. Not that any of it matters, our friendship—unlikely as it may appear—has been solid since we first met thirteen or so years ago.

That's not to say it hasn't been a challenge, especially these past years since I've moved back to Durango. Or maybe I should say, since I ran home to Durango, because that's basically what I did. Life as I knew it here in Denver blew up in my face, and everything and everyone I knew—including Thildy—had been part of that life, which is what put a strain on our friendship.

Thildy had continued to nurture our relationship with kind messages, sweet cards, and occasional phone calls when it was hard for me. So when she informed me she and Benjamin were finally tying the knot in a simple ceremony and she'd love for me to be part of her special day, I felt it was high time for me to pull my weight.

As promised, the wedding is a small affair, in line with Ben and Thildy's lifestyle which is no muss, no fuss. She looks like a pixie wearing a simple, vintage slip dress in a buttery silk and a halo of wildflowers in her hair, while Ben wears gray slacks and suspenders over a simple white dress shirt. My friend's sister, Hannah, stood up for her, and Benjamin's father did the same for him, keeping it all in the family.

I'd been honored when the couple asked me to memorialize their event with lively, candid pictures, rather than the standard posed portraits, even though I was well aware the request had a dual purpose. As sweet as she is, Thildy is no fool and knew exactly what she was asking of me.

Photography had been a serious hobby of mine since

high school, one I'd hoped one day could perhaps morph into something more. It had been another dream quashed in the shambles my life had descended into before I finally reached my breaking point. Asking me to dust off my camera had been my friend's not so gentle challenge to reclaim those parts of me I'd lost along the way. It had taken some convincing—on her part—and a few assurances, for me to accept both her invitation and challenge.

Over the past ten minutes most of the guests have left. Those remaining, mainly family members, are starting to take down the decorations in the barn. The Wagner family farm was the perfect venue for their minimalist wedding. It had felt a bit awkward at first, seeing Thildy's family again after basically disappearing years ago, but I shouldn't have worried, I was greeted like I'd just seen them last week. No uncomfortable mentions of a time or person I'd prefer not to be reminded of.

"Okay, that's enough," Thildy tells me as she walks this way after saying goodbye to a couple of friends. "Put that camera away, I've barely had a chance to talk to you."

"You were kinda busy getting married," I point out dryly. "Besides, I have a job to do."

"Right now, your job is to have a drink with the bride before she takes off for the islands," she counters.

Ben and Thildy's idea of a honeymoon is a two-week volunteer stint with a sustainable agriculture project in the Galapagos Islands. An all-inclusive resort in the Caribbean or maybe a chance to see Europe would be more my speed for a honeymoon, but to each their own. I know Thildy has been looking forward to this trip.

"Fine," I concede with a smile. "Just for a minute though, if I want to catch my flight."

"You know, you could grab the first one out tomorrow

morning and crash here," she tries to cajole me into changing my mind.

"I really can't. Work is crazy busy right now," I explain again. "I can't leave Mom in the lurch."

My mother has a busy law practice and I'm her office manager/legal assistant. Mom isn't getting any younger, and since she got a warning from her doctor last month her blood pressure was way too high, I've been trying to relieve her from as much of her load as I can.

"Fine," Thildy grumbles, "But Ben is already grabbing us some blueberry wine."

I try not to wince. I've tried her blueberry wine and to me it tastes like Kool-Aid on steroids, it wouldn't be my first choice, but it's her pride and joy so I say nothing. Instead, I sit beside my friend, who flopped down on one of the hay bales and is in the process of kicking off her shoes. She stretches her legs out in front of her and wiggles her toes.

"God, that feels good."

"I told you to wear your Birkenstocks," I remind her.

Her 'something borrowed' was a pair of her sister's high-heeled shoes. Not a smart choice for someone whose regular footwear is heelless.

"I know, but these looked pretty under my dress."

I shake my head and bend down to tuck my old Nikon in its protective camera bag.

"Oh shit," Thildy hisses right before I hear Ben call out an apology.

"I'm sorry, I tried to stop him."

Without looking up and before the sound of his voice reaches me, I already know who decided to make an appearance.

"I couldn't miss my favorite cousin's wedding now, could I?"

The sound of his voice elicits a physical reaction, and I have to struggle to keep the delicious field-to-table wedding dinner down. When I raise my head, I catch Thildy's look of apology. She'd assured me he was supposed to be in Lima, Peru for work at least another month and wouldn't be around for the nuptials.

I shouldn't be surprised; I remember very well Galen's habit of not being where he's supposed to be.

The first time I met him was when I was invited to celebrate Thanksgiving at the Wagner family farm. Mom had been up to her eyeballs in a trial at the time and encouraged me to accept the invitation. It was a large family gathering, but Thildy's older, suave cousin caught my attention right away.

I have to admit, I've always been drawn to shiny things, and Galen was no exception. Unfortunately, by the time I discovered what all that luster and glitter was covering up, I was in so deep, I couldn't see a way out. Not without extracting myself from the family I'd grown close to and distancing myself from my best friend, who doesn't even know the half of it.

But that was years ago, and I'm a different person now. Maybe this is a good opportunity to prove to him—or maybe even myself—he no longer has the hold on me he once did. A chance for me to dislodge that monkey from my back once and for all.

Determined, I twist my body to face him, carefully neutralizing my expression.

"Galen, this is a surprise."

"Lindsey, what an unexpected pleasure to find you here. You look even more breathtaking now," he gushes, picking up my hand to brush my knuckles with his well-shaped lips.

I fight the urge to grimace or pull away as he scrutinizes me closely with his penetrating eyes. It's what he would expect me to do, the reaction he's hoping for. He feeds on seeing me shaken and unbalanced, it makes him feel powerful, and in the past few years I've done little to rob him of that misconception.

That will stop now. It's time for me to show him the only person who controls me is me.

The moment he releases my hand I get to my feet, slipping the strap of my camera bag over my shoulder.

"That's kind of you." I smile and nod at him, before dismissively turning my back to address Thildy. "I'm going to have to get a rain check on that blueberry wine."

"Please don't run off on my behalf," the asshole says behind me.

"On your behalf?" I look over my shoulder at him, raising my eyebrow as high as it'll go. "Why on earth would I do that?" I follow my words up with a patronizing smile as I shake my head. "As I mentioned to Thildy, I have a flight to catch."

He's not that easy to shake off though, and quickly plasters on a smile. "Perfect, I'll give you a ride."

The moment I feel his hand grab a firm hold of my arm, I rip it free, dropping my camera bag in the process.

"I don't think so, I'll get myself there," I respond, distractedly rubbing my arm as a sudden rage has me continue. "And just to be clear, I revoked your license to put your hands on me without invitation years ago. Not that you had the right then, but I will not hesitate to call the police and have you charged with physical assault if you try again. Are we clear?"

He narrows his eyes on me and in their glare I recognize the sociopath he manages to hide so well, but his lips draw into a smile as he lifts his hands innocently.

"Still a little dramatic, are we?" he sneers, probably more for the benefit of our small audience. "I do believe you're overreacting a bit. The police? Really?"

I force a smile on my own face to hide the anger coursing through me.

"Oh, most definitely the police. And I'd be doing you a favor because you really don't want a run-in with my boyfriend, or his brothers, if he finds out you had your hands on me."

I'm not sure what prompted me to lie like that—or what caused the image of a certain arrogant biker to pop into my head as the words tumbled from my mouth—but although the boyfriend part is pure fiction, the rest of it is the truth. By merit of my mother's marriage to a member of the Arrow's Edge MC, I am, for all intents and purposes, part of the family. With the security of the club at my back, I manage to turn a reassuring smile to a shell-shocked Thildy, who looks as confused as I'm sure she feels. I don't doubt she has a question or two, but for now I want to get out of here.

"I hope you guys have an amazing time," I tell her as I pull her into a tight hug. "We'll talk when you get back."

Her arms close round me, squeezing hard.

"Yes, we most definitely will," she mumbles.

I have a feeling I won't be able to avoid sharing more than I'd ever intended to about what happened between Galen and me with my best friend. It's going to crush her.

Without another glance at Galen, I rush through my goodbyes for Ben and the rest of the family before finally climbing into my little rental car. I drop my head back, close my eyes briefly, and blow out a big breath, when a sharp knock on the driver's side window has me shoot upright in my seat.

He's peeking in, a smarmy grin on his face as he holds up my camera bag.

I lower my window because I'll be damned if I open the door.

"You forgot something."

"I see that."

I reach out but he moves the bag out of my reach.

"Everything okay?"

I glance beyond Galen and see Thildy's father coming toward us.

"It's fine, Uncle Eli," Galen quickly replies. "Lindsey just forgot something, that's all."

With that smirk still on his face, he hands over my bag. As soon as I have it in my hands, I toss it onto the passenger seat, close my window, and start the car. I manage to smile and wave goodbye to Mr. Wagner before I steer my rental down the driveway.

————

It's not until I'm sitting at the gate, waiting for my delayed flight home, that the full scope of what just happened hits me and I have to clench my hands in fists to stop the shaking, but at the same time, a little smile pulls at the corner of my mouth.

A delayed reaction.

Considering I hadn't been prepared to face off with the man I ran from four and a half years ago, I didn't do too bad. At the very least I showed him he no longer holds dominion over me, and that feels damn good.

I drain the Starbucks coffee I grabbed on my way to the gate and look for a garbage bin to dispose of it. I spot one between the men's and women's restrooms and get to my feet. It's probably not a bad idea to use the facilities while I can.

Grabbing my camera bag and my carry-on suitcase, I start heading toward the bathrooms, narrowly avoiding a collision with a man in a suit barreling past me. I clutch a hand to my chest, still a little jumpy I guess, but it's just another businessman hurrying to catch his flight. Except I notice this guy diving into the men's room. I guess catching a plane wasn't his reason for urgency. Still, I check the hallway carefully before I resume my trek.

To my surprise, the ladies' room isn't busy at all. No lineup, and I end up rolling my luggage into one of the larger stalls so I can quickly change. If I have to hang around the airport for a while, I'd rather do it in something more comfortable than the dress I wore for the wedding.

Feeling much better in a pair of joggers, my favorite "Nope, Not Today" T-shirt, and my comfy new Zenni sneakers, I wheel my carry-on out of the bathroom, only to have someone forcefully plow into me. My stuff goes flying and I land on my ass on the ground.

With a nose full of ripe man sweat, I panic and struggle to extricate myself from a tangle of limbs. Scrambling back, I press myself against the wall only to realize it wasn't Galen who took me to the floor—as I half expected—but the guy I saw running down the hallway earlier.

"I'm sorry," he mumbles, lifting his hands defensively.

Then he suddenly jumps to his feet and takes off, leaving me sitting on the floor, surrounded by the contents spilling from my luggage I guess I have to clean up myself.

Great. Another prime example of an asshole. I swear I attract them.

"Are you okay?"

An elderly lady stops and looks at me with concern.

"I'm fine," I reassure her as I get my feet under me and push up from the floor, glad to find all my parts still in working order, although my ass feels a little tender.

"Let me help you," she offers.

She's already bending down to pick up my purse, which thankfully hung on to its contents. Something that can't be said for my camera bag, which has spilled contents all over the floor. Embarrassed when I notice I'm drawing attention, I rush to shove my camera, littered batteries, lenses, and memory cards back in the bag. Taking my purse from the woman, I thank her and hustle back to my spot at the gate, eager to escape the curious looks.

The flight is blessedly short, a little over an hour, but because of the delay, it's still almost midnight before we land in Durango. Mom was supposed to pick me up—her vehicle is in the shop and I let her borrow mine while I was away—but I already shot her a text I'd be late and would grab a cab or an Uber from the airport. I got her standard thumbs-up in response.

I'm cranky, tired, and my hip is throbbing from where I hit the ground earlier. It'll probably be bruised, since the slightest bump will do that, and I limp a little as I make my way through the small terminal to the taxi spot in front. I'm ready for my bed and feel disheartened when I don't see any taxis waiting.

With a frustrated groan, I lower myself to the curb and press the heels of my hands against my burning eyes. It's been a hell of a long day and I'm running on the last of my fumes. The temptation to burst out crying is great, but that won't get me home and in bed any sooner, so I pull out my phone to order an Uber.

But before I have a chance to open the app, a dirty, old pickup truck pulls up. I hear a door slam, but I'm blinded by the headlights and can't see who gets out until I hear an angry voice from the shadows.

"What the fuck are you thinking, sitting out here in the dark? Jesus, you need a keeper; you don't have the good sense God gave a goat."

Of course, he shows up to witness another low point in my life.

Angry, I surge to my feet only to yelp at the stabbing pain in my hip. It only makes me madder and I let it fly.

"You know what? I don't need you or anyone else, Wapi, so you can fuck right the hell off!"

With that I grab my belongings and start marching in the opposite direction.

I don't get very far.

CHAPTER
TWO

WAPI

I take a few deep breaths to rein in my temper, which seems to flare exclusively in her vicinity.

I'm normally a pretty laid-back guy, but Mel's daughter has a tendency to get under my skin. Gorgeous, but way too high maintenance for my tastes, and she has an arrogant attitude about her that rubs me the wrong way.

Despite all that, I beelined it for the club truck and hauled ass the moment I overheard Paco saying something to Ouray about Lindsey taking a goddamn taxi home from the airport. I was on my way to bed, but I wouldn't have been able to sleep knowing she's out there somewhere.

Hell, the mere mention of her name would've been enough to keep me awake half the night. That's the kind of effect Lindsey Zimmerman has on me, and the reason I raced to the airport to prevent her from getting into a vehicle with some goddamn stranger in the middle of the fucking night.

"Jesus, you're a pain in my ass," I grumble when I catch up with her.

I unceremoniously take the carry-on suitcase from her hand and grab the strap of the camera bag from her shoulder.

"Hey," she yelps, shooting me an angry glare.

"Everything okay, Miss?"

I whip my head around to see a security guard wearing a yellow vest advertising that fact closing in on us.

Great.

A quick glance at the calculating smirk on Lindsey's face tells me exactly where her mind is going.

"Don't you dare," I warn her under my breath.

She only smiles wider before she turns to the guard, whose narrowed eyes are focused on me. She's enjoying this, knowing damn well the kind of predicament I might find myself in, depending on her next move.

"I'm fine, thank you," she tells the guy in a saccharine voice as she pats my chest with her hand. "My brother is a pussycat but can get a little intense when he's off his meds. Nothing I can't handle though. Not to worry."

Brother, my ass. I don't know why being labeled as such is more offensive to me than her calling me a pussycat or suggesting I need medicating. I growl my displeasure but still when, instead of removing her hand from my chest, her fingers curl into my shirt.

The guard's eyes dart between us before he finally addresses Lindsey, "Well...if you're sure."

She beams at him. "Absolutely." Then for good measure, she adds, "Really, he's a powder puff."

With one last glare at me, the guard moves back to the terminal. Then Lindsey releases my shirt and brushes past me on her way to the club truck. She's already buckled up in the passenger seat by the time I've tossed her luggage in the back and get behind the wheel.

"Very funny," I note, turning the key in the ignition.

"Oh, it's not funny at all," she snaps. "None of this is funny. I am so done with controlling apes suffering from overinflated egos and lack of communication skills. I swear, I've had enough."

Something tells me I may not be the only "ape" she's referring to, and that immediately sends up a red flag.

"Did someone bother you?"

I swear the question comes from a good place, but I seem to default to this angry snarl when talking to her.

"Aside from you, you mean?" she lobs right back.

Damn, no one could mistake Lindsey for meek. The woman can be a snarling cat. Not surprising, considering she was raised by Mel, who has the ability to make grown men shake in their boots. Like mother, like daughter, at least in attitude. In other ways those two couldn't be more different; Mel is as casual as they come, while her daughter seems snooty and hard to please.

Although, sneaking a sideward peek at her as I pull out of the airport parking lot, she doesn't look that high maintenance right now. She has her head dropped back, her hair gathered on top in a haphazard bun, and looks tired, almost weary.

"Hey," I prompt in a gentler tone. "Seriously, is there some guy somewhere who needs adjusting?"

The derisive laugh she barks out is not exactly the light-hearted chuckle I'd been hoping to elicit. She catches my questioning glance and shakes her head.

"You'll have to ignore me. What started off as a fun day has dragged on into a royally shitty one I can't wait to be over. You're simply the last in a series of questionable surprises."

I wince. I'm not sure what else contributed to her shitty day, but I realize I probably didn't make it any better.

I'm not normally an asshole, but around Lindsey it's almost a default mode. I'm also not a complete idiot and recognize I may have a bit of a hang-up when it comes to her. Guilt. Four years ago, she was abducted and got hurt while under my watch. It made me realize I had no business associating with her, no business harboring any kind of feelings for her, no business trying to protect her from the world.

And yet here I am. Again. It's an impulse I can't seem to curb and that ticks me off. Of course, the reality is I'm mad at myself for caring, but it's easier—and maybe safer—to take it out on her. Not fair, and it only adds to the feelings of guilt eating at me, but it's become a knee-jerk reaction.

Still, tonight I feel like I've just kicked a hurt puppy and need to apologize.

"Sorry," I start gruffly. "For the shitty day and…uh… anything I did to contribute to it."

She doesn't respond for the longest time and I resist glancing at her, focusing on the dark road ahead instead. When she does say something, her voice is so soft I have to strain to hear it.

"It's not you. I just need a good night's sleep."

The rest of the drive to her house is silent. I notice her SUV isn't parked in the driveway when I pull in.

"Where's your car?"

"Mom has it."

"Are you gonna need a ride into work in the morning?" I ask as I slip out from behind the wheel.

"Mom will swing by and pick me up."

I pull her suitcase and camera bag from the back seat and follow her to the door of her modest, two-story house, not too far from the college. Her place looks sharp. I know Paco—Lindsey's stepfather and my club brother—spent some time making some upgrades and doing renovations to the place after Mel moved in with him. He's also responsible for the cool rock garden in her front yard which, along with the new charcoal-gray color I helped paint the exterior, gives the house a clean, contemporary look.

I wait for Lindsey to unlock the door, flick on the lights, and disarm the alarm panel in the small entryway. The house has a state-of-the-art security system I know Paco insisted on, but that doesn't stop me from stepping inside.

"Wait here." Realizing that sounded more like an order than a request, I quickly add, "Please."

I do a quick scan of the main floor before darting upstairs to check the bedrooms. Satisfied all is secure, I head back down, finding Lindsey already in the kitchen.

"Feel better?" she asks with a raised eyebrow.

"Much," I admit as I catch her stifling a yawn. "I'll carry your suitcase upstairs and get out of your hair."

"That's okay, just leave it. I have to do laundry tomorrow anyway."

She reaches for the clip that is desperately holding together the bun on her head. Her honey-blond hair tumbles down in messy waves, and I know I have to get the hell out of here now.

Grunting, "Later," I stride to the front door when I hear her call my name, stopping me with my hand on the knob.

"Wapi?"

I glance back to where she remains standing at the kitchen island, her blue eyes, dark with fatigue, fixed on me.

"Thank you."

"No problem," I rumble, adding, "Lock up behind me," before I step outside.

There I pause, waiting for the sound of the lock snapping in place, before I continue to the truck. Once behind the wheel, I take in a deep breath and blow it out loudly. I wonder what the chances are I'll get any sleep tonight.

With one last glance at the house, I back out of the driveway and aim the truck toward the clubhouse.

———

Lindsey

"You look like hell."

I glare at my mother, who is scrutinizing me without apology, when I get into the passenger seat of my own vehicle.

"Gee, thanks, Mom. Sorry to disappoint, but this is as good as it gets with only four hours of restless sleep," I complain, taking a sip from my giant travel mug of life juice. An absolute necessity this morning.

"Rough night?" she asks, reaching out to tuck a strand of wayward hair behind my ear.

Both her tone and her gesture more reflective of the motherly concern she didn't quite manage to convey with her initial observation. That's my mother though; she has a heart the size of the universe, but zero bedside manner.

"Very rough," I confirm, as she backs into the street. "Don't get me wrong, it was a lovely wedding, I have lots of pictures to show you. Thildy was radiant and Ben was beaming. It wasn't until after the event things went to shit."

"You mean the delay," Mom states.

"Well…that was part of it, but I also had to contend with a parade of assholes," I grumble. "Some idiot bowled me over at the airport, then a snarling Wapi was waiting for me, but leading off the damn parade was the biggest asshole of them all."

"Don't tell me," Mom snaps, her eyes darting my way. "Wasn't he supposed to be in Chile or something?"

"Peru," I correct her, before indicating for her to keep her eyes on the road.

As she drives us to the office, I tell her everything that happened last night. I can tell from the way she white-knuckles her hold on the steering wheel from time to time, she's pissed on my behalf, but she lets me rant, which feels damn good.

These days I tell my mom just about everything. That wasn't always the case—not during my rebellious phase or the years I lived in Denver—but she was there when I showed up on her doorstep in Durango. I was at my absolute lowest and Mom turned out to be an amazing listener. However, she didn't mollycoddle me and didn't allow me to wallow in self-pity. In fact, she was tough and almost browbeat me into dusting off and getting back on my feet.

My mother might look a bit flaky—and people often underestimate her as a result—but looks can be deceiving. She is quite formidable and probably the strongest person I know.

"Is he going to be a problem?"

I don't need to ask who she is referring to.

"I doubt it. To what purpose? He can't have any doubt I

am done with him, so I don't see what he would stand to gain."

"You'd be surprised," Mom mutters. "Men like him don't like being made to feel redundant, and by the sounds of it, you made it abundantly clear he is. Stay alert."

"I always am, Momma," I reassure her as she turns into the Arrow's Edge MC compound.

I got a text from her before she picked me up this morning, letting me know her SUV was ready for pickup. Since Mom has a trial starting today, and I'm going to have my hands full catching up at the office and running her errands, it'll be more practical if we each have our own wheels.

Although it may have been time wasted given my mother's reaction when she saw me, I may have spent a few extra minutes getting ready, knowing we'd be stopping at the compound. I'm not looking too closely at why I felt the need to do that, but acknowledge a mild buzz of anticipation as I get out of the RAV.

"Mornin'!"

Brick steps out of the bay doors of the garage, wiping his hands on a rag.

"Morning," I call back as I make my way to where he is waiting.

"Where's Mel?"

"She's coming."

I glance back and see Mom still behind the wheel, talking on her phone. She's holding up one finger. Then the unmistakable rumble of a motorcycle has me turn toward the gate. The bike rolls through the gate and aims for the other end of the clubhouse, where all the bikes are parked side by side under a roofed overhang.

Even before he removes his half helmet, I recognize the

messy mop of dirty-blond hair. He casually runs a hand through it before he swings a leg over the bike, grabs a bag that was strapped to the back, and starts walking toward the clubhouse. I know he noticed me when he stops abruptly. For a moment my eyes lock with his gray-blue ones, before he ducks his head low and resumes his trek inside.

That mild buzz of anticipation turns a little sour in my stomach. It's seven thirty in the morning and pretty obvious he's only now getting home. Not that it's any of my business, nor should I care, but as I watch him disappear inside, I feel foolish.

"Was that Wapi?" Mom asks as she joins me.

"Was it? I didn't notice," I lie.

CHAPTER
THREE

WAPI

The clubhouse—which had been quiet when I walked in earlier—is abuzz with activity. Lisa is wrangling the kids, trying to get them fed and ready for the last week of school, something I usually help her with.

"Fun night?" she asks with a bit of a bite when she catches sight of me.

"I guess," I mumble, ducking past her into the kitchen to grab a coffee.

My night was of a more introspective kind up in the mountains. I couldn't settle last night when I got back to the clubhouse. I was craving solitude and the big open sky above me, both of which I knew I'd be able to find up on Baldy Mountain.

As much as I love being in Durango at the clubhouse with my family, I miss the sense of peace and balance I experienced when I was living off the grid in Alaska. Life was simpler, my needs minimal, and the only concern my own survival. It's been a struggle to find my equilibrium since I've been back.

I've been tempted to ride north again, spent some time thinking about it even last night while stretched out on a rock under the stars, but I'm not sure it would settle my restlessness. A lot of that has to do with the woman whose blue eyes looked at me with something close to disappointment just twenty minutes ago outside the clubhouse.

Lindsey wasn't the only reason I hit the road back then. I was still messed up after my sister's body was recovered from the Animas River, where she'd spent the previous twenty years submersed, still strapped in behind the wheel of her car. When you've had a traumatic childhood you've struggled to overcome, only to find out twenty years later even your fucked-up truth turned out to be a lie, it messes with you.

Lindsey definitely had been the trigger for my departure but, ironically, she is now the biggest reason holding me here. That's the clarity I reached after my night of introspection and communication with nature. My need to protect her from the world is greater than the urge to protect her from me. Whether I like it or not, her draw is strong, and rather than try to fight the pull, I intend to see where it might lead us.

"I'll take care of those," I tell Lisa, taking the stack of dishes from her hands as she walks into the kitchen.

"Actually, if you could grab the boys and do a school run? I've gotta take Finn to his dentist appointment."

Finn is the youngest of Brick and Lisa's three grandchildren, who all live with them. Both Brick's daughter, as well as Lisa's girl—Ezrah and Kiara's mother—died way too young. The way Brick and Lisa have forged a tight, cohesive unit, blending two households from different racial backgrounds, is a testament to what Arrow's Edge is all about; chosen family.

"Sure. What about Kiara?"

She's the only one of the kids currently living at the club compound—other than Finn—who is not yet in high school. This is her last week before she joins the others after the summer break.

"Lissie is driving Lettie anyway, so she's going to swing by and pick her up."

Yuma and Lissie live just down the road from the club with their two kids. Their son is in his first year of high school and their daughter just started first grade this year.

Currently we have only three boys living in the club dorm, but the total number of kids who are part of the greater club family is ever-growing. Not that long ago my brother, Honon, and my friend, Emme, became an instant family when two young kids landed, quite literally, on Emme's doorstep.

It's kind of funny, what was a club of mostly single brothers—who knew how to party hard ten or so years ago —we've turned into a collective family affair. Rather than throwing the infamous club parties of the past, we now host mostly PG-rated cookouts. Having never been big on those wild parties, I don't mind the change of orientation to family. It gives me a sense of belonging I missed growing up.

"Okay, boys. You have five minutes to grab your shit and get your ass in the van," I announce as I pass by the dining table, chewing the breakfast sandwich I snatched from the kitchen counter.

"You driving?" Booger asks with a bit of an edge, which isn't unusual for him.

"That's the plan. Got a problem with that?"

I raise an eyebrow as I turn to look at him.

The other kids gave him that nickname because he constantly sneezes and sniffles as a result of allergies. We would've shut it down right away, but the boy embraced that name like a badge of honor, so we left it alone. With a legal name of Frances Puffin, I can't really blame him, although I'm not sure Booger is much of an improvement.

He doesn't answer, but with a dramatic gesture lifts his hands defensively. Billy and Max, his two sidekicks, snicker beside him.

"Five minutes," I repeat, as I continue to Ouray's office in the back.

Our president is on the phone when I walk in, his dirty boots on his desk.

"I've gotta go," he tells whoever is on the other end. "And call parking enforcement to come and haul every last vehicle off."

"The gym?" I ask when he ends the call.

Among several other businesses, Arrow's Edge owns a boxing gym at the north side of town, as well as the yoga studio next to it. For the past few weeks people have been leaving their cars in the parking lot overnight. The occasional one wouldn't be an issue, but these vehicles all belong to the guests of the motel across the street.

The owner is having renovations done and two-thirds of his own parking lot is taken up by the contractor with a temporary field office and building supplies. Using our parking lot for overflow wouldn't have been an issue if the guy had the decency to ask, but he didn't. There already wasn't much goodwill on our part since the owner is not a fan of bikers and has repeatedly made that clear with unfounded complaints to the cops.

Now he's really pissing us off.

"Yeah, and Bubba is threatening to grab a few guys and cross the road to flex some muscle, so now I have to worry about him too," Ouray complains, rubbing his hands over his face. "I don't have the goddamn patience to deal with this shit today."

He drops his boots to the floor and reaches for a big bottle of Tums on his desk. Then he shakes out several in his hand and tosses them in his mouth all at once.

"I'll stop by the gym," I volunteer. "I was just coming in to tell you I'm taking the van today. I have to drop the boys at school and then I was going to pick up those tiles Yuma ordered, but I can do that after."

"I'd appreciate that." He loudly crunches the chewables, adding under his breath, "Fucking reflux."

I'm halfway out the door when he calls me back.

"You and me, we need to talk. A one-on-one at some point this week. Find some time and let me know, yeah?"

That sounds a bit ominous.

I nod, but as I walk through the clubhouse, I wonder why he'd need to talk to me alone. I can't think of anything, but the not knowing leaves me unsettled.

———

Lindsey

It's been a crazy morning, but by the time lunch comes along my desk is in pretty decent shape.

I'm about to head to the courthouse to drop off the report from a child psychologist Mom had been waiting for, and maybe on the way back to the office I'll pick up a power bowl from Sprouts, my new favorite restaurant.

Our client is Brian Dawson, the father of a nine-year-old girl whose newly remarried mother intends to move to Panama with her new spouse and take their daughter with her. It's a highly contested case in which the judge assigned a guardian ad litem to represent Samantha Dawson after attempts at mediation went south. Since the girl has developmental disabilities, he also ordered a psychologist to assist in determining the best interests of the child. That's the report we've been waiting for, since our client suspects his daughter doesn't want to go with her mother. According to him, she actively resisted the last few times he exchanged custody with his ex.

After giving the report a cursory glance, it looks like Brian's suspicions may have been well-founded.

———

"You're fucking kidding me," Mom bursts out as she flips through the pages of the report.

I quickly look around us, intercepting a stern look from a courthouse security officer standing guard in front of the doors. I shoot him an apologetic look, grateful nobody else appears to be close enough to hear.

The judge had just called for a brief lunch recess, and my mother was one of the last ones out of the courtroom when I caught up with her.

"Have you seen this?"

She holds up a drawing the psychologist submitted as part of the report. It's the same thing that stood out to me when I skimmed over the file. It's a child's depiction of a little girl, a woman, and a man.

The woman is standing away from the other two, clearly wearing a smile. The figure of the girl is much smaller and has no facial features at all, but what is most disturbing is the image of the man. He looks like a dark, menacing giant, looming over the girl, appearing to hold on to her. She made him look like a monster, with long fingers, a gaping hole for a mouth, and black spikes—or maybe horns—sticking out of his head.

"Yeah."

"Tell me that's not Brian," she hisses, jabbing a finger at the male figure.

"It's not him," I reassure her. "Brian doesn't wear glasses."

"Chris does," Mom growls.

The *Chris* she's referring to is Chris Menzies, the ex's new husband. He wears glasses, is at least six four or six five.

"I know. Why don't you join me for a quick bite at Sprouts?" I suggest.

Mom shakes her head as she stuffs the report back in the file folder and tucks it under her arm. Then she pulls her phone from her jacket.

"I can't. I have to find Cassie," she mumbles.

Cassandra Wilson is the little girl's attorney.

"I'm sure she has a copy."

"Yeah, but I want to talk to her before she takes it to the judge. We need to strategize." She glances up at me. "You go, I'll touch base with you later."

She doesn't give me a chance to respond and starts walking down the hallway, her phone pressed to her ear and her Chucks slapping the tile floor. My mother doesn't do business attire, and lives in her flip-flops three seasons out of the year. Believe me, I've tried to wrangle her into something a bit more appropriate, especially for court, but the Chucks were as far as she was willing to go. The suit she's wearing probably came from the men's department of a thrift store, but she makes it work for her.

I cross the road outside the courthouse, the restaurant is on the other side, down a block or two. It promises to be a warm afternoon and I briefly lift my face to the sun, enjoying the short walk.

I don't have to wait long since there's only one person in front of me when I walk up to the counter at Sprouts.

"For here or to go?"

"To go," I decide, smiling at the acne-scarred girl at the counter.

"What can I get you?"

"Could I have an ahi tuna bowl? Quinoa, baby kale, cucumber, edamame, radish, spring onion, a little red cabbage kimchi, and sunflower sprouts. Oh, and your roasted sesame dressing, please."

My mouth is already watering as I rattle off my favorite ingredients.

I just finished paying when my phone rings. It's Thildy, and I quickly step to the side, making room for whoever walked in after me.

"Shouldn't you be on your way to the Galapagos Islands?"

"We're at the airport as we speak," she states. "Our flight leaves in less than an hour."

"And you're spending that time calling me?" I tease with a chuckle as I glance out the window onto E 2nd Avenue.

"I have a reason. Actually, I have two. I meant to call you earlier for the first one, which was to apologize for last night, but *someone* told me to leave it alone."

"And yet here you are, doing it anyway." I grin at the sound of Ben's exasperated voice in the background. *"She probably already forgot all about it, and now you're bringing it up again."*

"Well, I feel bad about it, okay?"

"Guys…" I interrupt their first marital spat at my expense. "It's fine, either way. No need to apologize because I know better than anyone, your cousin does what he will and there isn't a damn thing you or I can do about it, except ignore it. So that's what I've decided to do, he's not worth the energy or the brain space."

"Smart woman," I hear Ben comment.

"Whatever," Thildy mumbles.

"So what was the second thing?" I ask. "You mentioned two reasons?"

"Right. The murder."

"Murder?" I echo, probably a little too loud.

"Yeah. A maintenance worker found a dead body in a stairwell in terminal B early this morning. I heard it was murder and it happened sometime last night."

"Are you serious?"

"Dead serious, pardon the pun. You left from B16, right?"

"Yeah."

I'm getting a little queasy.

"Well," Thildy continues with a little too much enthusiasm. "We're sitting two gates down from B16, looking at the caution tape right across from us. They have half of this hallway blocked off and there's a huge police presence here too. Creepy, right? Especially since you were here last night when they think it happened."

I'm not sure what to say, the thought actually makes me sick to my stomach.

"Do you know who died?" I find myself asking.

"The only thing I found out from the barista at the coffee shop was that it was a man. She didn't know anything else," she clarifies before adding, "Oh, I have to go, they're starting to board. I'll call you when we get back."

"Have a great time, you guys," I manage to get in before the line goes dead.

Jesus.

"Ahi tuna bowl?"

I swing around when my order is called out.

"Here."

I take a step toward the counter when a big hand wraps around my upper arm, right where another hand left bruises yesterday.

"Ouch," I yelp, pulling my arm free and rubbing it immediately, as I recognize Wapi. "What are you doing here?"

"Same as you. Lunch. What's this about a murder?"

I focus on the first part and ignore the second.

"You get lunch at Sprouts?"

"Never been here before, your mother just suggested I try it out. Now who got murdered?"

Of course she did. I have a thing or two to share with her, but first I want to get back to the office to check if I can find anything on the incident at the Denver airport.

Grabbing the paper bag with my lunch off the counter, I turn on my heel and head for the door. Behind me I hear Wapi's annoyed grumble.

"Fucking unbelievable."

CHAPTER
FOUR

WAPI

I left after she walked off, but got to her office first.

I'm waiting for her in the parking lot, leaning against the club van I'm still driving, when she walks up.

All I get is a little shake of the head when she passes me, but I follow her to the door of the office anyway.

"What do you want, Wapi?"

She plops the paper bag from the restaurant on her desk and I hold up my matching one.

"Joining you for lunch," I clarify, pulling one of the visitor's chairs up to the desk and sitting down. "Waiting for you to explain what the hell murder I heard you talking about."

"You know it's rude to listen in on other people's phone calls, right?" she snaps as she sinks down in her desk chair and wakes up her computer.

"Didn't take any effort to hear you yelling out *murder*. Hard to miss from six feet away," I point out.

Her eyes turn away from her monitor as she zooms in

on me, holding my gaze for a moment before apparently coming to a decision.

"Fine. That was my friend, Thildy, on the phone. It was her wedding I was at yesterday. Anyway, she's at the airport and apparently someone was killed there last night." A shudder appears to run through her before she continues.

Unfortunately, I'm sure it's not the first time something like that's happened. Denver airport is a pretty major hub, lots of people move through there daily.

I tell her as much.

"Yeah, except this happened about sixty feet from where I was waiting for my flight home."

"Did you see something?" I ask, instantly alert.

She shakes her head. "No. They found the body in an emergency stairwell this morning."

"Could've happened at any time, then," I point out. "If they didn't find it 'til this morning it's more likely it happened well after you flew home."

She nods, taking her lunch from her bag. "Probably."

I follow suit and reach into my bag to pull out the mystery container the girl at the restaurant handed me. I'd walked into the restaurant, and when I saw Lindsey standing off to the side, her back to the door as she was talking on her phone, I put in an order for whatever it was she was having. Unfortunately, when I take off the lid, I'm not exactly sure what I'm looking at.

"What the hell is this stuff?"

I poke a finger at what look to be green beans, raw fish, a frizzy clump of what I'm guessing are sprouts, and some kind of red cabbage slaw with a pungent smell.

"You don't know what you ordered?" Lindsey leans over the table to peek into my container.

I shrug. "I figured it was easier to have them copy your order."

A little smile tugs at the corners of her pretty mouth. "Those are edamame," she explains, poking the wooden fork in her hand at the green beans.

One by one she identifies the ingredients of my lunch which, frankly, doesn't really make it more appealing. Still, I'm no coward, and when she takes a hearty bite of hers, I feel compelled to try a mouthful of mine.

I brace myself—expecting it to taste like a mouth full of dirt and determined not to let on I hate it—so it takes me a minute to realize this is pretty tasty stuff. Clearly, I don't have as steady a poker face as I thought, because Lindsey starts laughing.

"Why were you even there? At Sprouts?" She has one of her perfectly shaped eyebrows pulled up high. "It clearly wasn't the food since, for a minute there, you looked like you weren't going to keep it down."

"It's actually not bad," I admit. "But yeah, I came looking for you. I called Mel about something but she was tied up in court. She suggested you'd be able to help me but that you weren't at the office. Then she mentioned where I could find you."

"What do you need help with?"

I just shoveled in another bite so have to cover my mouth with a hand before I answer.

"City bylaws. I need to know if I'm allowed to put up a fence or a barrier, and a gate of some sort."

"Where do you need a fence?"

While we eat our lunch, I explain the issues we're having with the gym parking lot.

When I got to The Edge this morning, Bubba was arguing with a parking enforcement officer and it took some time to get him inside so he could cool off. He was pissed because instead of towing the vehicles in question, the officer left tickets on each of the windshields, even though the parking sign we have up clearly warns unauthorized vehicles will be towed. After a chat with the officer, he assured me he would be by first thing in the morning and if the same vehicles were parked there again, he would have them impounded. He also suggested we talk to the motel owner again to see if we can come to some understanding, but I quickly disavowed him of that notion. I'm pretty sure both Bubba and Ouray are past any kind of *understanding*.

"So I figured it'd be less of a hassle to put up a gate or something. We have about sixty feet of our parking lot open to the road, which shouldn't cost too much putting chain-link fence up, but I need to know what I'm allowed to do and whether or not I need a permit."

Lindsey shoves her bowl aside and pulls her keyboard toward her.

"Let me have a look what I can find."

I guess I could've pissed around online myself to see if I could find answers—it's not like I'm computer illiterate—but I don't have a head for legal jargon, which is why I called Mel in the first place. I want to make sure I do things by the book because, although putting in the fence won't break the bank, I don't want the money wasted if I end up being forced to take it down again.

While Lindsey is digging up information, I grab the empty food containers and carry them to the small kitchen in the back, where I toss them in the garbage. Next, I fill the water reservoir of the Keurig on the counter, and grab a mug from the cupboard.

"Me too, please!" Lindsey yells from the front.

I spent enough time in Mel's office to know where everything is. Before I went on my lengthy road trip, I was assigned as security for Lindsey when they'd had some trouble here at the office, and spent more days than I care to remember perched on an uncomfortable visitor's chair, bored and more turned on than I'm willing to admit.

Of course, then Lindsey was snatched right from under my nose.

I shake my head to clear it. No use belaboring something I can't go back and change anyway. Instead, I focus on fixing us a couple of coffees and carry the mugs back to Lindsey's desk.

She's looking up at me with a triumphant gleam in her eyes.

————

Lindsey

He slides a coffee mug in front of me.

My favorite coffee mug, and the coffee is fixed exactly the way I like it with enough cream to turn it a light beige. Something we've had a few arguments about since Wapi prefers black.

Four years and he still recalls details like that.

For a second it makes me forget where my mind was at. Or maybe it's because he's standing beside my desk, looking at me funny.

"Thanks," I mumble, before I remember what I was going to say. "Oh, four feet, fifty percent transparency."

"What?" He seems confused.

"The fence." I tilt my computer screen so he can see it, it shows the relevant city bylaw I found. "Maximum four feet high and fifty percent transparent. They show some examples."

He puts a hand on the back of my seat and partially leans over me to get a good look at the screen. Dammit, he smells good. Like a fresh breeze, a hint of soap, and warm leather. That hasn't changed either, but other things about him sure have. I can't remember him having shoulders and arms like this four years ago. I'm having a hard time not imagining how those would feel wrapped around me. My body's response to his proximity is annoying.

God...I wish he wasn't an asshole.

"Permit?"

I almost jump out of my seat at his rumble.

"Sorry?"

"Am I gonna need a permit?" he repeats.

I scroll down the screen, leaning forward a little to escape the tempting warmth radiating from him. "It doesn't look like it."

"Good."

He raps his knuckles on my desk while giving my neck a squeeze with his other hand. Then he rounds the desk, sits down across from me, and pulls his phone from his pocket. While he talks to someone about work he wants started as soon as possible, I grab my cup of coffee and take a swig to hide the heat I feel creeping up my face.

It's not helping. I need some cold water to get this damn body under control. Ignoring his questioning glance, I get to my feet and head for the bathroom in the back. This is the reason why I've done my best to avoid him since he showed up unexpectedly last spring, after disappearing for three years. On those occasions I can't avoid being in the same room with him, I feel out of sorts and end up snapping and snarling.

Except, apparently, today. Hell, I think I actually might've smiled at him and I can't really afford to lose my resolve to keep him at a safe distance.

Four years ago, I could've sworn something was growing between us, but then he took off without a word. Worse, he bailed when I was in the hospital after surviving a horrendous ordeal. That hurt—a lot—and made me determined not to let myself become vulnerable again. I simply can't risk it.

By the time I return to my desk, Wapi is no longer on the phone. He's sitting at the computer in my chair.

"Why don't you make yourself comfortable?"

His head snaps up and his eyes narrow on me. Then he shoves the chair back and gets up, gesturing toward the seat.

"All yours, Princess," he sneers. "All I did was email the bylaw page you pulled up to my contractor. But no worries, I'll get out of your hair."

He moves for the door and is gone before I have a chance to react. Leaving me to feel like the asshole.

Damn him.

————

"That looks amazing, thank you so much."

I grin at Anika, who is standing behind me in the mirror and is running her fingers through the shiny waves she created.

This is what I needed after this long-ass day; some salon therapy, and some time with a friend, which Anika had quickly become after the first time I sat in her chair. She has a vivacious quality to her I was instantly drawn to. She's also brutally honest, funny as hell, and has a chip on her shoulder about men as big, if not bigger, than mine.

"I didn't think layers would look this good," I admit.

She whips the cape off, holding it away from me as she shakes it out.

"I told you."

She did. In fact, many times since I first started coming here. I'm lucky I take after my mom when it comes to hair, we have lots of it, but I've always been hesitant to do much more with it than trim the ends and throw in a highlight or two in the summer. It's been all one length for as long as I can remember. A little straitlaced and boring.

Not so boring now, with the feathered ends curling, creating a wind-tousled hairdo. It makes me look a little more free-spirited, not quite so buttoned-up. It makes me look—dare I say it—a little more like my mother's daughter. Nontraditional, uncomplicated, and effervescent. I like seeing myself like that, it feels liberating.

In an uncharacteristic gesture, I throw my arms around Anika and give her a big hug.

"Thank you. It's perfect."

"I know." Anika grins at me, patting my shoulder. "Maybe you should listen to me more. You know you're going to need some new outfits to go with that hair, right? Something that's not office attire?"

"Not all of my clothes are work clothes."

She cocks a hip and tilts her head. "Honey, you forget I've seen what you wear for a Friday night out, and believe me, this hair deserves better."

I don't bother reacting, walk to the cash register, and pull my wallet from my bag. Her assistant, Donna, rings me up.

"We're still on for the rodeo this weekend, right?" Anika reminds me as she starts working on her next customer.

The annual Ute Mountain Roundup is being held at the Montezuma County Fairgrounds in Cortez. A few weeks ago, Anika had to talk me into going, but I've actually been looking forward to it.

"You bet," I confirm, as Donna hands me my receipt.

I tuck it in my purse, wave goodbye, and head out to where my RAV is parked with an extra bounce in my step that wasn't there before. On the way home, I pick up some wonton soup and a couple of spring rolls for dinner because I don't feel like cooking.

At home, I quickly change into a pair of lounge pants and a T-shirt, scarf down my food at the kitchen island, and curl up on the couch with a glass of wine and my laptop.

Then I proceed to give my credit card a bit of a workout as I make an effort to spruce up my wardrobe.

CHAPTER
FIVE

WAPI

"Hey! You can't do that."

George Macias, the potbellied owner of the Oxbow Motel, jaywalks across Main Avenue as fast as his short legs can carry him. I cross my arms and lean against the back of the contractor's pickup, watching as he narrowly misses getting hit by a delivery truck. The man looks like a coronary waiting to happen, his face sporting an unhealthy purple glow.

"That's not legal," he complains as he indicates the rudimentary gate.

It's little more than two steel poles stabilized in concrete footers, a pair of steel-frame gate doors swinging between them, but it works. Two pins come down where the gate doors meet and sink into metal shafts Nick, the contractor, is just installing in the ground. A sturdy metal lock will keep the pins in place. At some point more permanent footings will be poured for the gate posts, but this is good enough to keep people out for the time being.

The low concrete curbs I decided on instead of four-foot fencing separating the parking lot from the street, were delivered and placed yesterday. When I showed up at a quarter to seven this morning, once again there were three vehicles illegally parked. I didn't bother calling parking enforcement again. With this gate up, we're once more in control of who parks here.

"Sure it is," I calmly respond. "It's on our parking lot.

"We'll see about that," he says, stepping into my space. Spittle is flying from his lips as he wags his finger under my nose. "I'll be calling my lawyer and I have friends on the city council I'll be contacting as well."

I shrug, unaffected. "As is well within your right to."

The fact I'm staying calm seems to aggravate him even more.

"You're nothing but a bunch of thugs and criminals. You think you're above the law and can just do as you please, but I'm not going to let you get away with that."

A little ironic what he's pointing the finger at us for is exactly what he is guilty of. By the way, that finger he's jabbing is coming very close to poking me in the chest. I look down at his pudgy hand pointedly before aiming my glare at him.

"You don't scare me," he spits out, despite abruptly jerking his hand back before he turns on his heel.

"Be careful crossing," I call after him.

I hear Bubba's deep chuckle behind me. "You scared the shit out of him."

"I did no such thing. I was showing neighborly concern."

That only makes him laugh harder.

"Right. That's why the guy is leaving skid marks all the way across the road. And you didn't even flex a muscle."

"I'm done," Nick announces, joining us. "All you need is a good padlock. I'll be back with my crew next week to pour the permanent footers."

"Good. What do I owe you?"

"I'll email you a bill when we're done here. It's easier."

I watch him get in his truck and drive off before following Bubba back to the gym where my bike is parked.

"I've gotta run, but I'll send one of the prospects to pick up a lock for the gate. You'll have it before you close down tonight." I swing a leg over my bike as I jerk my thumb over my shoulder. "And if that asswipe gives you any trouble, don't engage but let me know."

"Will do."

My next stop is the Brewer's Pub, one of our other businesses in town. For the past couple of months Ouray has had me take over the monthly check-ins with the brewmaster and the pub's manager. Most of our businesses can run themselves and don't need the club's daily input, but Ouray still likes to keep tabs and requires accountability.

When I came back to the club last year when our former president—and my surrogate father—was dying, I didn't know what the future would hold. I wasn't sure whether there'd still be a place for me at the club after I went nomad. But since then I've been kept so busy, I haven't had a chance to think about it much. Ouray has been funneling steady work my way, and lately it has been the kind of shit he usually would take care of himself.

I guess that should've answered the question whether the club still has room for me, but Ouray's request for a one-on-one meeting has made me wonder. That meeting is to take place after I drop in at the brewery, and I'm a bit nervous. Ouray hasn't been around the clubhouse as much as he usually is, especially this past week, something I know hasn't gone unnoticed by others as well.

————

"Take this."

Lisa shoves a tray with two bowls of soup, a couple of sandwiches, and two bottles of water in my hands.

"I want you to make sure he eats," she instructs me, keeping her voice low.

I'm a little puzzled but she's already disappearing back into the kitchen.

Ouray's office door is open. He's sitting behind his desk in his favorite position, his feet up on the desk, but his head is resting back and his eyes are closed. I hesitate on the threshold.

"Come in and close the door."

Guess he wasn't sleeping.

I walk in and kick the door shut behind me before I move to the massive conference table in front of the window to set the tray down. Then I sit down and dig into one of the bowls of soup. I'm not sure what has Lisa concerned about Ouray's appetite, but she wouldn't fuss without reason. I also know Ouray does not take kindly with any fussing, which is why I know there's no talking him into doing something he doesn't want to do, but if I sit down and eat, he might follow suit.

"Fucking Lisa," he grumbles behind me.

His boots loudly drop to the floor and his footfalls are heavy as he walks over. Then he sits down across from me and pulls the tray toward him.

I figure I'd leave the talking to him since he's the one who asked for this meeting.

I don't have to wait long.

"Fuck, man. Turns out I tempted fate a little too long. I knew I probably had high blood pressure, but I figured it was just a by-product of the job. I ignored it for the most part, started skipping my physicals after my doc began bitching about smoking and drinking, greasy foods, you know…all the things that make life worth living. Apparently, that wasn't a good idea."

"Your heart?" I guess, trying not to look as shaken as I feel.

"No. Not yet anyway, although if I'm to believe that quack I'm well on my way there too. Nah, turns out I have fucking prostate cancer."

My spoon clatters in my bowl. There aren't a lot of things that really scare me in this world, but that word is one of them. It scares the piss out of me. It's because cancer is a pariah, quiet and insidious, wreaking its silent havoc until often irreparable damage is done to its unsuspecting host. I don't fear when I can face things head on, but cancer tends to reveal itself by sneak attack.

"Cancer," I echo breathlessly.

"Jesus, don't look at me like I'm about to croak on the spot, I'm not fucking dying yet, brother," he grumbles. "Not unless my wife decides to help me along, which isn't outside of the realm of possibilities. She can barely talk to me; she's still so pissed. For years the woman has nagged me to go get checked out and I've been blowing her off. It didn't help I knew for a couple of weeks before I shared the diagnosis with her."

I can see how Luna would not have taken that well, but I don't bother pointing that out, clearly, he's living the consequences of that choice.

He waves his hand impatiently. "Anyway, enough of

that. Can't go back so we gotta go forward, which is why you're here. I started radiation treatments on Monday, which I go into Mercy for every morning, five days a week for the next eight weeks."

"Holy shit." I'm trying to follow along, but my mind is still reeling from the bombshell.

"The treatments wipe you out, mess with your bowels and bladder, which is more than you need to know. Short of it is, I need my energy and focus to kick this bitch, and I should probably spend some time groveling if I want my marriage to survive."

"What do you need from us?"

"You." He singles me out with a sharp look from intense eyes as he leans forward with his elbows on the table. "As you can see, Lisa suspects something is up," he adds as he gestures to the food. "But so far you're the only one who knows."

That puzzles me. I'd have thought Kaga, his right-hand man for as long as I can remember, or Paco or even Trunk would've been the more obvious choice to share this kind of news with.

Then he throws me for a loop.

"I'm going to ask you to step in for me."

I stare at him, slack-mouthed. I can't have heard that right. There are people far more qualified to do that. Heck, just about everyone else in the club would be more qualified than I am.

"The hell? Me?" I manage.

"Yeah, you. You've been picking up my slack for months now."

"But…what about the others?"

"Everyone else is where they belong, where they wanna be. You've been looking for your place, but I've always known where you were going to end up—where you ultimately belong—Nosh did too. You have what it takes to be a leader. I'm not gonna bore you with all the fucking reasons why, your head's big enough as it is, and this isn't a goddamn marriage proposal, but you need to know that eventually—when the time is right for me to actually hand over the gavel—I intend to put your name forward to take over leadership of the club."

Talk about being blown away.

I'm still wondering what the fuck just happened when I eventually walk out of his office. I barely acknowledge Lisa or my brothers as I stalk through the clubhouse and straight out the door.

Two minutes later I'm on my bike, roaring down to town with the wind whipping in my face.

He made me promise to keep his secret until Friday next week, at our next club meeting. He wants to talk to Kaga first, out of respect, but intends to share his condition and his plans with the rest of the brothers during the meeting.

They're going to be as shocked as I am. We had a tough few years already, losing first Momma—who was mother to us all—and then last year Nosh, the club's founding father. Two people intrinsically woven into the fabric of Arrow's Edge. Ouray is another whose name is synonymous with the club and what it stands for today. Discovering our president is fighting for his life, and there's not a fucking thing any of us can do about it, will shake everyone to the core.

In addition, I'm not so sure how the club is going to react when they find out he wants me to take over his responsibilities with Kaga in a supporting role. Hell, I just fucking turned thirty-five when most of my brothers are at least a decade, if not more, older.

The knowledge, the responsibility, and the secrecy

weigh heavily on my shoulders. As I'm crossing the bridge over the Animas River on my way to Baldy Mountain for another night with just my thoughts and the stars, I realize I'm not that far from Lindsey's place. I made a promise I wouldn't share with anyone in the club, but I figure technically Lindsey is not part of the club.

Last time I saw her she seemed friendly, softer, even a little flustered when I cautiously touched her, but next thing I know she was snapping and those pretty blue eyes had been shooting icicles at me. I'm not sure what the fuck happened from one minute to the next, but I didn't wait to find out and beelined it out of her office. I figured it was probably safer for all involved to go back to keeping my distance.

There's no one who keeps me off balance like she does, and yet something has me turn my bike into her neighborhood instead of going up the mountain to find some solace.

CHAPTER
SIX

LINDSEY

"Are you sure?"

Mom rolls her eyes at me.

"Yes, I am. Now that the judge has called a recess for two weeks, I've got nowhere else to be."

The judge in the Samantha Dawson custody case took one look at the psychologist's report on the girl and agreed with my mother and the guardian ad litem, a full investigation needed to be done into the possibility that poor child was being abused in some way by the stepfather. A more in-depth psychological, as well as a physical assessment were ordered but would require some time.

What was already a messy case, has become even messier, and a poor, nine-year-old girl with developmental disabilities is stuck at the center of all of it.

"Go on," Mom prompts me, flapping her hand to shoo me out. "Run your errands, have your fun, I've got this place covered."

It's just after three on a Friday afternoon and those tend

to be quiet in the office, so I don't think there'll be much to do anyway. Still, I feel a bit of guilt as I head for my desk to shut down my computer and grab my purse. The post office on Rim Drive is open 'til four o'clock. I'll have time to pick up the packages I received notifications about this morning. They're my online purchases from earlier in the week, and I'm more than a little excited I'll have them in time to wear this weekend.

On my way out the back door, I pop into the kitchen to turn on the small dishwasher, and stick my head in the door to my mother's office.

"Okay, I'm off."

Mom lifts her head, her purple reading glasses perched on the tip of her nose.

"Have fun, enjoy the tight asses in Wranglers, but don't forget Mason's soccer tournament on Sunday. You promised him."

I grin at my mother. "Anika said she was bringing theater binoculars for a better look. And tell Mason I'll be there and I'll buy him a donut at Durango Doughworks for every goal he scores."

Mom shakes her head, a faint grin on her lips.

"Spare me. That boy does not need added sugar, he already has more energy than he knows what to do with."

"Only because he's happy," I remind her.

Then I blow her a kiss and head out the back door.

Mason is my little brother. He's eleven and my mom and Paco adopted him almost four years ago. The poor kid witnessed his mother's murder and came into the care of the Arrow's Edge MC, like so many other kids with difficult or traumatic backgrounds.

It took Mason a while to get to a place where he wasn't distrusting of everyone, and plagued with nightmares. My mother and Paco were instrumental in helping him feel safe enough just to be a kid. It also means that, now in their fifties, Mom and Paco are getting a run for their money. That boy is definitely keeping them on their toes.

On my way to the post office, I stop at the Natural Foods Co-op and run in to grab a few things, since my fridge is almost empty. Some vegetables, rice noodles, coconut milk, and a small jar of kimchi. I doubt there will be many healthy choices at the rodeo tomorrow, but at least I can eat healthy tonight.

I'm almost giddy by the time I get home, dumping my groceries on the counter before I open my kitchen drawer for the scissors. I tackle the box first, pulling out the black on tan, embroidered, square-nosed cowboy boots. They cost a mint and I had taken a risk buying footwear online, but it was a reputable company with a decent return policy. I still can't stuff my feet into them fast enough.

Yesss. Perfect fit.

I run upstairs to check them out in my full-length mirror, belatedly realizing that might not be such a good idea in slippery new boots on wooden stairs as I almost lose my footing.

The boots look out of place with my pencil skirt and white dress shirt, but they are gorgeous. They are also far removed from anything I've ever owned before. Ironically, they'd look right at home in Mom's closet.

I kick them off, quickly shuck my work clothes, and slip into a pair of workout shorts and a T-shirt. It was warm outside today, a balmy eighty-two degrees. Maybe while I have the laundry going, I can sit out back with a glass of wine and a book. After trying on the rest of my purchases, I put in my first load before I start on dinner.

My favorite playlist is on in the background, my wok is

heating on the stove, I have a pot of water coming to a boil for my noodles, and I'm chopping the last of my vegetables when my doorbell rings. Wiping my hands on a kitchen towel, I walk to the front door, and check the spy hole to find Wapi on my doorstep. He looks a little lost, his hands deep in his pockets and his head hung low.

I should ignore him. Nothing good can come out of letting him in. I haven't seen him since he stomped out of the office earlier this week. Granted, I probably was snippier than I needed to be, but he rattles me. He makes me feel vulnerable and out of control, and that scares me. We seem to have this weird, volatile push-and-pull thing going on that can't be healthy.

He looks forlorn though.

Before I realize what I'm doing, I've turned the lock and am opening the door.

His head lifts slightly, looking at me from under his heavy eyebrows. His eyes appear almost navy instead of their gray-blue color. I'm sure it's partly the waning light, but there's something else there, something dark and painful.

"Can I come in?"

His voice matches the almost tormented look on his face he makes no effort to hide.

I step out of the way and wave him inside.

On the stove, the lid on my pot of water starts to rattle and I rush past Wapi to turn the burner down. The sesame oil and spices in my wok are starting to smoke a little and I dump in the sliced leeks, ginger, and garlic. The moment the veggies hit the hot oil they hiss and sputter, so I quickly flip them with my wok spatula a few times. Then I add in the julienned carrots, peppers, bok choy, and snow peas.

I can feel Wapi behind me.

"Smells good."

Without looking at him, I tilt my head to the fridge.

"Grab yourself a beer."

I drop rice noodles in the boiling water—about twice as much as usual—and close the lid on top. Those will be ready in three minutes.

"What are you drinking?" Wapi asks behind me.

"Red wine. Bottle is on the dining room table, glasses in the sideboard."

I give my bean sprouts a quick cold rinse, leave them to drain in the colander, then add the coconut milk and a healthy splash of lime juice to the wok and give it a quick stir.

"That smells amazing."

I feel an electrical charge skitter up my back to the base of my skull at the sound of his voice so close behind me. I swallow hard and clear my throat before I trust myself to speak.

"Bowls in the cupboard to the left of the sink," I croak.

I'm not exactly sure what I'm doing and, to be honest, I don't care to analyze it too closely right now. I simply listen to him move about my kitchen while I drain the noodles. Adding the bean sprouts and then the noodles to the wok, I give the whole thing a good stir before filling the bowls Wapi set on the counter beside the stove.

"You did something to your hair," he comments when I turn around and slide the bowls on the kitchen island.

I almost laugh. So much for Anika's well-honed mastery with the scissors. But then I get a good look at his face and control the urge. Something is troubling him.

"Dig in," I tell him instead, sliding onto the stool beside him and picking up the fork he put out.

Better to talk on a full stomach.

———

Wapi

"I can do those."

She takes the bowls from my hands.

"I've got it."

As numb as I feel, when I watch her walk to the sink, I don't miss the sway of her hips in those tight workout shorts, they don't leave much to the imagination. That much becomes clear when she bends over to put the dishes in the dishwasher. I quickly avert my eyes and drain what remains of my beer.

I'm about to get up and get out before I'm tempted to make a move I'm sure to regret, when Lindsey's voice gently reminds me why I ended up here in the first place.

"What happened? What has you upset?"

The question is like a warm hug without touching. Not that I've had a ton of experience with hugs in my life. As much as the club provided a home and represented safety for me, it wasn't a particularly soft and cuddly environment. I close my eyes and drop my head down to my chest.

"Wapi?"

When I look up, she's braced against the sink, facing me. Her blue eyes are pools of emotion I think I could easily drown in.

The next thing I know, I'm telling her about Ouray's condition and the conversation he and I had.

To her credit, Lindsey doesn't interrupt, even though I can see the shock on her face. She listens, casually moving through the kitchen as she grabs me a refill from the fridge and pours herself another glass of wine. Like the Pied Piper, she leads me to the living room and I follow without thought.

"I'm sorry to hear about Ouray. That must've been a shock."

We're sitting across from each other. I'm in the corner of the couch and she's sitting in the funky-looking round lounge chair opposite me, her legs tucked underneath her. I briefly envision myself in that chair with her curled up on my lap like that.

I don't manage much more than a grunted concession, having apparently run dry of words.

"That's a lot all at once," she observes. "Even though prostate cancer is very treatable and the odds are very much in his favor, I'm sure it's disconcerting to see someone you've always looked up to as strong, even invincible like Ouray, sick and weakened. On top of that, I'm sure those feel like some big, intimidating shoes to fill."

With just those few sentences, she not only identifies what I'm struggling with but outlines it in a way that doesn't feel quite as overwhelming as it did earlier.

As much as I was afraid it might be, it was not a mistake to come here.

"You could say that," I acknowledge.

She tilts her head and aims a pointed look at my boots on the floor. Then one side of her mouth curves up and her eyes sparkle when she finds mine.

"Have you seen the size of your feet?"

I glance down at my size thirteens and start laughing. Lindsey joins in. I haven't heard her laugh often, but I love the sound.

Before I realize what I'm doing I'm on my feet, instantly silencing her when she catches the look on my face.

"Fair warning," I alert her. "I'm about to kiss you."

I put my hands on the armrests to brace myself and lean down. Her eyes widen a fraction before they drop to my mouth. She makes a small sound in the back of her throat I don't even think she's aware of.

"Last chance," I whisper, pausing briefly before I close the distance.

There is no hesitation in the way she lifts her hands to my face, one sliding to the back of my head, the other cupping my jaw, as she invites me into her mouth. The strangled sound must be mine; she tastes fucking amazing and she kisses with attitude as her fingertips restlessly scrape my beard. Better than my best fantasy. I'm having a hard time keeping my damn legs under me.

The temptation is great to climb in that damn chair with her, but I realize all too well the moment I do that and my hands are free to roam and explore, this'll be like a runaway freight train and those can do a ton of damage. Not a risk I care to take. Not with this woman.

Putting one hand at the base of her neck, I end the kiss, staring down at her flushed face. I take in her swollen lips and the dark heat in her eyes as her pulse hammers against my fingertips.

She blinks a few times.

"Wow, that was…uh…"

"Yeah," I confirm in a rough voice before straightening up.

Goddammit, part of me knew it would be nearly impossible to walk away once we broke that seal. It would be easier if she were pissed at me now, but she doesn't look pissed. Not now.

"I should get going," I mumble, grabbing my empty can off the table.

I hear her get out of the chair and follow me into the kitchen, where I toss the can into the recycling bin under the sink. When I turn around, she's right behind me but I can't quite place the expression on her face.

"Are you running again?"

A lot is packed into that question, but the answer is simple.

"No. Not running. I'm...uh...treading carefully." I observe her closely when I add, "Too much at stake."

I can literally see the moment my words register. That strange expression appears to melt off her face.

"I see."

"Yeah."

I reach out to brush at a lock of hair she's trying to blow out of her eyes. Then I curve my hand around her neck and tug her closer, brushing her lips with mine.

"Thanks for your ear, Princess." I can tell she's about to take a chunk out of my hide at the nickname, so I quickly continue, "Great food, better company, but your beer sucks."

"What's wrong with my beer?"

The sharp ring of her doorbell saves me from answering.

Lindsey is already on her way to the door when I overtake her, getting to the peephole first. I immediately open the door.

"Evans," I greet the familiar cop. "What are you doing here?"

"Hey," he returns, apparently equally surprised at seeing me. "I'm looking for Ms. Zimmerman, actually."

Lindsey shoves me aside as she steps around me.

"Hey, Bill. What can I do for you?"

"Would you mind if I stepped inside for a minute? I'm hoping you might be able to answer a few questions for me."

"Sure." She steps to the side to let him in. "Would you like a drink?"

"No. I won't be a minute." He stays right inside the door. "I understand you were on a flight from Denver last Sunday night?"

She darts a glance at me over her shoulder.

"Yes, I was. Is this about that murder?"

"Oh, you know something about it?"

Evans seems curious, as am I. I hadn't been able to get much out of Lindsey when I first overheard her mention something, and nothing popped up on a murder at the airport when I looked online later.

"Not really, I just heard it from a friend who happened to be at the airport the next morning when the body was found. I meant to do a search online but things got busy, and then I kinda forgot about it," she explains.

"You wouldn't have found much anyway," Evans shares. "For now, the public line is it was an unfortunate accident. The victim was part of an ongoing investigation by the Denver Police Department."

I'm not sure why, but I don't like where this is going.

"Be helpful if you got to the point, Evans," I prompt the detective. "I'd love to know why you'd think Lindsey would know anything about this."

I ignore Lindsey's heated look and aim my own glare at Bill Evans. It clearly doesn't intimidate him—I don't think very much does.

"I don't. Ms. Zimmerman just happens to be the seven-teenth name on my list of passengers on that flight who are local to Durango. After I leave here, I have nine more to go."

Then he calmly fishes a sheet of paper from a file he has under his arm and focuses his attention firmly on Lindsey.

"If you wouldn't mind taking a look at this picture, and tell me if you've ever seen this man."

I get a glimpse of a guy who looks like a nondescript, middle-aged, office stiff as Evans hands her the picture. Lindsey sharply sucks in air the moment her eyes focus on the image. My hand instinctively curves around her shoulder.

"Is that the dead man?" she asks breathlessly, looking up at Evans. "He ran into me, knocked me on my ass outside the airport bathrooms."

"Are you sure it was this guy?"

Evans seems incredulous, clearly not expecting her to actually recognize the guy.

"Yeah, I'm pretty sure that was him. That was the second time I saw him. I'd caught him running down the hallway earlier. He almost bumped into me that time too. Same guy, both times. Suit, middle-aged, sweaty. That's all I know, really."

"Did you notice if he was carrying anything? A brief-case? A folder?"

"I don't think so. I don't recall seeing anything on him."

"Was he with anyone? Did you see him talk to anyone?"

Lindsey shakes her head, and I don't miss the slight shift of her body closer to me.

"Not that I remember."

"So that is the victim?" I echo her question from earlier to give her a break.

The cop's attention shifts to me, not missing the propri-etary hold I'm keeping on Lindsey.

"Yes."

Lindsey's entire body sags against me at his answer.

"Who was he?" she asks warily.

"A Denver accountant, and that's all I can tell you. And Lindsey," he adds. "I'm sorry, but I have a feeling Denver PD may want to talk to you."

"But that's not going to happen tonight," I assert, pinning him with a pointed look.

"No," he concedes. "It'll probably just be a phone call sometime tomorrow."

"Wonderful," Lindsey mumbles. "There go my plans for the rodeo."

I wait until Evans takes his leave before I turn to her.

"What's this about a rodeo?"

CHAPTER
SEVEN

LINDSEY

"This is she."

"I'm sorry to interrupt your Saturday morning, Ms. Zimmerman. I'm Detective LaVine with the Denver PD."

The man sounds like James Earl Jones; deep, smooth, and resonant. One of those voices you can happily listen to reciting a grocery list.

He puts me instantly at ease.

"Detective Evans told me to expect a call. At least I'm assuming that's what this is about?" I check as an afterthought. "The...uh...dead man at the airport?"

"It is," he confirms. "I understand you had an encounter with the victim at the airport last Sunday night?"

"More of a run-in, I would say. I didn't exactly talk to him or anything."

"I see. Would you mind telling me exactly what happened? Start from the time you got to the airport and walk me through."

It actually helps my recollection to start by describing every step. LaVine occasionally asks a question, like; "Was there a big lineup at security? Did you stop to grab a coffee?" All of it serves to relax me and it works, because when I get to the part of the actual incident, I'm able to share a few details I don't think I mentioned to Bill last night.

"He actually apologized," I share.

"Can you remember exactly what he said?" LaVine prompts.

"All he said was, *I'm sorry,* before he took off."

"Which direction did he go?"

"I think he ran toward the escalators, but I can't be a hundred percent sure. Two seconds after he took off, an elderly lady stopped to help me."

"Did you see where she came from?"

"At the time I assumed she came out of the bathroom behind me but, to be honest, I can't be sure. I don't remember seeing her in there," I elaborate.

LaVine continues to probe for details but, other than describing what the woman looked like, I don't have much more to tell him. Then he has me go over the entire thing once again but nothing new popped up.

All last night—after I almost had to shove Wapi out the door—I'd already spent replaying the collision outside the terminal bathrooms in my head, trying to remember bits and pieces, but nothing I could come up with seemed that useful.

Still, LaVine seems satisfied with what I was able to tell him.

"Appreciate your help, Ms. Zimmerman," he rumbles.

"Lindsey," I correct him. "Call me Lindsey."

"Very well, Lindsey, my name is Mike. I won't take up

any more of your time. If I have any more questions, I will give you a call."

"Yes, for sure."

"Oh, and as I believe Detective Evans already mentioned, this is part of an ongoing investigation—a particularly sensitive one—so I'd appreciate it if you didn't share what we discussed, or at the very least be selective about who you talk to. For the sake of the investigation as much as for yours."

"Of course," I answer before I have a chance to register his words of caution.

It hits me after he's already hung up the phone, it's probably not a bad idea to be a bit careful. After all, someone killed the guy and might think I know something. Of course, I don't, but me talking to the police might make it look like I do.

Good thing I have great security, which is what helped me convince Wapi to go home last night. Of course, I still barely slept since my mind was churning, so I finally gave up and got out of bed at six thirty, to already find a message from Wapi on my phone, which I'd left charging in the kitchen.

That was kind of sweet, actually. He wanted to know how my night had been. When I mentioned I hadn't slept that well and was thinking of scrapping the rodeo he'd questioned me about last night, he recommended I hold off on cancelling, suggesting I might welcome the distraction after I talk to the Denver PD.

Now I'm glad I did. I feel much better after talking to the detective and am actually looking forward to going. Bonus, there's still plenty of time for a nap before I have to get ready.

I can't wait to see Anika's reaction to my new wardrobe.

———

"Holy hell, look at you!"

I grin as I sink down into the passenger seat of Anika's Miata. She insisted on driving her little convertible.

"You know my hair is going to be a mess by the time we get there, right?" I point out when she pulls away from my curb.

Anika is wearing a cowboy hat, the one thing she wasn't able to talk me into adding to my wardrobe. She has it secured with a leather strap under her chin. Of course, I'll be the one looking like a mop by the time we get to Cortez.

"A mess? We're going for windblown," she says cheerfully. "Or maybe just-fucked. Either way, you'll turn heads."

She snickers at her own joke.

As soon as she turns onto US-160, she burns rubber.

"You're going to get us pulled over," I have to yell to be heard.

"Don't worry. I know where all the speed traps are," she assures me.

"That's great, but I didn't get a new haircut and this rockin' outfit so I could look awesome in my coffin," I point out.

Immediately her foot lets up on the gas, as she darts me an apologetic glance and mouths, "Sorry."

The actual rodeo doesn't start for another forty-five minutes or so, but the overflow parking lot at the fairgrounds is already filling up. Anika manages to snag a parking spot and then makes me wait while she puts up the soft cover.

"Wouldn't it have been easier to not put it down in the first place?" I question her.

"Of course," she agrees as she gives my hair a flip. "But then you wouldn't be looking this fabulous."

The line at the gate moves quickly and within minutes we're through. It's much busier than I thought with quite a crowd. Anika grabs my wrist and drags me to a food stand boasting Navajo fry bread tacos. No amount of objecting keeps her from ordering me one. Delicious as they are, they're massive and messy, and I'm pretty sure I'll end up wearing half of it on my new, pale blue, embroidered, bohemian top.

Half an hour later, I sit down in the front row with a cardboard container barely holding the Navajo taco, a large plastic cup with beer, and a healthy stack of napkins I was able to stuff in my purse. Next thing I know, the first strains of the national anthem start playing over the sound system. Lucky Anika hadn't quite made it into her seat yet.

There is no way in hell I'll be able to get back on my feet without accident, with my hands full. So while the fresh-faced young girl in the pink cowboy hat massacres not only "The Star-Spangled Banner" but also "God Bless America," I stay seated and scarf down as much as I can of my food, ignoring a few angry glares.

By the time the ear torture is over, I've managed to eat half of my taco without spilling a single crumb. Most people around me are sitting down except Anika, who is leaning over the railing, looking at something.

"Is that who I think it is?" she asks, nodding to a few people still standing half a row down from us.

I don't recognize anyone and am about to tell her that when two of the boys take their seat, leaving two individuals standing. One of them is looking at me.

I have no trouble recognizing him.

———

Wapi

"Where are you going?" I ask as she tries to slip past me to the stairs.

She turns to face me, pointing at a spot on her blouse, but my eyes get hung up on the peek of cleavage the generous V allows.

"Nice. You look great."

She does. The boots, the worn jeans, the flowy top, and the fuckable hairdo. She looks hot.

"Excuse me, that's not where I'm pointing," she schools me. "I need to put some water on this, you made me spill my taco," she clarifies.

"I did?"

Seems like a bit of a stretch, given that I was here and she was sitting all the way over there, but I like the sound of putting water on her blouse. It'll only improve the view.

"You startled me. What are you doing here anyway?" she asks, narrowing her eyes on me.

I lean my hip against the railing and cross my arms, smirking at her.

"Watching the rodeo, like everyone else."

She crosses her own arms and grins back. "Let me guess, this was a last-minute decision?"

Her eyes sparkle, drawing me in.

"Maybe," I concede, taking a step closer.

"It wouldn't have anything to do with me being here, would it?" she probes.

"It's a distinct possibility."

I take another step until I'm flush against her. Then,

with the tip of my finger, I lift her chin and take her mouth. It's so damn easy to get lost in this woman, I almost forget where I am until a couple of whistles go up behind me.

Then someone yells, "Not the kind of bucking I thought I was in for tonight. Sit the hell down or get a damn room!"

Releasing Lindsey, I snap my head around to pinpoint the smart-ass. Instead, I catch sight of Booger and the other two I decided to bring, snickering in their seats. So I shoot them a glare instead.

At that moment Lindsey makes her escape, darting down the stairs. I point a finger at the boys. "Do not move." Then I take off after her.

I just catch sight of her slipping into the bathrooms and resign myself to wait outside. I lean my back against the wall and get comfortable, but I don't have to wait that long before she reappears. She tries to hide a smile when she catches sight of me pushing off from the wall.

"You know, I could probably find my own way back."

"I'm aware," I tell her, touching the wet spot on her shirt before lifting my hands to her face. "But I just needed another taste without the audience."

I keep the kiss short and sweet. An appetizer for later.

"I'll come by after."

She tilts her head. "I'm sorry, I must have missed the question in there." Then she glances past me toward the rodeo arena. "And you're making me miss the cowboys."

"Fuck the cowboys," I grumble, giving her hair a little tug. "If I show up later, will you be home?"

"Probably. Unless I get a better offer," she teases, before brushing past me toward the stairs.

"You'd better be," I call after her. "Or I'll come looking for you."

At the base of the stairs, she looks back, a smirk on her face.

"*Yippee ki-yay.*"

CHAPTER
EIGHT

LINDSEY

"Holy shit."

Anika elbows me in the ribs when I take my seat beside her.

"Someone's been holding out on me."

I glance down the row to where Wapi is just taking his seat.

I'm not the only one looking, there's no denying the man has appeal. You'd think he'd look a little out of place at the rodeo, with his tattoos, torn jeans, and that slouchy beanie he wears a lot of the time, but put a western shirt on him and swap that beanie for a Stetson, and he'd fit right in. He's just a different kind of cowboy.

"Not really," I answer Anika.

"Oh, come on," she mocks. "Last I knew you could barely stand to be around the guy, and here you are, in a freaking hot lip-lock in front of an audience. Heck, less than a week ago you were sitting in my chair, lamenting on how big of an asshole he is. You have to agree, it's a bit of a shocker."

"He *was* an asshole," I explain. "That is, until last night, when he stopped being one."

She huffs beside me. "You're not giving me much to work with here, girlfriend. What changed?"

Not much, to be honest. Other than him showing up on my doorstep, choosing to turn to me to look for solace. But that's not mine to share.

"We ended up sharing a meal last night, and then we shared a kiss. There isn't much more to report. I'm not even sure what to make of it myself," I admit.

Anika straightens in her seat to take in the action in the arena.

"Well, there goes my plan to pick us up a couple of cowboys to party with," she grumbles.

I refrain from pointing out the likelihood of that would've been slim to none anyway, I'm sure she knows that already. Instead, I bump her with my shoulder when a long-legged cowboy passes in front of our seats, his fine, Wrangler-clad buns flexing at eye level.

"Yummm," she mumbles, and I snicker.

I may not be interested but that doesn't make me blind.

———

Wapi

Fucking dumb, punk kid.

I finish filling out the insurance form and hand it back to the nurse.

"Please take a seat in the waiting room. We'll let you know when we have an update on Frances."

Goddamn Booger.

I should've thought twice about bringing those knuckle-heads to the rodeo. I thought it would be something fun, something new for them, and—needless to say—providing an excuse for me to go.

Now I'm stuck at the hospital in Cortez because that little punk wanted to show off to his buddies.

The three of them had left to get drinks and were gone a while, which I didn't think much of since the lines were long. Maybe ten minutes after they left, Billy came running back to our seats, panic on his face.

It had been Booger's idea to sneak to the back of the rodeo grounds where they keep the livestock. The idiot thought it would be fun to piss off one of the bulls and ended up getting his forearm crushed between the fencing and the animal.

By the time I got to him, the EMTs—there on standby for the rodeo—were already tending to him. From what I could see, the kid's arm is a mess with an obvious open fracture. He went in the ambulance, and I followed in the pickup with the other two.

I already called the clubhouse and talked to one of the brothers, Mika. He's on his way to come and pick up Billy and Max. Ouray wasn't at the clubhouse and I decided not to bother him. What would be the use? This is the kind of stuff I'll be dealing with once I step in for him anyway. I'm already here so I'll handle it.

The two other boys are looking a bit pale around the gills when I join them in the waiting room. I'm sure they got an eyeful of Booger's mangled arm. *Good*. I hope they remember this next time someone has a harebrained idea, but I'm not holding my breath. Teenagers have proven not to be the smartest.

"Is he okay?" Max asks, when I take a seat beside him.

"Did you see his fucking arm?" Billy snaps at his friend.

"Hey," I intervene. "First of all, watch your language. You're not at the clubhouse. And no," I address Max. "I'm pretty sure he'll need some surgery."

I'm proven right half an hour later, when the ER physician stops in to report he's called in the orthopedic surgeon. Mika arrives shortly after and I'm relieved when he takes the boys off my hands. Not long after a nurse comes to get me and shows me into a small room where a miserable Booger is looking small and vulnerable in the hospital bed.

His tearful, "I'm sorry," when I walk in instantly deflates the anger I had no intention of hiding from him.

"Oh, I'm sure you are, kiddo. Can we agree this probably earns top billing on your growing list of questionable decisions?"

"I guess," he mutters. "I thought it'd be funny."

"Which part? Trespassing into an area you're not supposed to be, or pissing off an already-angry bull and then sticking your arm in his pen?"

He turns his head away from me and shrugs. Despite the time Trunk—our resident psychologist—and Lisa spend working with him, he is still that messed-up street kid we picked up almost a year ago.

I soften my tone a bit. "You know you don't have to try so hard, huh? Billy and Max aren't your friends because of the stupid shit you pull, but despite of it. Right now, they're scared shitless on your behalf. You don't have to *earn* friends; you just need to meet them. As with family, you don't *earn* them either, they're simply there."

His eyes come to me. "I don't got no family," he proclaims defiantly.

"Really? Then what the fuck am I? You think I'm hanging out at the damn hospital on a Saturday night for fun, when I have a beautiful woman waiting for me?"

Which reminds me, I should let her know I likely won't make it tonight.

"The chick from the rodeo?" Booger pipes up from the bed.

I shoot him a pointed look. "Woman, and yes. Let me be clear, if you were anyone other than family to me, I'd be knocking on her door right now and not sitting beside your sorry ass in a hospital bed."

Despite the shitty situation he got himself into, Booger wears a satisfied little smirk when he lays his head back on the pillow and closes his eyes. I'm hoping this time he may have gotten the message. He looks to be sleeping, maybe from medication he's getting through the IV, and I'd love to get hold of Lindsey but I don't want to disturb the kid.

I send her a message instead.

Sorry. I'll have to take a rain check. Will call later.

I haven't heard anything back by the time they finally come to get Booger for surgery, so I head outside to give Lindsey a call and grab myself a coffee. It sounds like it might be a long night.

My call is immediately bumped to voicemail, meaning either she's talking to someone, or her phone is turned off. I leave a quick message.

"Hey, it's me. I'm still hung up in Cortez. One of the kids I

had with me at the rodeo got hurt and was taken to the hospital. Looks like I'll be here a while. Anyway, you're probably sleeping already so I won't bug you anymore tonight."

Shit, and now I can't get the vision of Lindsey in bed out of my mind.

This is going to be a really long night.

———

Lindsey

I wave at the Mazda Miata's retreating taillights before I shove my key in the lock.

That was a fun night, and not only because Wapi showed up, although those few kisses definitely set the tone. I actually enjoyed the atmosphere, the excitement. I may have winced a few times, and definitely squeezed my eyes shut when one of the bull riders got his hand stuck in the ropes as he was getting bucked off, but I got swept up in the collective adrenaline surge.

That's probably why I'm so tired, stumbling into the house. I toss my purse on the bench, quickly tap my code into the alarm panel, and throw the deadbolt on the front door. Next, it takes me a good five minutes and a whole lot of cursing to get my feet out of my brand-new boots. Then I walk into the living room and flip on the standing lamp next to the couch, it makes the house look cozy and I'm not a fan of having overhead lights on everywhere.

Since I don't really know when Wapi will get here—he was already gone when we left the grandstand—I rush upstairs to freshen up and throw on some lounge clothes. I have no idea what his intentions are for tonight, but I want to be ready for whatever happens.

Halfway up the dark stairs my feet suddenly fly out from under me. I land on my hip and do a face plant, hitting my forehead on the edge of a step, as I slide down a couple of them. What the hell was that? It felt like I stepped on something but I have no idea what that would've been, it's too dark for me to see anything.

In the bathroom I strip out of my clothes, and check my face and hip in the mirror. The bruises from last weekend haven't faded much yet and are now a yellowish green. I'm sure in a day or two I'll be sporting some new ones in blue and purple, making for a colorful palette. My forehead is already sporting a bit of a goose egg where I hit the step. *Lovely*. I guess I could try to cover it up with makeup, but I doubt it's going to do much to hide it, so I simply don't bother.

After washing my face, and other odds and ends, I pad into the bedroom reaching for the switch, only to realize the light on my nightstand is on. I must've forgotten to turn it off, which is funny, because I could swear I'd left without making my bed, yet it appears I did remember to do that.

I leave my hair loose, dress into a French terry lounge set I found at Target last summer, and head back downstairs, this time a little more careful where I put my feet.

I'm actually a little nervous. I feel I'm on the precipice of a vast unknown territory. I try to look ahead but can't get a clear picture. It's like standing on the edge of nowhere and feels a little unsettling.

Wine will help. I make a beeline for the cabinet in the dining room to grab a glass and a new bottle. Other than the occasional glass of wine—and the rare beer I had earlier —I'm not a big drinker. However, this is the third bottle I'm opening in the six days since I came back from Denver. I'm not sure what that implies, but it seems to coincide with shifts in my otherwise predictable and balanced life this past week.

With my glass in hand, I walk into the pantry, hoping I have some of those cheese crackers left. Sadly, I don't, but I do find a small individual pouch of chocolate-covered raisins. That should work, it's all grapes. I set my loot on the small side table in the living room, fetch my phone from my purse in the entryway, and get comfortable in my oversized barrel chair.

Immediately a new message from Wapi pops up and, as I read it, my mood drops. Disappointment replaces the buzz of anticipation as I shake half the pouch of chocolate raisins in my mouth. Damn him once again.

Will call later?

He gives me whiplash. A few hours ago, he gave me a hard time about being home tonight so his majesty could drop by, and now he's going to be a no-show? Well, screw him, maybe I won't be home if he ever calls.

"I just dropped you off," Anika points out when she answers my call.

"He's not coming."

"Wapi," I clarify snippily. "He said he was going to come and now he's not. He sent a message; said he'd *call later*."

"Okay—"

"He's got another think coming if he assumes I'm going to sit here like some kind of whimpering wallflower waiting by the phone for his call."

As if conjured, I hear the beep of an incoming call. A quick glance at the screen shows Wapi's number.

"That's him now," I share with Anika, and I add stubbornly, "I'm not going to answer."

"But how do you know—"

I'm rambling, I know it, but I can't seem to stop the tumble of thoughts.

"Am I wrong? He gets me all ramped up, I'm looking forward to it, and then he blows me off. I don't want to get caught in a situation where I'm little more than a doormat, there for someone else's convenience. Not again. Is it me? Do I have—"

"Okay, that's enough," Anika firmly interrupts. "Now you listen to me. You are overreacting because you're disappointed and scared Wapi has the power to make you feel that way. You being pissy at him says nothing about him and everything about the massive suitcase of baggage you drag along with you. So, cut it out, call the guy back, and give him a chance to explain what happened, like an adult."

Abruptly the call ends and I sit there for a moment, stunned at the dress-down I just received at the hands of my happy-go-lucky friend.

Ouch. I feel about three feet tall right now.

I reach for my wine and take a hefty swig. My phone vibrates on my lap, notifying me of a voicemail message. I listen to it on speakerphone. It's Wapi, and his message makes me feel even smaller.

As much as I hate to admit it, I totally overreacted like some kind of drama queen. I'm so grateful Anika slapped some sense into me before I made myself look like an absolute bitch.

First taking another fortifying sip of wine and setting my glass aside, I dial Wapi's number, holding my breath until I hear the sound of his voice.

"I thought maybe you were in bed already."

"Not yet. Tell me what happened," I prompt him.

"The short version is that Booger—he's one of the club kids—managed to get his arm caught between a bull and a fence and is now in surgery to screw all the broken pieces back together."

"Oh no, that sounds horrible. I'm so sorry."

"He'll live, and hopefully has learned his lesson. Anyway, one of the guys came to pick up the other two boys, but I'll be staying here tonight. I hope you understand."

Ashamed, I close my eyes and bang the heel of my hand against my forehead.

I intended to say "of course", but instead, "Ouch," comes out.

"What did you do?" he asks instantly.

"Oh, I just accidentally bumped my forehead. When I got home, I rushed upstairs and fell, slid down a few steps, and banged my head. Got myself a couple of new bruises and an impressive goose egg on my forehead."

"You should get yourself checked out. You could have a concussion."

"I'm fine. Honestly. Just a little accident-prone, I guess. Nothing a good night's sleep won't fix."

I can hear him groan.

"Are you okay?"

"I'm fine," he assures me. "You should get some rest. I'll be in touch tomorrow."

"Okay. Goodnight, and best of luck for the boy," I add. "I hope he's going to be okay."

"Night, Princess."

Feeling a whole lot better, I tuck my phone in my pocket, grab my glass and the empty wrapper, and take them to the kitchen. Then I go back to turn off the lamp in the living room and head up the stairs.

I'm several treads up, when my right foot touches something slippery. I glance down but can't see a damn thing, it's too dark. Fishing my phone from my pocket, I turn on the flashlight and shine it down.

It's difficult to see against the dark grain of the wood, but there appears to be a damp spot on the right side of the tread. I reach down and touch it. It feels oily. Then I sniff my fingertips. It smells just like my orange furniture oil.

Hmm. Since I, for obvious reasons, am not in the habit of using it on the treads, I guess I could've spilled some carrying it upstairs. However, it's been well over a month, probably more, since I've polished my bedroom furniture.

Weird.

CHAPTER
NINE

LINDSEY

As I approach the field I wave at Paco, who is standing by the dugout.

He's probably giving Mason some last-minute instructions, blatantly ignoring the coach standing five feet away. For a guy who, for most of his life, was able to avoid any kind of commitment other than to his club, Paco sure took to parenthood like he was born for it. That, and he makes my mom ridiculously happy.

He lifts his head when I walk up to him, tugging down my ball cap.

"Hey, Linds."

"Morning, Paco." I rise up on my toes to kiss his stubbly cheek. Then I peek around him to where Mason is sitting on the bench, tying his cleats. "And how's our mini-Ronaldo doing?"

Mason looks up and shoots me a gap-toothed grin. He lost his incisors a few months ago, but the adult teeth have only just come peeking out.

"Ronaldo is history, it's Messi now," he corrects me.

"Ah, I see. I stand corrected."

I know zero about soccer, other than the ball has to go into the net. The only reason I'm familiar with those two particular soccer players is because they're not hard to look at. Plus, I have a healthy appreciation for what soccer does for the gluteus maximus.

"Where's Mom?" I ask Paco.

He points over to the bleachers, where I catch sight of her pacing back and forth in front of the bottom bench. She's clearly talking to someone.

"Any way you can talk her off that damn phone?" he wants to know. "Stubborn woman doesn't know how to slow the fuck down. Pardon my French."

"You know Mom, but I'll do my best." Then I lean over the fence to ruffle my brother's hair. "Break a leg, buddy."

"Linds! You say that to an actor, not a soccer player," Mason returns, mortified.

"Oops, sorry!"

I wink at Paco as I start walking toward the bleachers, hearing his deep chuckle behind me. Mom acknowledges me with a quick nod but continues to pace and talk.

It doesn't take me long to figure out she's talking to Cassie Wilson, and Mom is not happy. Something about our client, Brian, not having access to his daughter, but it sounds like the guardian ad litem won't budge. Not surprising and probably standard procedure any time abuse is suspected. Especially when the child in question doesn't have the developmental capacity to give some clarity on the situation. Cassie's first responsibility is to ensure the girl is safe, and right now that means from her father as well.

Mom knows that too, but her job is to fight for her

client's best interests. She's a passionate lawyer—dedicated —so she fights, gets carried away, and digs in like a damn terrier, hoping to wear her opponent down. Except Cassie isn't really her opponent, and instead of gaining ground, she may be alienating an ally.

When the whistle sounds to announce the kickoff, I've had enough.

Walking up behind her, I snatch the phone from her hand and immediately pivot out of her reach, walking away from the stands.

"Cassie? Hi, it's Lindsey, Mel's assistant. I'm so sorry to interrupt."

"Oh…hey, Lindsey." She sounds startled.

"Like I said, I'm sorry to interrupt, but Mel forgot she had a previous engagement and she's already late." When I look at my mother over my shoulder, she's wearing a mutinous expression. "Unless something comes up that needs to be addressed before tomorrow morning, is it okay if she catches up with you then?"

"I had a few things lined up for today as well, so yeah, that works for me."

I end the call and sit down beside Mom, handing her back her phone.

"You do know where your paycheck comes from, right?" she snaps, shoving her phone in her pocket.

"You bet," I return without hesitation. "And I'd like those paychecks to keep coming, but they won't if you end up giving yourself a stroke or a heart attack. The doctor said for you to slow down. Making work-related phone calls that get your blood pressure up on a Sunday morning at your son's soccer game does not qualify as slowing down."

"Hear, hear," Paco mumbles as he approaches with a

tray of coffees he must've picked up at the concession stand.

"Watch it," Mom warns with a growl.

She's pissed, but not pissed enough to refuse the coffee he hands her. He hands over mine with a wink that doesn't escape my mother. Paco is a good man, but before he digs himself an even bigger hole, I change the subject.

"Hey, did you hear about the boy? The one who got hurt by the bull?" I ask him. "You wouldn't happen to know how he is, would you?"

"Booger? Yeah, I heard about it this morning when I called the clubhouse. Dumb kid. He needed surgery, but should recover. Lisa mentioned he should be released either later today or tomorrow."

"Boy? What boy?" Mom wants to know. "Who are you talking about?"

I let Paco explain.

"Poor kid," she observes before turning to me. "Hey, weren't you there last night? At the rodeo?"

"I was, but I had no idea that happened until after I got home."

She narrows her eyes on me the way she used to when I was a teenager. She's like a human lie detector. "Then how did you find out about it?"

I recognize the trap I inadvertently opened myself, but there's no avoiding it.

"I spoke to Wapi."

"Really…last night? After the rodeo? Did you call him or did he call you?" she pelts me with questions.

"Mel, this isn't the Spanish Inquisition," Paco cautions under his breath.

I shoot him a grateful smile. "It's okay."

"Hey," she digs in with a shrug. "I'm just curious,

because I could've sworn she hated him a few days ago. It's hard to keep track."

"I didn't hate him. I *don't* hate him. It's complicated."

"No, it's not," Mom fires back. "It's simple, but you're just too chicken and letting your past dictate your future."

Yeah, my mother doesn't hold back and isn't afraid to call it as she sees it. Regrettably, she's also frequently right.

As she is in this case, and I really don't like acknowledging it. So instead, I ignore it and go back to her original question.

"I called him, after he messaged me. We had plans he had to cancel because of the accident. That's all."

"That's all," she echoes, giving me a look from under her eyebrows.

"Yup."

"So you're dating him," she pushes.

"Mom, please. I'm not sure what we're doing yet. Can we just leave it at that?"

She raises her hands, palms out, but when she picks up her coffee to take a sip, I see a smile play on her lips.

My mother is something else.

———

Wapi

I wrap a towel around my hips and walk into the bedroom to find Paco sitting on the edge of my bed.

Mika was back at the hospital earlier this morning to relieve me. When I got back to the clubhouse, I only stopped to give Lisa an update on Booger's condition before beelining it for my bedroom. I fell asleep the moment my head hit my pillow. I was out cold until one thirty.

Paco must've come in while I was in the shower, which is a bit of a surprise. We tend to be pretty respectful of each other's space, unless there's an emergency. Given that he's calmly sitting on my damn bed, I doubt an emergency brought him here.

"Why don't you come right in," I tell him, turning my back.

I pull open a dresser drawer and grab a clean pair of jeans. Then I drop my towel and bend over to step into my jeans.

"Jesus Christ, Wapi," Paco grumbles. "Goddammit, I'll never be able to unsee that."

I tuck my junk away and close the buttons on my fly, then I pull a shirt out of the drawer and turn around to face him.

"Think how easily that could've been avoided with a knock," I point out, slipping the shirt over my head.

"Yeah, yeah. Trust me, I'll think twice next time, but this is important."

"What is?" I ask, bracing myself with my ass against the wall as I wrestle on a pair of socks.

"Lindsey."

He doesn't need to say more, I know exactly why he's here. Not sure how, but he's clearly picked up on the fact things have changed between me and his stepdaughter.

"Right," I respond by way of confirmation, crossing my arms.

"Brother, what are you doing? Or wasn't it you who skipped town when that girl was still recovering in the fucking hospital after being abducted and tortured four years ago?"

The question is not unexpected, nor is it undeserved. I did do that, and I'm prepared to own up to it but don't get the chance. Paco continues his tirade as he surges to his feet and starts pacing the room. Every word hitting it's intended target.

"You told me you weren't the right guy for her and here you are sniffing around again. Dammit, Wapi, I watched that girl struggle to come back from the blow you inflicted. Especially since she'd barely had a chance to get over the first asshole who'd eroded her trust and self-confidence, and coincidentally, that cocksucker has also just decided to have another go at intimidating and badgering her."

What the fuck? How come I didn't know about this?

"Who?" I bark. "What's his fucking name?"

"Right, that tells me you have feelings for her but you had those four years ago too. So that brings me back to my original question; what are you doing? It took Lindsey forever to smile again, brother, so forgive me if I invaded your goddamn privacy, but I'd like some reassurance this time you're sure you know what you're doing. Because I'm telling you right now, if you hurt Lindsey again, you will live to regret it."

I'm gonna fucking do everything in my power to make sure no one and nothing can harm Lindsey, and that includes me.

"Need his goddamn name, Paco," I grind out.

He stops in front of me, one hand rubbing his neck as he studies me for a moment.

Then he shares.

"He was briefly in Denver last weekend at the wedding Lindsey was there to attend. He's Lindsey's friend's cousin.

You may want to keep that in mind before you go chase the guy down. Mel says Linds took care of him herself. You know Mel, she'd be the first to go after him and rip him a new asshole, if she had any doubt her daughter couldn't handle herself. Just to say, laying harm on the guy, as tempting as it may be, could do more damage than good."

I'm already pulling on my boots, but Paco blocks my way when I grab my keys and try to leave.

"Did you hear me?"

"I heard you," I confirm.

He grins in my face. "Then where the hell are you off to in such a hurry?"

I shoot him a level look.

"Lindsey's."

He shakes his head. "She's not home, brother. She took Mason to Durango Doughworks to celebrate his win and load him up on sugar. Like the kid needs it," he adds mumbling, but I'm already halfway out the door.

————

The boy sees me first.

"Hey, Wapi."

I ruffle his hair but my eyes are on his sister, who is watching me with a guarded expression from under the brim of her hat.

"Hey, Mase. I hear you won?"

I slide into the booth next to Lindsey, slip my hand under the table, and give her knee a squeeze.

"Yeah, we won the whole tournament. I scored two goals in the final," the boy boasts with a grin.

Reaching my free hand over the table, I give him a fist bump.

"Good stuff, kid." I glance at the empty plates on the table. "You didn't leave any for me?"

"Can I get you guys anything else?"

A girl, maybe fifteen or sixteen, holding a coffee pot interrupts us. Her eyes are on Lindsey.

"Just the bill, please," she answers.

"And what about you? Is there anything I could get you?" she directs at me with a flirty smile.

My stomach suddenly growls, reminding me I haven't eaten anything since pulling a small bag of peanuts from the vending machine at the hospital sometime in the early morning hours.

"Yes, actually, a black coffee and half a dozen donuts to go." I pull a few notes from my wallet and hand them to the girl. "That should take care of any outstanding bills."

"You didn't have to do that," Lindsey mumbles as the waitress collects the empty dishes from the table and leaves to fill my order.

When I don't respond, she turns to the boy. "Why don't you go wash your hands and we'll get going."

Mason's no fool and glances from his sister to me and back, before getting out of the booth. As soon as he's out of sight, I twist in my seat to look at Lindsey.

"Paco alerted me you were looking for me." She taps her phone, which is face down on the table. "He also said you know about Galen."

I take in a breath to reply when she lifts a finger.

"Just so you know," she continues, "I'll be having words with my stepfather about interfering in my life, as well-intentioned as it may have been. As for my ex, I don't wish to waste another moment, another word, thought, or spark of energy on that man. I may or may not share that story with you at some point, but that will be by my choosing, and it's not now."

I hear her, but what she's asking of me is counter instinctive and not easy. However, if I read anything into what little information Paco provided, her asshole ex was at the very least controlling, and I'd be no less if I force her to talk about what happened. That definitely won't get me the girl.

"What are your plans after you leave here?" I ask instead, and see it catches her by surprise.

"I'm dropping Mason off at Mom and Paco's and then I'm heading home to finish up on some laundry. Why?"

"Well, I plan to check in with Booger, who should be on his way back to the clubhouse with Mika as we speak. Then I intend to pick up a few groceries and come over to your house to cook you dinner. Do you like salmon?"

"You're gonna cook for me?" She treats me with a little smile.

"That's the plan."

"Okay. And I love salmon."

I tip her chin up and drop a kiss on her lips.

Of course, Mason picks that moment to saunter back to the table.

"Gross." He makes a face to illustrate how he feels about that. "Hey, does that mean my sister's your old lady?"

CHAPTER
TEN

LINDSEY

The moment I walk in the door, I toss my ball cap and purse on the bench and race upstairs.

I have no idea how long I have before Wapi shows up, and I'm in serious need of a shower.

Last night I was so wiped, I forgot to set my alarm and when I woke up this morning, I had to hustle to make it to Mason's game in time. The tangled mess of hair I woke up with has been hidden by my hat all morning, but it needs a good washing and some serious work. So do some other parts of me.

I'm not in the shower long, but I feel much better when I walk into my bedroom, wrapped in a towel. Instead of wasting time blow-drying my hair, I opt to twist it up in a bun. It can dry like that and I'll have my hands free to maybe do a little tidying.

Starting here in the bedroom.

My rushed exit this morning left the room a bit of a mess and I haven't opened the curtains in days. I don't often bother with those, because I just have to close them again at night, and it's not like I spend a lot of time here other than sleeping. Don't get me wrong, I have no idea how tonight is going to go—I'm not even sure I'll be ready to make that step—but I like to be prepared for all eventualities, which means opening the curtains.

I get dressed, and then straighten my bed, briefly contemplating if I should change the sheets before dismissing it. I washed them on Friday. Scooping up the few clothes I tossed on the bench at the foot end of my bed, I head into the walk-in closet and flick on the light. *Dammit.* I forgot about the burned-out bulb. Something else to add to my list but it'll have to wait, I don't feel like hauling out the stepladder.

I give the bedroom a final once-over, making sure it's tidy. Despite the ample light now streaming in through the window, it looks pretty clean. Then I grab my wet towel and dirty clothes and head downstairs, where I toss the clothes in the laundry room next to the kitchen.

There are only a few dishes in the sink I quickly wash by hand. I'm generally a tidy person, although I try not to get hung up on a little mess. There was a time the sight of even a speck of dust, or having anything out of place, would have my anxiety shoot through the roof. Years of conditioning had done that. Nowadays, I'm a little more relaxed and am okay leaving some things until I get to it, but it still makes me feel a little uneasy.

By the time my doorbell rings, the house is in good shape and I've been trying to kill time going through some of the pictures I took of Thildy and Ben's wedding. My camera bag has been sitting at the bottom of the closet in the entryway since I got home last weekend and hadn't been touched. Since my friends will be back from their honeymoon in just a week, and I'd really like to have at least a good selection ready for them to see, I figured I'd get started on that while I waited.

But now I toss my laptop aside, launch myself off the lounger, and rush to the door. At the last moment I stop to peek through the spy hole to confirm it's Wapi. I take a deep breath in, reach up to pull the clip out of my hair, and give it a ruffle with my fingers before I open the door.

For a moment I hesitate, freaking out a little when I see him standing there, two brown bags in his arms, and a hint of a smile in his eyes.

"Is it okay if I come in?" he asks dryly.

I realize I'm blocking his way and hustle aside.

"Shit, yes. Of course. Sorry."

"You didn't have your deadbolt set," he comments as he walks past me toward the kitchen.

"Sorry?"

He tosses me a look over his shoulder. "Your front door, you didn't have it deadbolted."

I stop and swivel around to the front door.

Hmm. He's right, I didn't have the lock on. I'd been in a rush when I ran in the door earlier and clearly forgot.

In fact, now that I think about it, I never deactivated the alarm either.

I glance over to the keypad and notice the light is green. Shit, I must've forgotten to arm it this morning when I ran out.

"Lindsey? What's wrong?"

I hear Wapi walk up and turn to face him.

"Nothing. You're right, I forgot to turn the deadbolt when I got home. My bad."

I'm pretty sure if I were to admit I never had the alarm

on either, he'd be giving me an earful instead of the stern look he tosses me.

Stupid. It's not like me to forget things like that. More evidence I'm a little off my game this week.

I plaster on a smile and try to move by him but he hooks an arm around my waist, pulling me flush against him. I instinctively lift my hands to his chest and tilt my head back.

"Hi," he rumbles, one side of his mouth twitching.

"Hey." I sound a little breathless.

Holding my eyes, he takes my hands and pulls them up higher. Then as I slip my arms around his neck, he slowly runs his hands down my body, ever so slightly brushing the curve of my breasts in passing. It's enough to draw a whimper from my lips, which is quickly swallowed by his kiss.

The man can kiss.

His arms band around me at the small of my back, nearly lifting me off my feet, and making sure there isn't an inch of space between his body and mine. I hang on to his neck for dear life.

I'm not exactly small at five foot six and a hundred and sixty-three pounds, but in his arms—the way he holds me —I feel like freaking Tinker Bell, dainty and delicate. Even the way he carefully sets me back on my feet makes me feel cherished, although I'm not too thrilled when he lifts his head.

"Tamari salmon, roasted asparagus, and smashed baby potatoes sound okay?" he asks, walking back to the kitchen where he starts pulling groceries from the bags.

"Sounds amazing. I'm surprised you picked asparagus though." I note the six-pack of beer and the bottle of red he pulls from the second bag. "It's a pretty risky choice. People either hate them or love them. Like pineapple on pizza," I suggest.

"Pineapple on pizza should be outlawed," he states firmly as he puts his beer in my fridge. "But I know you like it, the same way I know you like asparagus."

He closes the door and turns around, eyes on me, before he adds, "I pay attention."

———

Wapi

Every so often I glance over at Lindsey, who is curled up in that chair again.

She offered to help me in the kitchen but I told her I had it handled, and suggested she relax while I got dinner going.

She looks engrossed in whatever she's doing, occasionally mumbling to herself, which is pretty cute.

Using the back of a spoon, I squash the slightly cooked potatoes and sprouts on a baking tray, drizzle them with oil, and toss them with freshly ground black pepper and sea salt. Next, I slide the tray into the oven, beside the large salmon fillet already cooking. Then I check the counter to make sure I have everything ready, before giving my hands a quick wash, and joining Lindsey in the living room.

She hears me approach and drops her head back, turning to the side to look at me.

"It already smells good," she shares.

I brace my arms on the back of her chair and bend down to brush her lips. I catch sight of a picture of a woman's profile on her computer screen. It's black and white, beams of sunlight playing over her features. There's no mistaking the sheer joy on the woman's face.

"That's a beautiful shot," I comment. "Yours?"

I remember the camera bag when I picked her up from the airport last week.

"Thank you. It's hard to take a bad picture of Thildy, she's a beautiful soul."

To illustrate, she flips through a few more images of the same pretty woman, who looks more like a wood nymph than a bride. In some pictures she's joined by a tall man, who looks at her like she hung the moon and carries the answers to the universe.

"Thildy is my best friend, and that's her Ben," Lindsey clarifies.

"You're good," I tell her, as I round the chair.

"It's just a hobby," she dismisses with a shrug, but the fleeting, pleased look doesn't escape me.

Plucking the computer from her hands, I deposit it on the side table and lift her out of the seat. Then I sit down with her on my lap.

I like the feel of her there, but I recognize the error of my ways when she starts to shift restlessly. My cock is hard and her movements are sweet torture, skimming the line between pain and pleasure. I lift her up and shift my hips slightly so there's enough room for her to fit snuggly beside me. There's only so much temptation I can resist.

"Those look like more than just a hobby, Lindsey," I volunteer, trying to stay on subject as I stroke her smooth leg with my hand. "They could easily be professional. Have you ever considered doing this as a career?"

Her bitter laugh is unexpected, and I think it caught her off guard too. She glances at me a little sheepishly.

"I might have at some point," she admits. "But after my second year of college, I switched from a major in photography to a two-year paralegal program."

"Why?"

She shrugs, looking down at her hand plucking at the armrest.

I can't imagine she would, but still I ask to be sure, "Did Mel put pressure on you?"

"No." She shakes her head firmly. "Mom is all about following our own path."

Then a light goes on. "Don't tell me it was that guy."

"Okay, then I won't," she comments glibly.

I lightly pinch the skin of her leg. "Smart-ass. But since we're talking about him—"

"You were," she corrects me. "I was doing my best to avoid it."

I grin at her tart response; I love her edge.

"Fair enough. So can I safely assume he hasn't bothered you since?"

"Yes. Oh, and before you ask, I did talk to the Denver PD yesterday."

Just then the timer on the oven goes off.

"Keep talking," I tell her as I lift up her legs and slide out from under her.

She ends up following me into the kitchen, and while I pull the salmon out of the oven and loosely cover it with tinfoil to settle on the stove top for a few minutes, Lindsey relays her conversation with the Denver detective.

"Did this Detective LaVine tell you anything about this ongoing investigation?"

She shakes her head. "No, other than to warn me not to discuss anything we talked about with anyone."

Red flags immediately go up. It could be the detective is

simply being cautious, *or* he has reason to think someone other than the police might have an interest in Lindsey's run-in with the dead guy. Meaning, she could be at risk.

"You're talking to me," I point out.

"Yeah, but you already knew and you're the only one who does. I haven't mentioned anything to anyone else."

"What about Mel or Paco?"

Keeping quiet about it seems like the smart thing to do, however, telling her mother or Paco should be safe. Plus, it wouldn't hurt to have a few more people close to her alert.

"Are you kidding?" she exclaims, grabbing the wine bottle to top up her glass. "I'm not going to worry Mom unless it's absolutely necessary. She's had to worry about me enough over the years. And Paco? He'd just overreact. No," she answers with a firm shake of her head and a pointed finger aimed at me. "I'm not telling them and neither are you."

At least not until after I talk to, not only Bill Evans, but especially Detective LaVine. I need to know if there is a valid risk for Lindsey, and if so, how serious to take it.

"Fine," I concede for now.

However, if law enforcement tells me she could be at risk, I'll have no qualms about breaking my word and telling whomever necessary to help keep her safe.

"But you have to promise to be better about locking the damn door and setting the alarm, whether you're here or not," I add.

"Okay, *Dad*," she mocks with a roll of her eyes.

Hardly, even though it's tempting to put her over my knee.

"There's nothing fatherly about what I want to do to you, Princess," I warn her, catching the flash of heat in her eyes.

EDGE OF NOWHERE 111

Fuck yes, I can't wait to go there. But that won't be tonight. Oh, I plan on doing a little more than kissing, but I'm not going to rush this. Now that I finally have my head on straight about this woman, I'm not about to risk fucking it up.

There is too damn much at stake.

———

"Wapi…"

My scalp stings as her fingers tug sharply at my hair.

"Mmm," I hum around her nipple.

"More…"

She's pulling at the back of my shirt, and I feel my resolve fraying. Already I have her top half gloriously naked, my mouth on her tit, and my hand down the front of her stretchy pants. That's further than I intended to take it tonight, but Lindsey is not shy about what she wants and is currently grinding herself on the two digits I speared her with.

I can't retreat now, not without getting her off, or she'll have my balls, I'm sure. I rock my fingers deeper, press my thumb on her clit, and close my teeth on her nipple for a gentle bite.

She goes off like a fucking rocket on the Fourth of July. The walls of her pussy clamp hard on my fingers as she bucks in my hand. I want to feel her come on my cock like that so hard it hurts.

Releasing her nipple, I glance up at her blissed-out face as her body goes slack against me. Gently, I remove my hand from her pants, smiling at her small whimper of displeasure. Her eyes are mere slits, but when I slide my fingers—slick with her cum—in my mouth, her nostrils flare wide. She likes that.

I groan when her taste overwhelms me, tempting me even more. But rather than throw my resolve out the window, I cling to the very last thread of it as I push myself out of the chair. I grab her shirt from the floor where I dropped it, and help her cover herself up.

"You're leaving?" she asks as I grab my wallet and keys from the side table where I threw them. "Now?"

"For now," I correct her. "But I'll be back, one little taste of you is not enough. Not even close."

She follows me to the door where I kiss her deeply.

"Lock up behind me, please."

I catch her eye roll and wait outside the door until I hear the lock slip in place. Only then do I walk to the driveway.

I'll be going to bed with her scent in my nostrils, her taste on my lips, and my hand wrapped around my dick.

CHAPTER
ELEVEN

WAPI

"Not bad."

Ouray comes sauntering up to where I'm talking with Heidi outside the Jooba Yoga Studio. She's the studio's manager.

"Heidi," he mumbles in greeting before indicating the new barriers and gate. "Guess that solves the problem. Good call, brother."

"Thanks, but it's not done and I'm afraid it doesn't solve all our problems. We still have that asshole across the street to deal with."

Agitated, I run my hand over my beard. It's been a shit show so far, and I've been wasting time on fucking George Macias when I had other plans for today.

"The cocksucker..." I belatedly realize Heidi standing beside me. "Pardon my French."

She waves me off. "I've heard worse."

"Anyway," I continue to explain to Ouray. "He had the cops and a city inspector here first thing this morning,

ordering the contractor to stop pouring the permanent footings until a permit was produced. I had to stop by city hall
to get that shit resolved but by the time I got back here,
Nick had left already. And now he doesn't have time to
finish it until fucking next week."

Of course, I'd just been about to leave when Heidi called
me over because, apparently, she's been having some
plumbing issues in the studio. So, it looks like I'll be stuck
here longer playing handyman. *Awesome*. But I've bitched
to Ouray enough. It kind of defeats me taking the weight
off him.

He claps me on the shoulder. "So it gets finished next
week. Big deal. Pick your battles, brother."

"Right. What are you doing here anyway?"

"Had business in town," he says, darting a glance at
Heidi before his eyes come back to me.

I realize belatedly he probably had a radiation treatment. I nod my understanding.

"Was gonna see if Bubba wants to grab some lunch," he
continues, jerking a thumb over his shoulder toward the
gym. "Tag along if you want."

"Nah, I've got some stuff to take care of."

Hopefully the issues at the studio won't take me that
long because I still haven't had a chance to get in touch
with Bill Evans.

I did shoot Lindsey a message this morning to check on
her. She sent one back a few minutes later, saying she was
fine but in a rush to get out of the door. I reminded her to
set the alarm, to which I received a rolling-eye emoji.

She definitely doesn't make it easy for anyone to look
after her. Fiercely independent, which means I'll have to tread
lightly. She probably wouldn't be happy if she knew I plan to

talk to law enforcement, but she doesn't need to know. At least not unless what the cops end up telling me makes it necessary to take some security measures, because I have no intention of letting Lindsey get hurt on my watch again.

I watch Ouray head for the gym before I follow Heidi into the yoga studio.

It's almost four by the time I get on my bike, the smell of shit still clinging to me. What I'd hoped would be a simple job with a plunger ended up with me having to take the entire goddamn toilet up to get to the blockage. Some stupid idiot had tried to flush a towel. Heidi mentioned she'd had problems with that toilet for the past week, so I assume that's how long that crap had been stuck in there. Had I known it would be so involved, I'd have called a plumber. At least those guys get paid to poke around in shit piles.

I could've had a shower at the gym next door, but that would've defeated the purpose since I don't have a clean change of clothes with me, and driving all the way to the clubhouse is not an option.

I called and caught Bill Evans, who was just walking out of the police station. When I told him it was urgent for me to talk to him, he said he'd wait for me in the parking lot. I turn my bike in that direction and hope the wind will blow most of the stench off me.

He gets out of his vehicle when I pull my bike in beside him.

"Jesus, man. Did you just crawl out of a septic tank?"

Bill buries his nose in the crook of his elbow.

"Don't get me started. Just stay upwind of me," I suggest.

"What's so urgent?" he wants to know.

"Are you aware Lindsey got a call from a Detective LaVine?"

He nods, a guarded look on his face. "I am."

"He warned Lindsey not to talk to anyone. Why is that?"

"It's an ongoing investigation."

He shrugs, like that's supposed to be an answer. He might as well have said "no comment." It's about as informative. But I do notice he looks a little uneasy.

"Come on, man. There's gotta be something more you can tell me. Is there a concern for her safety? If so, why? A warning without qualifying the threat is like tying a blindfold on someone and telling them to drive safely."

"Fuck me," he curses under his breath. "Okay, I'm going to give you a hypothetical scenario and you can draw your own conclusions. Let's say there's a suspicion of large-scale development fraud, and the police have an inside informant who promises to deliver them tangible evidence. Evidence that will make their case against certain major players. Now, let's suppose the informant never shows up with the evidence, and is found dead the next morning. His pockets are pulled inside out and his phone and wallet are missing. Later it's discovered his car and his apartment have been broken into and tossed."

"They're looking for something," I suggest.

Evans shrugs. "Possibly. Or maybe they found it and want to make sure there's nothing else incriminating. Or maybe one thing has nothing to do with the other."

"Or," I add the option. "They may have watched him collide with Lindsey and suspect it was more than an accident."

"Unless…" Evans suggests. "They don't know about the

collision but could find out if the incident for some reason became public knowledge."

So noted. A lot of variables but the overall storyline makes me very uneasy and one term he used stands out.

"When you say *major players*, what are you talking about? Big money? Big power? Big politics? Organized crime?"

"Hypothetically?" He starts walking to his vehicle and pulls open the driver's door, turning his head. "Take your pick."

Jesus.

————

Lindsey

"And?"

I follow Mom into her office, where she dumps the leather satchel she uses to carry her files on her desk.

"Julie Menzies apparently snapped when she found out from her lawyer she wouldn't be able to see Samantha." My mother walks around her desk and drops down in her chair, leaning back. "She ended up firing the lawyer, and in today's hearing, she got into it with the judge and was slapped with contempt of court. She's going to spend forty-eight hours in jail and will have to pay a fine. It's starting to look better and better for Brian."

Mom wears a satisfied grin but I still feel a bit conflicted.

"I guess that's good," I concede, planting my hip on the corner of her desk. "Although I do hope Samantha's mother gets her shit together. I'm sad for the girl, it's no fun to be stuck between battling parents. She's going to need them both if it turns out her stepfather has been molesting her."

My mother scrutinizes me with a pensive expression on her face. She can probably guess I'm thinking of the years of acrimony between my parents after their divorce. My father was a fair-weather father, which to me translated into a fun parent, albeit a mostly absent one. When he did show up, he would spoil me rotten and take me on adventures. I was a kid, I loved my dad, and it was hard to know Mom was always mad at him. As an adult, I know she had every reason to be pissed, but as a kid it made me feel torn.

At the time Dad was a NASCAR driver and traveled a lot. We didn't really have much of a relationship through my teenage years, and he was not even on the radar while I was in college or with Galen after. Since then, however, my father retired, moved to Montana, and we've reconnected, talking once a month or so. Not much, but something.

Which reminds me, I haven't talked to him in a while.

"You're right. Let's not forget that poor girl," she agrees, before adding, "Are you coming down with something? You look tired."

I'm sure I do, I didn't sleep much and had bags under my eyes this morning. There's no amount of concealer that could completely hide those.

"I don't know. Maybe a cold?" I suggest, pushing myself up from the desk. "I have that draft agreement done on the Harris file. Did you want to look it over now, or first thing tomorrow?"

"Tomorrow." She checks her watch. "I'm meeting Paco and Mason at the Backyard Edge for an early dinner. First day of summer break for Mase, and the boys are leaving tomorrow on their annual camping trip."

Paco and a few of his Arrow's Edge brothers started this

tradition a few years ago, taking their kids camping for a few days to herald in the summer. The club is big on family, and part of me wishes I'd grown up in an environment like that. I'm glad Mason gets to experience it though.

"Why don't you join us?" Mom interrupts my thoughts. "Unless you have other plans?"

No other plans, and since I haven't been in touch with Wapi since early this morning, I'm not sure whether he has any that involve me, but if that's the case, he should've communicated them to me.

"Sure. It's been a while since I've had their brisket."

I follow Mom to the restaurant, where Paco and my brother are already waiting. I wave at Sophia, restaurant manager and wife of Tse, who happens to be one of my stepfather's good friends and part of the Arrow's Edge MC family. Tse and Sophia also live just up the hill from Paco and Mom's place. They're neighbors.

The Backyard Edge is one of the MC's Durango businesses. These days Arrow's Edge is securely woven into the fabric of this town. Over the past fifteen years or so, the club has grown into a substantial contributor to the local economy. It wasn't always that way, and some of the older guard in town still look at the club with suspicion, but even those stick-in-the-muds can't resist the draw of the Backyard Edge's brisket they serve here. The place is about packed, even this early on a Monday night.

"Excited about summer?" I ask Mason, ruffling his hair as I take the seat beside him. "Your camping trip?"

As much as he pretends to duck out of the way of any kind of public affection, the barely contained smirk on his face tells me he's not as averse as he'd like us to believe.

"It's okay," he mumbles nonchalantly.

"Whatever…" I bump his shoulder. "Well, in that case

you stay and help Mom at the office and I'll go camping with Paco."

I grin at his little-boy snicker. For all his aloof, teen posturing, he's still a little kid.

"You in a tent?" he mocks me.

"Yeah, why not?"

"Bugs. Duh."

"I can handle bugs," I lie. It wouldn't be the first time I call Paco over to my house to kill a spider.

"As if," Mason returns. "You were afraid to get into the treehouse last time because of a daddy longlegs."

"Yeah, well, he was looking at me funny," I joke, and Mason dissolves into giggles.

Our bantering is interrupted by one of the servers approaching to drop off our drinks. While we wait for the food, Sophia stops by the table for a chat. This time, when asked if he's looking forward to his upcoming trip, Mason nods enthusiastically.

As per usual, the brisket is melt-in-your-mouth. I inhale my food and, like every time, end up eating too much.

"God no, no dessert for me. I wouldn't know where to put it. I'm going to need to sleep off this food coma," I announce.

No one else wanted any either so Paco settles up, refusing to take money from me, which I'm still grumbling about as we walk out to the parking lot.

"Just don't get eaten by a bear or anything, okay?" I tease Mason, hooking an arm around his neck.

He does his best to avoid the kiss I'm trying to press to his head, but he still manages to wrap his spindly arms around me for a hug.

"Be careful, okay, buddy? Listen to Dad and don't do anything stupid."

I tell Mom I'll see her in the morning and wave at Paco before I get into my SUV.

I've barely pulled out of the parking lot when Wapi calls.

"Where are you?"

"Hello to you too," I return sharply. "I had dinner with my family and now I'm on my way home. Why? Where are you?"

"Damn. I'm on my way to Alamosa with Honon."

"Alamosa?" I echo.

"Yeah. We got a call about a young kid out there in trouble. I was hoping to catch you at home to tell you I'll be out of town in person, but you're obviously not there."

"I'll be there in ten."

"Couldn't wait around, Linds."

"No, of course not," I reassure him, dismissing the pang of disappointment I can't help feel.

"If everything goes smoothly, we should hopefully be back some time tomorrow, but I'll touch base with you in the morning regardless."

"Okay."

"And, Princess? Do me a favor, don't forget to set your alarm and lock your doors the moment you walk in."

I roll my eyes, realizing instantly he can't see my reaction.

"I can look after myself, Wapi," I remind him.

He comes back with, "Humor me. Don't make me worry about your safety when I'm hours away should something happen."

His tone is sharp but I recognize the plea underneath. Now that I'm older and wiser and see things more clearly, I realize Wapi may well still be carrying some guilt about what happened to me four years ago. Not that he has anything to feel guilty about, other than perhaps the disappearing act he did after.

I think it's inherent with these men, this need to protect what they care about, and I don't doubt Wapi cares about me. I know he's worried.

"Okay, I promise I will be extra careful."

Ten minutes later I walk into my house, close and lock the door, and tap my code into the alarm panel. For good measure I shoot Wapi a text.

Locked in. You can relax.

Immediately my phone buzzes with an incoming response.

Thanks, Princess.

Kicking off my shoes, I pad barefoot to the kitchen. It's a beautiful night and I plan to enjoy the remaining daylight with a book and a drink on my deck.

Maybe that'll help me sleep since I didn't sleep that well last night. I was restless, rolling around, and when I would finally doze off, something would startle me awake, only to start the whole rolling around thing over again. I ultimately gave up around three thirty, turned on the lamp on my nightstand, and read until I saw the sun come up. Hopefully, I'll do better tonight.

I pour myself a glass of wine, and then run upstairs to grab my book from the bedroom. It's where I left it on the nightstand, right beside the lamp I apparently forgot to turn off this morning.

I swear, for someone who thrives on being organized and in control, I've become a bit of a mess. Forgetting things is a bit annoying, but a bit of loosening up isn't all bad. Last night with Wapi I willingly threw control out of the window and the result was heavenly.

The alarm beeps twice to alert when I open the back door. It's gorgeous out, not too warm, and I opt for the lounger. Setting my glass, phone, and the book on the small wicker table, I sit back and take in the view. The rear of the house faces the hillside which, at this time of year, is still coated in the soft green of early summer. The sun sets at the front of the house, but the mornings provide me with gorgeous sunrises back here. Both early in the morning, but also at this time of night, it's not unusual to see deer, an occasional elk, or even a bear back here.

I take a sip of my wine, and am about to open my book when my phone starts ringing. No caller ID, so I contemplate letting it go to voicemail. But what if it's that Denver detective?

I quickly answer, and immediately realize my mistake.

"Alone tonight?"

I ignore the shiver running down my spine.

"What do you want, Galen?" I snap.

He's quiet for a few beats, making me feel very uncomfortable, and I wonder if I should hang up. Before I have a chance to, he speaks, making every hair on my body stand on end.

"You're looking beautiful tonight."

CHAPTER
TWELVE

WAPI

"Check the shed."

It's unlocked. I poke my head inside to find a lawn-mower, rakes, and a wheelbarrow, but no sign of ten-year-old Zach Burkhart.

"Clear," I call over my shoulder at Honon, who is on hands and knees checking under the back porch.

We've been going through the neighborhood around the nursing home where Zach's grandmother saw a glimpse of him outside her window earlier this morning.

It's a shit show.

Ms. Burkhart explained she'd raised her grandson from the time he was five when her daughter died of a drug overdose. Last week, the old woman fell and broke a hip. She spent a couple of days in the hospital before she was moved to the nursing home. Not only is she facing a lengthy recovery, but she's losing her small, two-bedroom apartment and won't have a home to return to, even if she recovers.

She was pressed to come up with a solution for Zach, who's been by himself at the apartment since she got injured. Ms. Burkhart shared she grew up in foster care herself and had little faith in the system. She'd heard of Arrow's Edge through an old friend of hers, who had told her the club took in boys. She'd lost touch with her friend over the years but had kept the club's phone number.

The friend's name was Lettie Hendricks, later became Lettie Wells, or better known to us as Momma.

The poor woman had not even been aware, when she called the clubhouse and spoke with Lisa, that Momma has been gone for quite a few years already.

Unfortunately, last night when she tried to tell the boy we were on our way to pick him up and take him back to Durango with us, he took off before she had a chance to explain things. We've been checking the apartment, as well as a few places his grandmother told us he might be at, but weren't having a lot of luck. Then this morning Ms. Burkhart called to let us know she was pretty sure she'd seen Zach outside her window, ducking into the trees.

We've been going around the neighborhood all morning, trying not to stand out like sore thumbs. The old woman doesn't want to involve the police, afraid if they end up finding her grandson he'll be swallowed up by the system and she'll never see him again.

"He can't be far," Honon mumbles when we sneak back into the alley behind the houses.

"Night's falling, maybe we should go back to the apartment? See if he shows up there?" I suggest, following Honon down to the end of the block.

"I don't know. I don't think so, I have a feeling he's not going to take that chance. Especially knowing we're likely out looking for him."

He's probably right, but I'm at a bit of a loss where to go from here.

We stop when we hit the sidewalk and when I glance to my right, I can just see the parking lot of the nursing home. Beyond it the street ends at a narrow strip of green space bordering the Rio Grande, which runs right through Alamosa.

"How deep is the river here?"

"Don't know. What are you thinking?" Honon asks, stepping up beside me to follow my line of sight.

"I'm thinking Zach won't want to be too far from his grandmother. She's the only safe place he has." I point in the direction of the river. "There's a golf course just on the other side of the river. You can probably see the nursing home from there. Lots of places to hide during the day and no one's around at night. In the dark, you'd be able to see the lights on at the home."

Honon starts moving.

"Let's go see if we can find any shallow areas."

We find it just north of where the river meanders. A section where the water is shallow enough for a bank to form halfway across to the other side.

"What do you think?" Honon asks, but I'm already pulling off my boots and socks and rolling up my jeans.

"Wouldn't it be easier to grab the truck and drive around?"

"Scared of a little water?" I tease him, grabbing my boots as I dip a foot in the surprisingly cold water.

I ignore his grumbles and while he's still taking off his boots, I start crossing the Rio Grande. It sounds more adventurous than it really is, and I end up with one wet pant leg when my foot slips on a rock, almost landing me on my ass in the river. Behind me Honon chuckles until I hear splashing and a muttered curse.

Dark sets in, and we are quickly losing light out on the golf course. It doesn't help the fairways and greens are surrounded and separated by treed areas. There is no easier way to do this than just walk, keeping an eye out for hiding spots.

"It's like a fucking needle in a haystack," Honon grumbles. "We should've waited for daylight. My fucking tank's running empty, brother. Gonna need some sleep at some point. Not like we got any last night."

While he is complaining loudly behind me, I hear a rustle overhead and just catch a glimpse of a sneaker disappearing in the leaves.

The kid is up in the damn tree.

I stop and turn to face Honon, which means the kid should just be able to see the back of me.

"Are you going to be bitching and moaning all night?" I ask Honon, trying to signal him with my eyes. "You're gonna drive me up a tree."

I know he clues in when he puts his hand on his neck, and pretends to stretch it, rolling his head back and from side to side.

"Twenty minutes," he feigns pleading. "A catnap, that's all."

He sits down under the tree, his back against the trunk.

"Fine, I'll come back for you in a bit," I play along.

I keep moving through the woods, occasionally glancing back, as I find myself a vantage point from where I can keep an eye on the boy.

I've been waiting, shielded behind a tree trunk maybe fifty feet or so away, for close to twenty minutes. I'm starting to wonder if the kid is going to stay up in that tree all night, when I see some movement. If not for the boy's white shoes, I might have missed him.

When his feet touch the ground I'm already on the move, but Honon is closer and faster. He's already holding the struggling kid.

"Relax, Zach, we're here to help," I assure him. "Why don't we go see your grandma and get this cleared up. Okay?"

———

"I can look after myself until you get better, I promise."

When I glance over at Honon, I note he's having as hard a time listening to the boy's pleas as I am. Zach's face is red and tears are streaming down his cheeks, and his grandmother is fighting to keep her composure.

"Zacharia, my boy, I'm not gonna get better if I have to worry about you alone out there," she tells him on a sob. "I'll call you whenever I can."

"We'll get you a cell phone," Honon promises the boy. "You'll be able to call whenever you like."

Ms. Burkhart is now full out crying and can't do much more than nod. It's time to bring this to an end.

"Zach," I draw the boy's attention. "Your grandma needs rest, buddy, and we should get on the road."

I briefly contemplated Honon's suggestion to get a hotel for the night and head home in the morning, but I'm eager to get back to Durango. Even if Honon is making me drive his damn truck, and it'll be after three in the morning by the time we get back to the clubhouse.

"Will I see you again?" he asks his grandmother.

Seeing her inability to answer, I do it for her.

"Of course you will. I'll drive you myself."

After tearful hugs and promises to be in touch, Honon is finally able to coax the boy into the hallway, but the woman holds me back.

"Thank you for stepping in," she mumbles, dabbing at her tears with a tissue. "That about killed me."

"We'll look after him," I promise. "He'll be well taken care of."

"I hope so." She points a shaking finger at the door. "'Cause that boy is my life."

————

Lindsey

I'm pissed. I'm so angry I'm giving myself heartburn.

I admit, Galen had me freaked out last night. He made it sound like he had eyes on me and I went running inside like a scared rabbit. At least I managed to tell him, "Fuck you," and hung up the phone before I knocked over my wineglass in my rush to get inside. Of course, when I had a minute to think about it, I realized nothing he said actually proved he could see me, or had even seen me at all.

I'd reacted as if I'd never spent four years building myself back up from the decimated pieces he left of me. That's what got my blood boiling. It's the same kind of games he always played, but I'd hoped I'd be wiser now.

It's fucking embarrassing I'm apparently not.

Another virtually sleepless night had me snapping at Mom this morning. Of course, that doesn't fly far with my mother, so we spent most of the day avoiding each other. She'd already been out of sorts because Paco and Mason left on their camping trip this morning. I guess I could've told her about my insomnia and Galen's stunt last night, but with her high blood pressure I didn't want to risk stressing her more.

So, we didn't talk, and she never came back to the office after lunch. More reasons for me to lie awake and fret tonight. To add to that, Wapi shot me a text earlier that he's stuck in Alamosa a bit longer than anticipated and he'll let me know when he gets back to town. I end up staying late at the office, tackling a few projects I've been putting off, just to keep my mind occupied and my body busy, hoping to tire both out.

Unless I can get some rest, things are just going to keep spinning out of control, and I'm done with it. Tonight, I'm going to sleep, come hell or high water.

When I get home, I head straight upstairs to change into my running gear. I haven't been for a run in almost two weeks and I can tell. Running is a great way to get rid of some of the tension, especially if you follow it up with a nice warm bath.

That's next on the list. A light meal, a bath with a glass of wine—or maybe I should skip the wine and take some melatonin instead—and then to bed with some mindless TV in the background.

Back downstairs I dig up my running shoes from the hallway closet, and tuck my driver's license, a credit card, and a small canister of Mace in the small pocket in the waistband of my leggings. I find my earbuds in the pocket of the running jacket where I'd left them coming home from Denver, and grab my Apple watch from the charger on the TV stand. I strap it on, pop in my earbuds, and as an afterthought put on the jacket and zip it up. It can get cool out once the sun is down.

Finally, I turn on the standing lamp in the living room, pull up my favorite playlist, set the alarm, and close the door behind me before setting off down the street.

The sun is already disappearing behind the ridge when I turn onto the trail running behind the neighborhood. It's actually a network of trails, with several loops heading both north, into the hills, and south toward Fort Lewis College. I pick a four-mile trail that starts on the hillside, while I still have light, and then by the time it gets too dark will loop back through the neighborhood. It shouldn't take me much more than forty-five minutes or so, even at a leisurely pace. I'm not doing this to win any races.

I'm not even ten minutes into my run when the music stops. A quick check reveals my watch ran out of juice. Already. It's an older model but I only use it for running so I don't have to carry my phone, so I just haven't bothered upgrading it. I guess I'll have to now; it's barely holding a charge.

Unfortunately, without the music, it takes me a while after that to find my rhythm back, but once I do my thoughts settle down. The fresh air, the wonderful silence, and the steady thump of my feet impacting the hard ground serve to put me into the zone. A state of trance where my heart beats and my breath flows to the cadence of my surroundings, and were time has no meaning.

My feet follow the trail by rote, and before I know it the night is dark and I'm turning up my driveway. Stopping in front of the door, I lean over with my hands on my knees to catch my breath, noting a few aching muscles. That warm bath is going to feel so good. Straightening up, I blow out a big breath and reach for the door.

A strange smell hits me when I walk in and automatically sniff my armpits. I definitely reek, but I don't think that's it. I move to the alarm panel to disarm it, noticing too late the light is already green.

Before it has a chance to register, I hear a moan and automatically swivel around to the source of the sound.

Behind the couch in my living room I catch sight of a man, lying in a pool of blood.

I'm frozen. There's a fucking man in my living room. Is he dead? I can't wrap my head around what I'm looking at. Is this some kind of hallucination? Except the man moans again, turning his head in my direction.

Galen?

Something is wrong. Something is really wrong.

I curb my instinct to go check on him and am already starting to retreat to the entryway, when I hear the sound of footsteps above me. My heart stops and I reach behind me, searching for the door, but my eyes stay fixed on the stairway, and the man who suddenly appears.

I have never seen him before and I'm not about to wait around to find out who he is.

Instead, I whip around, yank the front door open, and bolt down the street.

CHAPTER
THIRTEEN

LINDSEY

I run, fueled by fear and adrenaline.

There's not much thinking involved, but as luck will have it, I had the presence of mind to turn toward the college instead of into the hills. I don't actually have a plan, other than to get away as far as I can.

I live on the fringe of town, nothing but mountain behind me, and neighbors spaced out along my street. I'm running down the middle of the street through my neighborhood, afraid to look behind me. Instead, I peel my eyes for anything or anyone who could help, but I don't see a sign of life. Not until I turn the next corner.

Halfway down the street, a silver SUV is turning into a driveway on the left side. My chest is tight with panic, as my body automatically veers in that direction, and I run up on the narrow sidewalk. A vehicle means people, and people means safety.

From a distance I watch as the driver's side door opens and am about to call out, when I hear the squealing of tires behind me. A quick glance over my shoulder reveals a black pickup making a sharp turn into the street. Something about the way the vehicle is encroaching on the wrong side of the road as it speeds up has the hair on my neck stand up.

I pump my legs faster, running full speed toward the confused man who just exited his car.

"Watch out!" I hear him yell.

Then a loud kathunk, followed by a grinding sound behind me. I don't need to look to know the pickup just climbed the curb and is targeting me.

The blood rushes in my ears as I make a sharp left, spotting a narrow passage between two houses. Blindly darting down the dark alley, I shoot up a quick prayer I'm not getting myself trapped. When I get to the back of the houses, I see the narrow path continues between the backyards, opening up to the hillside in the back.

Thank God.

Before I turn right at the back of the fence, I risk a quick glance back. A man is just coming out from between the houses. I can't really tell if it's the same guy I saw back at the house, but that stops to matter when splinters of wood explode inches from my face.

My feet are already eating up ground before my brain registers I'm being shot at. I run on instinct, my body zigzagging along the back of the yards, ducking out of the way of any bullets. I only heard two more, but by now I'm panting loudly and my heart is pounding so hard, I can't hear anything else.

A few yards up ahead a copse of trees border the property line, so I force my legs up a gear and aim for the much-needed coverage they provide. I can't afford to stop moving though. I have no idea who these people are but if they're not afraid to start shooting at me in the middle of a residential neighborhood, I have to believe they are not particularly worried about hurting innocent bystanders. I can't put other people at risk, so I keep running, in the hope someone will have called 911.

Once in the trees, I finally risk a glance over my shoulder, catching sight of the man who is clearly struggling to keep up. It fuels a new surge of energy but that doesn't last long. By the time I see the lights from the college athletic fields in the distance, my legs are burning. The pain is one thing, I can run through it, but there's nothing I can do about the heaviness setting in and slowing me down.

I remember reading somewhere about a softball tournament being held at Fort Lewis, and I wonder if that is this week. It would explain the lights and the full parking lot near the diamonds. If I can make it down there, I might be able to get lost in the crowds, hide in the bathrooms. Hell, I might even be able to find a police cruiser controlling traffic.

I'm not sure how I managed, but I finally reach the college grounds. I'm barely running now, just getting one foot in front of the other as I move toward the athletic fields. I pull the hood of my jacket over my head to cover my blond hair and occasionally check behind me, but I no longer can see my pursuer. Oddly enough, that doesn't bring me relief. I'd almost rather know where he's at, because I don't for a second believe he's given up.

It looks like people are starting to leave, a few vehicles pulling onto Rim Drive as I walk onto the parking lot. My aim is the pathway leading from the parking lot to the small building that houses locker rooms and bathrooms, where I see a group of people.

Passing by a few buses parked along the edge of the

parking lot, I catch sight of a black truck pulling in on the other side. It looks exactly like the one trying to run me down earlier.

My God, he must've gone back to pick up his vehicle and somehow still managed to track me here.

I quickly turn my back, hoping he hasn't seen me, and start retracing my steps. But about two hundred feet away, walking on the sidewalk along Rim Drive, is the man who shot at me.

There are *two* of them.

With nowhere else to go, I duck in between two buses. The one on my left has the doors to the storage compartments open, a few large bags on the ground beside it. I don't need to think twice and climb into the one closest to me.

It's pitch black, so I have to feel my way around. I touch several bags that were already loaded up and, without making too much noise, crawl over to get behind them. I press myself in the farthest, darkest corner, and curl into a ball, making sure no one looking in will be able to see me behind the duffel bags.

Then I close my eyes and do something I'm not prone to…I pray.

Time becomes abstract when you don't have a watch or a clock to measure it by. As a result, I have no concept how much time has passed when I hear someone walking up outside. Next thing I know there's a rustling noise and then a loud thud, reverberating around me, as another big bag is tossed into the storage compartment, and then another.

Then I hear talking.

"Excuse me, did you happen to see a woman, blond hair, wearing athletic clothes, purple jacket, baby-blue running shoes."

I can't place the voice, and I'm not really able to detect

any strong accent either, although if I were to venture a guess, I'd say Midwest.

"Who wants to know?"

That must be the bus driver, or whoever was loading the bags. Bless him.

"FBI. Special Agent Miller. So did you? See the woman?"

Wait. FBI? The FBI is shooting at me?

"Have you looked around? Every damn woman you see is wearing athletic clothes, half of them are blond. What's this woman done anyway?"

The response he gets chills me to the bone.

"Murder. The woman is wanted for murder."

————

Wapi

I'm grateful when I finally turn into the driveway to the compound.

That was a long fucking drive and Honon and the boy were asleep before we hit the mountains. Since I didn't exactly have anyone to talk to so I could stay alert, I ended up drinking not only mine but Honon's large coffee we picked up on our way out of town. I'm fucking bouncing in my seat now and I seriously need to piss. Then I want to have a shower and make sure the kid is settled in for the night.

Next, I'm heading over to Lindsey's and I don't give a flying fuck it's a little after three in the morning. Closer to four by the time I get there, I guess. I texted her before we hit the road to let her know we got the boy and are on our way back, but she never got back to me. It's possible she was already in bed and turned off her notifications, but I still want to make sure she's okay.

I'm not surprised to see lights on in the clubhouse. Lisa is probably already in there waiting for us. Honon gave her a heads-up and knowing Lisa, she set an alarm. She's Momma to all the kids, and exactly the kind of person Zach needs when he wakes up and finds himself in a strange place.

What does surprise me is seeing Ouray's SUV parked in front of the clubhouse at this hour. I have an uneasy feeling in my stomach, but that could also be the coffee. Pulling into the spot next to him, I catch sight of Ouray watching me through the window.

That uneasy feeling turns into a knot. Definitely not the coffee.

I turn off the engine and check the back seat to find the boy still asleep. So is Honon beside me.

"Honon, wake up."

I slap him on the shoulder and he finally startles awake.

"What?"

"I think there's trouble," I inform him, jerking my chin at the window where our president's face is just visible. "I don't know what's going on but I'm gonna run inside, if you can take care of the boy."

I drop his keys in the cupholder, get out of the truck, and head inside. Not only is Ouray in the clubhouse, Brick is sitting at the large dining table with Lisa.

"Need a word, brother," Ouray announces. "Let's go in my office."

Yeah, this is not good.

"First, I need to piss like a racehorse."

I head to the back to use my own bathroom. I want to

splash some water on my face and grab a clean T-shirt. I'm feeling a bit rank and I have a feeling this night is not over yet.

I do my business, wash my hands and face, and dump the shirt I was wearing in the hamper. Then on my way out I grab a fresh shirt and am pulling it over my head when I walk into Ouray's room. Brick is standing by the door, his arms folded over his chest. Standing up from his seat on the couch is Bill Evans.

"Okay, I'm not getting good vibes here. What the fuck is going on?" I glance from Brick to Ouray, who is leaning on his desk.

"Have you heard from Lindsey tonight?" Evans asks.

My blood turns cold as I glance from face to face, not liking the solemn expressions on any of them. Immediately I pull my phone from my pocket and check my messages.

Nothing.

"Not since earlier today. Or yesterday. Whatever. Why are you asking?"

"Last night dispatch received a report of a pickup truck chasing after a running woman. That was followed by several calls from the same neighborhood about shots fired. Lindsey's neighborhood."

Oh, fuck no. This is not fucking happening.

"Lindsey?" My voice sounds more like a croak.

"We're looking," Evans confirms my fears.

The reason for Brick's looming presence by the door becomes evident in the next moment when I try to exit the room. Not that I'm about to let him stop me from looking for her.

"Wapi, stop!" Ouray bellows when I try to shove past Brick. "Sit your ass down and fuckin' listen. There's more."

More?

I swing around on Ouray, thrown by how poorly he looks, but only for a moment before my fear finds a way out in anger.

"How long has she been gone, huh? Why didn't you fucking call me?"

"And then what, brother? You guys were already on your way home. Not like there's anything you coulda done except maybe kill yourself on those mountain roads in the goddamn dark," he snaps back.

I drop my head and press the heels of my hands against my forehead. I want to fucking scream.

Instead, I take in a deep breath and turn my eyes to Evans.

"Tell me."

He gives me an assessing look before he nods and continues.

"I sent officers to check her house. Door was open and we found a guy in the living room, in a pool of blood."

It's like a punch to the gut. I'm having a hard time computing everything.

"What the fuck? Dead?"

Evans shakes his head. "Last I knew he was hanging on, but he's got two holes in his body and lost a crapload of blood, so I'm not sure for how long."

"Who was it?"

He pulls out one of those little notebooks and flips through it.

"Guy by the name of…Wagner, Galen."

"Son of a bitch," I spit out, shoving my fist in my mouth and biting my knuckles to stop from putting it through a wall.

"You know him?" Ouray asks.

"Lindsey's asshole ex."

"Did you ever meet him?" Bill wants to know.

"No. Paco gave me his name. He mentioned the guy recently started bothering Lindsey again, and—"

"Again?" Evans interrupts.

"Did I mention he's an asshole? What the fuck was he doing there?"

"We're hoping he'll eventually be able to tell us. Or Lindsey," he adds as an afterthought.

"She wouldn't have invited him in, that's for damn sure," I promise him. "Not a chance."

"Do you know if she owns a firearm?"

"Lindsey? You're kidding me, right?"

I shoot an incredulous look at Evans but he just raises an eyebrow.

"You think she shot him? Lindsey?" I bark out a bitter laugh. "Then who the fuck was trying to run her down in the street?" I shake my head, agitated. "This is bullshit. Has anyone even talked to Mel?"

"Luna is already with her," Ouray answers. "Paco is on his way back, and the other brothers will break up camp in the morning and roll out."

"Tony Ramirez should be there right now, talking to her. We're not sitting still, Wapi," Bill volunteers.

"Glad to hear it, but I don't plan to sit still either." I challenge each of the three men with a glare. "So don't try to stop me."

CHAPTER
FOURTEEN

LINDSEY

I startle awake with a loud clang and it takes me a second to realize where I am.

It quickly becomes clear as more and more light comes into my dark corner of the luggage hold.

How the hell did I not only get myself in a situation like this, but manage to sleep through it better than I have for days?

It seemed like a good idea last night to hide in here, but then the door suddenly closed, shutting me in the dark. I panicked, especially when the engine started, the sound down here so loud I could feel the vibrations through my body. The only thing that kept me from yelling out, as I felt the bus start moving, was the knowledge somewhere out there were a couple of men, claiming to be FBI, who clearly would not think twice about killing me.

Somewhere along the way I fell asleep, my arm curved under my head serving as a pillow, and the rumbling of the engine becoming white noise to block out everything else.

My bladder is about to explode and my arm is numb. I'm dying to move, but I'm waiting for a moment when whoever is unloading takes a break. Which I hope they'll do, otherwise I'll be left with the choice to either make a run for it, or have the door closed on me and stay locked in here for God knows how long.

I can see it's light outside, which could mean it's daytime, but maybe it's artificial light. I can't tell, so I have no idea what time it is, or more importantly, where the hell I am. It feels like I've slept for a while, so it's possible I'm not in Durango anymore. The only way to find out is to get out.

That moment comes soon enough, when I hear someone call out, "Hey, is this yours?" followed by footsteps moving away from the bus. I don't allow myself to think and scramble over the few bags I was wedged behind. Unfortunately, the arm I slept on is virtually useless, and I'm blinded by the lights after however many hours in the dark, so I'm not exiting the bus soundlessly.

I hear another, "Hey!" but this time it's yelled, and I know it's directed at me. I dart a squinted look in the direction of the voice and see someone rushing toward me. I turn the other way and run.

Feels like I've landed in the middle of some kind of thriller, but I have no clue what the plot is. I know someone is after me, but I have no idea who, or why. So, until I have a chance to sit down and figure out what the hell is going on, I can't afford to trust anyone.

As I dart around the corner of a brick building, I glance behind me to see if the driver is coming after me, but I don't see him. I do catch a glimpse of several other buses so I'm guessing this is some kind of bus station or depot. This is definitely not the Durango Transit Center though.

The street I end up on is not familiar at all, and I scan every sign and building to get a bead on my location. I find it painted on the window of a coffee shop which boasts the name Best Brew Santa Fe.

Wow.

That is not next door.

I keep moving to get as much distance between myself and the bus, while I try to come up with a plan of action. Last night I did a quick inventory and know all I have on me is an Apple watch with a dead battery, a pair of earbuds, my driver's license, and a credit card. I'm so grateful I have a habit of slipping those last two in my pockets in case of an emergency when I go running. They will come in handy.

I'm a little worried using my credit card though. If those men actually are FBI, it wouldn't take much for them to flag any credit card use. I think I'm going to have to—I'll need money—but I have to be smart about it. I need a plan in place, then find an ATM, pull out the maximum cash advance I can get, and then quickly move to a different location.

One thing I'm going to need is one of those pay-as-you-go phones, I don't think they can trace those. I'll need clean clothes, food, a toothbrush, and then I have to find a safe place.

But first I need to find a bathroom, I can't hold it anymore.

Across the street is a large plaza with big box stores, including a Walmart. I should be able to get whatever I need there, a bathroom first and foremost.

The relief is incredible, and I groan audibly. A snicker sounds from the stall to my right.

"Sorry," I mumble.

I hadn't been aware someone was there.

"No need to apologize. I completely understand the feeling." It sounds like the voice of someone older. "These days I'm afraid to go anywhere unless I know it has a bathroom I can access."

The voice is followed by the flushing of a toilet. I briefly consider waiting until she's gone, but to what end? The woman doesn't know me from Adam and I'm looking pretty non-distinct, although I might be a little smelly. By the time I flush and exit the stall, she's already drying her hands.

She's an older woman with a sweet smile that reminds me of my mother, and for a moment I'm tempted to ask for a hug, because I could really use one right now. The poor woman would probably run from the bathroom screaming assault, and I really don't want to draw attention to myself.

"Have a wonderful day," she offers me over her shoulder as she walks out.

Only a brief and superficial interaction, but after she leaves, the bathroom feels lonely. I wish I could talk to my mother, but I'm not sure that's a good idea. I plan to let her know I'm fine, but Mom is going to insist I talk to the cops, when I'm not yet sure I want everyone to know where I am. Including law enforcement. My mother trusts in the law and those who are sworn to uphold it, but I prefer to be sure.

I shop for what I need, having it already in a cart so that I can haul my ass out of here once I pay for it. Next, I find the ATM machine, pulling out $2,500 dollars, which is about the thirty-five percent of my credit card limit I can take out in a cash advance, and pay for my purchases.

By the time I get outside, I have the beginnings of a

plan, and use my new phone to call for a taxi. Then, while I wait, I dial a number I'm glad I have memorized.

Twenty minutes later I walk up to the Delta desk inside the airport terminal and buy a ticket.

————

Wapi

"Find her."

Mel looks haggard—showing the toll this is taking on her—and at the same time determined, but I can see she's battling to keep that stiff upper lip.

I bend down and drop a peck on her cheek, because an actual hug might break the fragile hold she has on her emotions. Fuck, it might break mine.

"I will."

I know better than to promise anything unless it's a sure thing, but I need to make myself accountable and she needs to hear it.

I step outside, bolstered by her faith in me. Luna is just tucking away her phone and turns to me.

"Anything?" I ask, hoping the call she went outside to answer has offered some news.

"Wapi, the DPD is already out there looking, going house to house through the neighborhood. My team is being briefed as we speak and then they'll be on the case. You need rest, I know you do."

"Appreciate the concern, Luna, but what I *need* is to be out there looking for Lindsey," I assert firmly. "Now, was there anything helpful you can share?"

She sighs, lightly shaking her head. "The vehicle trying to run her down was a black Silverado extended cab. Officers were able to collect the feed from several security cameras in the neighborhood, and one of them showed the truck climbing the curb. It also shows a woman darting through a front yard and ducking in between two houses, and a man getting out of the passenger side of the truck, chasing after her. The truck is seen heading south, toward the college."

Then that's where I'm heading.

I step around Luna and start down the steps when she calls my name. I stop and turn around.

"That was almost eight hours ago. She could be anywhere."

Maybe, or she could be hiding out in the trails going down the hill from the college. Maybe she's waiting for daylight. It would be the smart thing to do; wait for the streets to get busy. It's coming up on six now, and already starting to get lighter.

"Call me if there's anything new," I tell Luna.

She shakes her head, clearly not happy with me, but that doesn't stop me from joining Honon, who is waiting for me by the bikes.

He insisted on tagging along. I told him to stay with the boy—we're the only friendly faces the kid knows—but Ouray vetoed it and insisted Honon stick with me. Lisa assured me she had Zach, and with a promise to the boy we'd be back, we came straight to Mel and Paco's house.

"Fort Lewis," I announce, swinging my leg over my bike.

Honon nods his understanding and is right behind me when I turn my bike toward the road.

I'm still fucking sick to my stomach, but I feel better

actively doing something. As much as it scared me to hear her phone was found in her kitchen, smashed to pieces, it gives me hope to know she managed to get away. At least that's what I'm telling myself.

She is smart, resourceful, and I know she can run like the wind. She *has* to be okay, I'm simply not willing to consider anything else.

I slowly cruise Rim Drive, around the college, keeping my eyes peeled for any sign of a black truck or Lindsey. We passed one police cruiser turning onto E 8th Ave heading downtown, and another was sitting in the main parking lot by the library, but nobody is out here pounding the pavement. The campus looks pretty abandoned.

I pull into a small parking lot near the entry to the trail and get off my bike. Honon pulls in beside me.

"What are we doing?"

I point down the hillside. The vegetation is mostly brush, no taller than six or seven feet in places, but it's pretty dense.

"I think she may have come in this direction. I wanna search the trails. Not hard to hide in there."

"That's literally a needle in a haystack, brother," Honon complains.

"Beats sitting around with my finger up my fucking ass waiting for someone else to find her," I snap. "You can stay or go, I don't care, but if I don't keep moving, I'm gonna lose it."

Honon lifts his hands.

"Then let's get moving."

———

The sun is up and Durango is well awake when I return to my bike.

Honon left a while ago, needing to get home to help Emme get the kids up and ready for the day.

I've had a call from Paco, who just arrived home and wanted to know if I had anything to report. I got in touch with Evans and Luna, but neither had more to report. Either that or they weren't sharing.

To be honest, I wasn't holding out much hope after the first forty-five minutes, but having no fucking idea where to go next, I just kept looking.

But a few minutes ago, I noticed a listing on the electronic information board up at the sports field of the championship game of some kind of softball tournament, which apparently took place last night. There would've been a lot of activity I would imagine.

Then just now I caught sight of a campus police car drive by, and that got me thinking about the security cameras all over campus. The cops or the FBI probably got a hold of those already.

I brush myself off and swing a leg over my bike, pulling out my phone.

"Like I told you earlier, I'll call you when I have something," Luna starts.

"Did anyone pull the security feed at the college?"

It's quiet on the other end for a moment.

"I'm pretty sure Green's got it back at the office. Why?"

"Because it looks like there was some kind of softball game here last night. That would mean a crowd."

"That's right. Four Corner State Softball Championship was being held here. Yesterday was the last day." She pauses. "Let me call Green and find out whether he's gotten around to checking that footage. For either the truck or Lindsey," she adds.

"I have a better idea," I propose. "Why don't you tell him I'm on my way. If she was in that crowd, I'm more likely to pick her out."

It gives me something constructive to do, and I'll be right at the source should any information come in.

I don't wait for her answer—I'm pretty sure she'll try to disavow me of the idea anyway—and end the call. Then I start my bike and head for the FBI office on Rock Point Drive.

I have to cross downtown Durango, which is slow going at this time of the morning. I make a quick stop to pick up a coffee and a box of donuts. I haven't had a damn thing to eat since last night, and I burned off most of my adrenaline on the trails at the college. I need fuel.

I ignore several calls from Luna and by the time I get to the FBI office, she's already there, waiting for me.

And she's pissed.

"You're a pain in my fucking ass, Wapi."

Suddenly the adrenaline I've been coasting on drops, taking all the fight out of me, and is replaced by bone-deep fatigue.

"Linds is out there, Luna."

"And we're all working on finding her," she replies, the sharp edge gone from her voice.

"But she's mine to protect."

She sighs, shaking her head as she steps aside and waves me in.

"*Jesus*. You guys and your overinflated sense of responsibility."

CHAPTER
FIFTEEN

WAPI

"There."

Luna scoots her chair over and leans in to see where I'm pointing on the screen. You can just see the front of the pickup truck come into view. The time signature at the bottom of the screen is five past ten.

"Are you sure it's them?"

"Keep watching."

On the screen, the truck can be seen slowing down and then stopping, a figure getting out at the passenger side. It's pretty clear he's a man, dressed in dark clothes and wearing a ball cap. He crosses the road and walks toward the parking lot, appearing to scan the crowd starting to exit the sports fields.

"He's looking," Luna comments.

"Yeah, and watch the truck, it's heading toward the other parking lot entrance."

It's the third time I'm watching this, but this time I'm

paying particular attention when the man on foot suddenly stops. I freeze the feed.

"He's seen something."

I nod in agreement. "He's looking toward the parked buses."

I zoom in on the area and forward the video in slow motion. The angle is not ideal, the camera is located on a lamppost on the opposite side of the road, and you can't really see in between the parked buses.

"Jasper," Luna calls out to the FBI's tech specialist. "Is there a feed for the parking lot by the ball diamonds other than the one we're looking at?"

"Give me a sec."

While he looks, I rewind the clip again, this time letting it run. You can see the guy from the truck walk up to the back of one of the buses, appearing to talk to someone just out of sight on the side of the bus, not in view of the camera. A few minutes later he reappears on the path toward the pavilion before disappearing altogether.

"Roosberg," I hear Luna answer her phone. "He is? Good. Stay there and as soon as he wakes up, make sure you're the first one in the room with him. Call as soon as you know more."

Then she turns to me. "Wagner is out of surgery. He should survive."

I can't decide whether that's a good or a bad thing. It's hard to imagine Lindsey responsible for putting those holes in him, but who the hell knows?

The AirDrop screen pops up asking to accept a new video file.

"That's from a camera outside the locker rooms," Green clarifies from the other room.

"Here, let me," Luna says, bumping me out of the way with her chair and pulling the keyboard toward her.

In no time she has both feeds up on the screen, side by side, and forwards both to the ten-o-five time stamp. The new camera view hides part of the parking lot behind the trees, but on the left side of the screen you can see the front of the parked buses. From this angle you look through between the two remaining buses to the parking lot beyond.

Slowly she forwards both feeds through time. You can't see the truck from this new angle, however, right before the suspect freezes and appears to stare at something on the original video, you can see a figure darting between the buses and disappearing into the open cargo hold of the first bus in line. The same bus where the man later goes to talk to the driver, who is loading bags into that same baggage hold.

The bus eventually drives off, taking the stowaway along.

"Son of a bitch," I mutter, feeling overwhelming relief and a healthy dose of pride.

I'm still not sure what the fuck happened at her house, but Lindsey wasn't exaggerating when she said she could take care of herself.

"New Mexico license plate," Luna announces, leaning close to the computer screen where she's zoomed in on the rear of the bus as it eventually drives out of the parking lot.

"Any way we can find out what city the teams were from?" I prompt her.

"There should be some kind of roster of teams available."

She minimizes the video screens and pulls up a browser. In no time she's navigating around the Four Corner State

Softball Championship website. We find the answer on the results page. Teams playing in last night's finals were the Angels from Aurora, Colorado, versus the Rockets from Santa Fe, New Mexico.

Bingo.

I'm already out of my chair and heading for the door when Luna calls out behind me.

"Where the hell are you off to?"

"Santa Fe."

"Jesus, Wapi. How do we even know if that bus drove straight back to Santa Fe? The team may have stayed at a hotel on the road. There's no way of knowing."

"Do you know what it costs to rent a bus like that?" I offer, pausing by the door. "For a regional ball club that would be a good hit to the budget. They're not going to spend more than is necessary on a bus *or* on overnight stays."

She doesn't argue, which I take to mean she concedes my point. Instead, she makes a suggestion.

"Let me get Jasper on this. We can probably track exactly where that bus went."

I lift a hand. "Do what you need to do, but I'm not waiting around for that."

I got a glimpse of the green logo and name on the rear of the charter bus; *Shofur*. It's a distinct enough name and shouldn't be too hard to find.

Out of respect for Ouray, I dial his number to check in as I climb on my bike.

"What's going on, brother?" he asks.

"She's managed to get into a charter bus heading for Santa Fe." I explain quickly how we discovered it.

"You're going after her."

It's a conclusion rather than a question, and fuck if I

don't feel guilty. I was supposed to lighten the man's load and now I'm bailing on him. I'm torn, I have a responsibility to the club, but right now that conflicts with my feelings for Lindsey.

"Go," he adds before I have a chance to answer him. "Go after her. I can fucking hear you thinking, I know where your mind is because that's where mine would be. But, kid, we're fine here, your brothers have your back. Go find your woman."

Not known for his telephone etiquette, Ouray abruptly ends the call, and I start the engine, turning my bike toward the New Mexico border.

I don't get very far—I'm about five minutes outside of Aztec—when my phone vibrates in my pocket with an incoming call. At first, I think maybe it's Luna calling, but when I have to stop at a red light coming into town, I pull out my phone and quickly check call display.

It isn't Luna, but an unknown number. Normally I ignore those, but I don't now.

"Hello?"

"Is this Wapi?"

It's a guy's voice I don't recognize.

"Yeah, who wants to know?"

"Are you alone?"

Behind me a car honks and I see the light has turned green. *Fuck.*

"Who the hell are you?" I ask him, trying to maneuver my bike closer to the side of the road.

"Are you alone?" the guy repeats.

He's starting to piss me off.

"I'm in the middle of traffic and, unless you fucking tell me who you are and what you want, this conversation is over."

I'm about to end the call when I hear the man mumble, "He's a charmer."

Then suddenly there's another voice in my ear.

"Wapi?"

―――――

Lindsey

I hear my name called and I turn in the direction of the voice.

He's hanging out the driver's side window of an older pickup truck, waving at me. Other than his choice of vehicles, he hasn't changed much. I dart across the small parking lot and get in the passenger side, from where I'm half hauled across the center console and enveloped in a bone-crushing embrace.

"Easy, Dad," I grumble, before adding, "We should get out of here."

Not that I think anyone could've followed me here, but after eighteen or so hours on the run, I feel I can't afford to let down my guard. I'm pretty sure someone will have figured out I ended up in Santa Fe on that bus, and it wouldn't be that hard from there to discover I hopped a Delta flight to Salt Lake City, since I had to use my driver's license as identification. However, I hope I was able to lose my trail, since it was my father who arranged for the private charter to fly me from Salt Lake to Kalispell, Montana, where he lives.

"Are you going to tell me what is going on that has you on the run?" There's a sharp edge to his tone, even as he pulls the truck out of the parking lot of the small airport. "You're scaring me, Linds. Telling me not to let anyone know, not even your mom? What the hell is going on?"

When I called him from Santa Fe, all I'd shared was that I was in trouble, that it was life or death, and that I needed a place to lay low for a bit. The charter flight had been his idea, and the fact I didn't balk at him paying for it, when I've refused taking any money from him since college, must've made it clear how serious my trouble was. Or rather *is*, since I don't think this is over by a long shot.

"I'm not even sure, Dad. It's all very confusing."

"Start at the beginning," he prompts, patting my knee with his hand. "We've got a bit of a drive ahead anyway."

The beginning would have to be Thildy and Benjamin's wedding, so I begin there. Of course, that requires me to explain Galen, and the kind of relationship I escaped when I left him. Those aren't things I'd usually discuss with my father, but I figure he should have the full background. He didn't hesitate to come to my rescue so I feel I owe him as much. Dad may not have been a very active parent in my upbringing, but that doesn't mean he's not a protective father.

"That piece of shit," he interjects angrily. "You should've told me. If I'd known, I would've—"

"Right," I interrupt him. "Which is exactly why I didn't tell you then, but I'm telling you now. Besides, you can save your anger because what I was coming to in my story, was that I came home from a run last night to find him in a pool of blood in my living room."

That takes enough of the wind out of Dad, so I can fill him in on the rest. The incident at the airport, the dead man in the stairwell, the visit from the Durango PD, and the subsequent phone call with Detective LaVine with the

Denver PD. Finally, I fill him in on what happened last night, how I ended up in Santa Fe, and why I haven't contacted anyone back home.

"FBI? Are you sure?" he questions.

"No, I'm not sure. Of anything, to be honest. I haven't been able to wrap my head around anything that's going on, but I do know I don't want to worry Mom, she has high blood pressure."

"Your mother does?"

I can feel his eyes on me, and when I turn there is genuine concern on his face. I know they fought like cats and dogs, but I don't think Dad ever really got over my mother.

"Yeah."

"She needs to slow down. I always told her that intensity will be the death of her one day," he grumbles.

"Can we please not talk about Mom and death in the same sentence?" I caution him. "I have enough doom in my life to focus on right now."

"Sorry. Forget I said anything," he quickly mollifies me. "But to your point, isn't your mother going to worry if she doesn't hear from you anyway?"

"Sure, but I wanted to have a plan in place first," I explain. "And I don't want anyone to know where I am. Not until I have a better idea of what the hell is going on."

"So, what is your plan?" Dad wants to know.

I've been wracking my brain to figure out what to do from here. I'd rather stay out of the way and let people I trust dive into this. People like Paco, who has connections and the skills to dig around in a nonintrusive way. Normally, I'd say I trust the Arrow's Edge family, but connections are deep between the club and law enforcement. The president is married to an FBI agent, and I know for a fact the man's loyalty would be to his wife first and foremost. Same with Paco, who will always choose Mom's well-being over everything and anyone else, which is the way it should be. To be honest, for the rest of the club I don't really know where their loyalty would fall, making it a safer option just to stay out of sight for a while.

There is one person, however, who—I know instinctively—will have my back without question. He's the person I need to get in touch with.

"I need a pee break, a coffee, and your help making a phone call. In that order," I tell him.

He pulls into the parking lot of a place called The River Coffee Company. Dad walks in with me, going up to the counter to put in his order and a latte and something to eat for me, while I use the facilities.

One glance in the mirror shows the dire need for a proper shower, a good night's sleep, and a decent brush, which I forgot to buy at Walmart earlier. As it is, I have my plastic bag with a toothbrush and toothpaste, a package of cheap underwear, one of sports socks, and a change of clothes, but nothing else. What's left of the money I took out of the ATM is tucked into the zippered pocket of my jacket. What I have has to last me, so I don't really want to waste it buying things I can do without. I'm sure Dad would give me money if I asked, but he already arranged for the charter, and I don't like asking.

"Eat here or in the truck?" he asks when I join him at the counter, just as the barista calls out his name.

"Truck. We need to make a call."

It's a call I dread, because he's going to be pissed, but at the same time I look forward to hearing his voice.

After taking a fortifying sip of my brew, I hand Dad my pay-as-you-go phone and tell him to make the call. I don't want to risk him identifying me should he be in the presence of others, so it's safer if my father makes sure he's alone before handing me the phone.

"Wapi?" I mention his name, after Dad makes sure he's alone.

"Jesus, Linds, I've been worried sick. Are you all right? Where the fuck are you? Who is that guy?"

I bark out a nervous laugh at the barrage of questions. All fair.

"I'm unhurt, confused, that was my dad, and I need your help," I try to tackle them all at once.

"Whatever you need. Are you still in Santa Fe?"

Wow. Didn't take them long to find out that's where I ended up, which worries me a little. How long will it take for them to track me to Salt Lake, and from there here to Kalispell?

"I need you to let Mom know I'm okay, and I will be in touch at some point. But please don't tell her I'm with my father. I don't want her to know where I am."

"Which is?" his voice comes back sharply. He sounds angry.

"Wapi…can you call Mom?"

"Princess, I'm fucking well on my way to Santa Fe and I *will* find you, but it'll make it a lot easier if you just let me know where you are."

That does something to me, like a fist twisting in my chest. I realize, unless I tell him, he will use whatever he can to find out where I am, and that might not work in my favor.

"I'm in Montana."

"*Jesus.* How the fuck did you get there? Never mind," he immediately follows it up with. "You can explain to me later, I've gotta get on the road. As it is it's gonna take me a full day driving if I don't take fucking breaks," he grumbles.

"Don't—" I try to stop him, but he's not listening.

"Give me an address."

"Look, I have no idea—"

"A fucking address, Lindsey," he barks.

"Give me that phone," my dad says, even as he grabs the phone from my hand and hits speaker. "This is David, Lindsey's father, and I'm not on board with you yelling at my daughter."

"All due respect, sir," Wapi comes back immediately. "I can't protect your fucking daughter if I don't know where she is."

"She's with me, she's safe."

"Maybe for now, but for how long? Whoever has it in for her will come sniffing around at some point, and then what?"

I hadn't really thought that far, I was in too much of a hurry to get out of Dodge, but he makes a good point, if someone is eager to get their hands on me, eventually, they'll chase down my father.

"And you think you can do better?" Dad challenges him.

"I know I can," he answers confidently. "I'd give my life for your daughter."

Dad throws me a questioning look, but I'm too busy gasping for air after Wapi blows me out of the water with that last comment.

"What is she to you?" my father demands to know.

Wapi's answer is as simple as it is complicated.

"Everything."

CHAPTER
SIXTEEN

WAPI

"What do you mean, you can't tell me?"

It doesn't surprise me Mel is snarling like a pissed-off momma bear

"I can't tell you in part because I don't know."

That's a bit of semantics, I may not know exactly where she is, but I know it's somewhere in Montana. Her father told me he had an idea for a safe place but needed to clear that first. He'd send me the information as soon as he could firm things up, but that hasn't happened yet, so I effectively don't know at this moment.

"If I find out you are lying to me, Wapi, I swear I will—"

"I'm keeping her safe," I interrupt. "And if that means keeping information from you, I will. You can waste time threatening me all you want, but I'm not even clear on what the hell is going on, so I'm going to ask that you trust me—trust your daughter—until we have answers and it is safe to share them." I take a deep breath to calm myself down, since my own blood is still racing. "Now, I gotta go, Mel. The sooner I can get to her, the faster you'll have answers."

It's silent for a few beats before she's back.

"Promise me, Wapi. Promise me nothing will happen to my girl."

The only emotion Mel tends to show is anger, so I'm a little thrown when I recognize tears in her voice.

"As soon as I have my eyes on her I'll let you know," I assure her.

Without waiting for her response, I silence my phone and tuck it into my saddlebag. I don't need to be distracted by the phone calls and messages I'm sure are forthcoming once the word spreads. In fact, it probably wouldn't be a bad idea for me to pick up a cheap, unidentifiable phone. I don't want anyone tracking me.

Instead of heading back through Durango and risk bumping into someone, I continue to Farmington. There I stop at a Cellular One store to pick up a phone and immediately send a message with my new number to the phone number Lindsey called me from. I receive a thumbs-up within a few seconds.

I wasn't on the phone very long earlier and would've liked to have spent some more time talking to Lindsey, but not with her father right there, listening in. Besides, I'd much prefer to get on the road and be able to see her face-to-face. To that end, I run into a grocery store for a couple of things to sustain me so I can stop as few times as I can get away with. My bank happens to be next door, and I'm able to withdraw a good chunk of cash to last me a while. I'd prefer not to use any cards if I can help it.

Finally, I stop at the post office, pack my old phone in packaging material I can buy right there, and ship it back to Durango. It would've been quicker to toss it, but that would mean losing the thousands of pictures I always meant to download but never did. The entirety of my three years on the road is held in that phone, which served as the only witness to my solitary adventures.

Feeling safely disconnected, I then turn my bike onto a route that carefully avoids Colorado, briefly cuts through Arizona, then through Utah, Idaho, and finally into Montana. It'll be a long fucking haul, but it won't be the first time I drive across several states in one trip.

Despite my optimistic intention to drive through with only bathroom stops, my lack of sleep over the past few days catches up with me after the little over seven hours it takes me to get to the outskirts of Provo, Utah. My eyes are so gritty and my ass so numb, I'm afraid if I push it, I'm going to end up a skid mark on the asphalt.

To be safe, I check into a motel for a few hours of rest.

My room is the end unit, as I requested of the barely interested teenager manning the desk when I walked into the office. The far end will give me the option to park my bike around the side and out of view of the road. I should be able to slip out of here virtually unseen in a couple of hours.

As soon as I enter the utilitarian room, I first head to the small but blessedly clean bathroom to rinse the road off me with a quick shower. I get dressed in the same clothes I was wearing before flopping down on the double bed closest to the door. Pulling out my cheap phone, I shoot a quick text to the only phone number listed in my contacts.

In Provo. Catching 2 hours of sleep. Any word on location?

The last I ask because the address I was promised has not yet appeared in my messages. I set the alarm on my phone and intend to wait for a response but, already being horizontal, I can't hold off sleep for long.

When my alarm wakes me two hours later, a short message is waiting for me.

Happys Inn, Montana. Mesg 1hr out.

I suspect the request for a one-hour warning was her father's idea, and if I had to venture a guess, I'm not going to find Lindsey at Happys Inn. Can't really blame the man, if I had a daughter in trouble, I wouldn't trust me that easily either.

Thankfully the nap did me good, I feel a ton better. Refreshed, and ready to hit the highway. I make a stop down the road from the motel to fill up my tank. At the attached twenty-four-hour coffee shop, I buy a breakfast sandwich and a travel mug I have them fill with coffee. All fueled up, I hop on the I-15, which should take me all the way up to Butte, Montana.

The benefit of driving through Utah at night is avoiding the midday temperatures, which can get uncomfortably high. The roads are nice and quiet too, which means I make good time. The sun is only just starting to rise in the sky when I hit Butte, Montana, around eight in the morning.

I have to pee and wouldn't mind some fresh coffee, so I might as well gas up again too. My Harley Dyna will do a hundred and eighty miles on a tank of gas, maybe two hundred if I squeeze it. That means I've already had to stop to fill up twice on the almost five hundred miles it took to get here since leaving Provo. If I'd known I'd be driving clear across the country when I left Durango, I might've grabbed a club vehicle to get more miles out of a tank, but that might also have meant being easier to track.

I pull up the GPS on my phone to check how much longer. Looks like I'll be hitting Happys Inn at around two this afternoon, taking at least two more fuel stops into account. My fucking ass is already numb, but I'm not going to stop now.

It's actually closer to one fifteen when I roll into Happys Inn. Not the town I was expecting, it's basically a gas station, convenience store, and bar rolled into one. That's it. A small collection of buildings, but nothing that looks like a town by any stretch of the imagination. I'm surprised at the number of vehicles parked in front though. More popular than I would've expected.

I pull my bike into an empty spot, but before I can dismount, I hear my name called. Owner of the voice is a guy, I'd guess late fifties, with gray hair poking out from under his black Stetson. As much as he tries to blend in with the locals, he stands out like a sore thumb. My gut says I'm looking at Lindsey's father.

"David Zimmerman," he says, confirming my guess.

I swing my leg over my bike and rise to my full height, which is about half a head taller than the other guy, despite the obvious heel on his far-too-shiny cowboy boots. That explains the slightly oversized hat as well. Lindsey's father is about her height, which kind of makes sense, considering he used to be a race car driver from what I understand. Those guys aren't quite as small as jockeys are, but most of them tend to be on the slighter side to make crawling in and out of those tight cockpits a bit easier.

I peer beyond him to see if I can spot Lindsey, but the pickup truck he probably got out of is empty.

"She's not here."

My eyes snap back to the older man.

"Where is she?"

"She's safe."

———

Lindsey

"You have got to be shitting me."

He shakes his head, regret on his face.

"I swear, I had no idea," he repeats. "Not until I received a letter from a lawyer three years ago informing me Gemma had died."

Gemma, the name of the woman he'd had a brief affair with while my mother was pregnant with me. The woman who subsequently ended up pregnant by my father as well. He must have some powerful swimmers. According to my father, he'd broken it off with her and never knew she had his child until the lawyer notified him.

"That's why you moved to Montana," I accuse him.

He doesn't bother denying and nods. "In large part, yes. It was news to him too and after the paternity test confirmed he's my son, I wanted a chance at some kind of relationship with him."

I can't help it, I snort. My father's never been big on building, let alone maintaining relationships. I should know, I'm the one who has to remind him he has a daughter regularly.

I think that's what upsets me most about this, not that I turn out to have a half brother no one knew about, but he apparently is worth my father moving across the country for. Not only that, but he's known for three years and never bothered telling me.

I didn't think Dad had the capacity to hurt me anymore.

Guess I was wrong.

And now he wants to dump me on his bastard son's doorstep for safekeeping. Well, fuck that.

"Stop the truck."

I can feel his eyes on me but I refuse to look.

"Come on, sweetheart, don't be like that."

"Dad, I swear…"

I take in a deep breath, determined not to react emotionally. I'm not fifteen anymore. Besides that, I have bigger problems right now.

"You can't simply drop me on this man's doorstep," I try again.

"I'm not, he's expecting you. He's known about you for a while."

Oh, wow.

My father really doesn't have a sensitive or considerate bone in his body. It's not that he's a bad man, he's just… utterly clueless. Mom is going to have a shit fit when she finds out. Better make sure Paco is close by when she does. He's the only one who can calm her down when she blows up.

So, my brother knows about me. I wonder why he's never made the effort to reach out?

"Here we are."

My eyes snag on a sign hanging over the entrance to a

driveway he's turning the truck into. The name isn't familiar. When the trees clear on either side, it's quickly obvious this is some kind of horse farm. It's a beautiful place, the house a large stone and log construction with a porch spanning the entire front. The views are gorgeous with the mountains as a backdrop.

Instead of pulling up to the big house, Dad turns to the left, where I notice several cabins tucked into the trees. A tall man is standing in front of one of them, his arms crossed over his chest. I can't quite make out his face, the cowboy hat he's wearing is tugged low and casting a shadow.

When he lifts his head and I can see his eyes, they're fixed on me through the windshield. I'm shaken to the core and I wish Wapi was here, with his hand pressed to the small of my back to let me know he's there. I've never needed him more.

I'm so mesmerized by this stranger, I don't even realize my father is out and around the truck, until he pulls open my door.

"Come on out, sweetheart. Meet Dan."

He's darker than I am and I look for something familiar in his features. I don't see it until one side of his mouth jerks up in a barely-there smile, revealing a dimple that matches my father's exactly. He must've inherited his height from his mother's side of the family because he's easily as tall as Wapi.

No sooner has his name popped in my head when my phone beeps with an incoming message from him.

"I'll take care of that," Dad declares, sliding the phone out of my fingers. "You guys get acquainted."

Then he promptly walks off.

"Hi." I awkwardly hold out my hand, which is immediately swallowed up by his much larger one. "I'm Lindsey."

He chuckles and the sound is surprisingly deep. "I figured as much. Mine's Dan, but I'm sure that's not news to you either."

I drop my hand and snort harshly, unable to stop myself from commenting, "Well, it was ten minutes ago."

"Touché," he returns with a tip of his hat. "Although, for the record, it's all pretty well fresh for me. I'm still trying to come to terms with the fact I actually have a father, let alone a sister."

He makes a fair point so I swallow my bitterness, recognizing we're all victims here of a sort.

"I can't imagine that was an easy discovery," I concede.

Then I focus my attention on the property.

"What is this place?"

"This is my home. Welcome to High Meadow."

CHAPTER
SEVENTEEN

LINDSEY

The cloud of butterflies in my stomach is growing by the minute.

My father left a while ago to meet up with Wapi and he could be here at any time.

When we were at my dad's place last night, Mom had called him. She wanted to know if I'd been in touch, which meant she was digging. Apparently talking to Wapi and getting his reassurances I'm safe wasn't enough. That's when Dad suggested finding another place to stay. He knows Mom as well as I do and is aware she can be a terrier when she puts her mind to it, so it's probably safer for everyone if my father gets back to his regular routine to avoid raising suspicion.

This morning, Dan strongly encouraged my father to trust I'd be safe here at the ranch. He brought up the fact no one associated with me is aware of any connection to High Meadow, and to ensure it stays that way, it would be smart for Dad to keep his distance.

I could tell my father wasn't happy and got the sense he really wanted to play a more active role in keeping me safe when he hugged me goodbye. That went a little way to soothing the lingering burn of betrayal. I know over time my heart will heal and I'll be able to rationalize my father's decisions, but for now the hurt is real.

After Dad left, my newfound brother showed me into the farthest cabin. Smaller than the rest, this one was set well back into the trees, making it hard to spot for someone driving onto the property.

From the front door you enter a main space to the left; one big square room with an open kitchen at the rear, a small island, small dining table with four chairs, and a sitting area at the front. The furnishings are dated, but the stone fireplace makes the whole thing look cozy and warmly rustic. To the right of the front door are three sets of doors, two are bedrooms—one with a queen and the other with bunkbeds—and the third is a small bathroom with just a shower.

I got comfortable while Dan went to take care of some things, but he promised he'd be back soon. Getting comfortable meant putting away the meager possessions I acquired in Santa Fe and hauled in a plastic Walmart bag across the country. The toothbrush, paste, and deodorant are on the counter in the bathroom, and I left the clean underwear and T-shirt in the top drawer of the dresser in the main bedroom. That's all there is. I wasn't going to drag my dirty, smelly running gear on the plane with me so I discarded all but my shoes and my jacket in the airport washrooms, where I changed into clean clothes before catching my flight.

A knock has me up and running to the door, but it's not

Wapi on the doorstep. It's Dan, and he has his hands full of bags.

"Supplies," he mumbles as I step aside to let him through.

He dumps the bags on the kitchen island. "A few basic groceries and some clothes, courtesy of Alex."

"Who is Alex?" I immediately ask.

"Jonas is my boss and owns High Meadow. Alex is his wife. And in case you're wondering," he continues, "I told them you're my sister and you needed a place to hide out. They probably assume it's a domestic situation. Our dad told me only marginally more, but I have a lot of questions I'm hoping you'll be able to answer for me at some point."

I feel guilty. These people have possibly taken me in under false pretenses. Well, I guess technically not false, since I did escape what was definitely a situation in my home, but they should probably know the danger might not just be to me. Am I putting them at risk now too? That's the last thing I want.

"I'm so grateful, to you and, uhm, the owners, and the last thing I want is to put you in harm's way. So, I think as soon as my ride gets here, I should probably be on my way."

"And that'd be monumentally stupid," he doesn't hesitate to inform me.

"Excuse me?"

"You heard me." He leans a casual hip against the island and crosses his arms across his chest. "No one's going to look for you here."

"You don't know that. These people, I don't know how far their reach goes. Hell, I don't even know why they're after me, but I do know they don't think twice about hurting people to get to me."

Memories of Galen twitching in a pool of blood on my living room floor flash back, sending shivers down my body.

Dan takes a step closer, placing a hand on my shoulder.

"The reason I know you're safe here is because I know *we* can keep you that way."

I can't help the snort that escapes me. "I'm sorry, but you work on a horse farm."

He grins, flashing a set of strong teeth—*yowza*, my brother is nothing to sneeze at—and proceeds to explain how qualified these people are.

First, he points out with some pride this isn't just a horse ranch, but a breeding facility. Then he tells me about High Mountain Trackers, a highly trained mounted search, rescue, and recovery team working from High Meadow as its base. The ranch's owner, Jonas, originally formed the team with fellow special ops veterans, but in recent years has expanded the team with new members from different backgrounds. That includes Dan himself, who was apparently first hired as a ranch hand.

"Let me guess, you always wanted to be a cowboy," I observe, half teasing.

I'm actually quite impressed and the urge to run out the door doesn't feel as pressing. If these people are former special ops, they're better equipped than I am to deal with whomever is after me. They still shouldn't have to though.

"Not exactly," is his response. "I always wanted to be a doctor, but sometimes life's needs take you in different directions."

There's a weight to his words which, added to the vast discrepancy he describes between his dreams and his reality, makes me curious.

"I sense a story there."

He nods as he casually moves to the door.

"There is. For another day though. I'm more concerned about you taking off, leaving me to chase after you. I've gotta get back to work, but tonight I was hoping to introduce you to Jonas. I'll leave up to you what, if anything, you choose to share about your situation, but I don't normally keep things from my team."

He opens the door and steps outside.

His message is clear, he'll lie for me if he has to, but he'd rather not. Oddly enough, instead of annoying me, it warms me to think he's willing to back me up. This is the kind of thing I used to wish for when growing up; a sibling to have my back. A few hours ago, I didn't even know I had one.

On impulse I step out after him and grab his arm. When he turns, I pull him into a quick hug, and he wraps his arms around me without hesitation. I'm surprised, both at myself and at Dan's easy display of affection. My mother wasn't exactly a hugger when I was growing up, and as far as I know, neither is my father. It's a trait Dan must have picked up from his mother.

The sound of a motorcycle catches my attention and I take a step back to see Wapi pulling up. His eyes are locked in on me and don't waver as he gets off his bike and stalks right over. Without introductions, he tags me behind the neck and I don't resist when he takes my mouth in a bruising kiss.

"When you're done mauling my sister…" Dan interrupts, causing Wapi to abruptly end the kiss.

"Your fucking sister?"

———

Wapi

I lean my forehead against the tiled wall of the small shower and let the water pelt the back of my neck. Feels good to wash the road off me.

I had no idea who the fuck Lindsey was snuggled up with on the front step, but I'm glad I chose to stake my claim by kissing her instead of flooring that cowboy. It would've been awkward whaling on the guy who turned out to be her brother.

A fucking brother she didn't know about. I was already pissed at her father for holding me up with his stupid questions, but I'm even angrier now. Not only did he cheat on Mel, he kept the product of his infidelity a secret. I don't care it came as a surprise to him too, he's since had years to come clean with both Lindsey and her mother, but chose not to.

The brother, Dan, introduced himself and shook my hand, but didn't stick around, leaving it to Lindsey to explain the situation to me. Which she did, while putting away a few bags of groceries. I had more questions I wanted answers to, but she suggested I grab a shower while she made us something to eat, and promised to tell me all she knows after.

Rinsing the shampoo I found in the shower from my hair and beard, I turn off the water and grab the towel Lindsey found me in the closet in one of the bedrooms. I dry my body before giving my hair the same treatment, noticing once again I should probably get a haircut. I pull on the same pair of jeans but leave off the shirt, it smells ripe, which would defeat the purpose of the shower. I may have a clean shirt in my saddle bags.

The scent of melting cheese hits me as soon as I exit the bathroom. Lindsey is by the stove, stirring something in a pot on the burner. She does a double take when she sees me, and a blush spreads on her cheeks when I catch her staring.

"That grilled cheese I smell?"

"Uhm, something like it. It's called croque monsieur, a fancy word for a grilled ham and cheese sandwich. I'm warming up some canned tomato soup as well, hope that's okay. Dan dropped off only a few things."

She's rambling a little. It's cute, especially since Lindsey is usually so tightly controlled. I'll admit I'm getting a kick out of rattling her cage a little. She's been rattling mine since I first met her. At least this feels a little more balanced now. Maybe I should quit wearing shirts around her altogether.

I close in on her and I know she's aware when her shoulders pull up to her ears.

"You know I could see if Dan has a shirt you can borrow," she mutters.

Chuckling, I press my lips to a small patch of her exposed neck. "I can go find him if it bothers you so much," I tease her.

She ducks out of my reach and starts digging around the cupboards for soup bowls.

"Oh, I don't care."

She lies, but I'm not going to call her out on it. At least not right now, I fully intend to later but could use something to eat first. I'll need the energy for where I'm hoping that particular conversation will end. Besides, I'd feel better if she could fill me in on all the pieces I'm missing, and I could update her with what I know.

After that, I'm eager to see where this leads.

While we eat, Lindsey tells me everything that happened to her over the past—almost—two days. After she does, I understand why she felt a little conflicted as to whom she could trust. The fact she had enough faith in me to get in touch makes me feel better.

"Is there any way we can find out how Galen is doing?"

As far as I'm concerned, the asshole doesn't deserve her attention. He was clearly stalking her, had found his way into her house, so I feel he got what was coming to him. But this happened in her house, and I'm sure that night was traumatic enough for her without someone actually dying as a result.

"I'm sure we can—"

A knock on the door cuts me off. Lindsey starts to get up but I motion for her to stay, and move to the door myself.

"Am I interrupting something?"

The woman standing on the doorstep wears a smirk as she unapologetically checks me out. The thick gray braid over one shoulder and the fine lines fanning out from her sparkling eyes betray her as middle-aged. She has a paper bag in her arms.

Before I have a chance to respond, she boldly moves past me into the cabin.

"I'm Alex," she directs at Lindsey, who's gotten to her feet. "Sorry to barge in, but the guys were called out to find a missing hiker, and I have an appointment I can't miss. I didn't want you to show up at the house and find no one there." She sets the paper bag on the table. "I brought over a few more things you might find use for. Dan mentioned you both traveled light."

"I really appreciate that," Lindsey thanks her, looking a little flustered. "I'm sorry, I don't want to be a bother."

The older woman waves her off. "Nonsense. You're not a bother. Stay here as long as you need."

She's about to walk out the door when Lindsey stops her.

"My name is Lindsey, and that's my friend, Wapi."

Friend, *my ass*. Friends don't kiss the way she kisses me.

"Nice to meet you, Lindsey." Then Alex turns to me. "Wapi? That sounds Navajo to me. Lucky, right? Funny, you don't strike me as Navajo."

"I'm not. At least not as far as I know. How I got the name is a long story," I share.

She smiles and nods, reaching for the door.

"I'd love to hear it but I'm afraid it'll have to wait. I'm already late." She points at the bag. "Check in there, I think there are a couple of shirts that might fit you."

Then she gives me the once-over again and smirks.

"Although, I'd hate to spoil that view. Have a good night."

With that she pulls the door shut behind her.

When I turn to Lindsey, she's trying to hide a grin.

"What?" I want to know.

"She's right, it *would* spoil the view."

I'm across the small cabin in three strides.

CHAPTER
EIGHTEEN

LINDSEY

He stalks toward me and my skin tingles before he even touches me.

I know what's coming and I'm ready for it. The moment he is close enough I jump him, throwing my arms around his neck. I'm not sure who initiated what, but the next second his tongue is in my mouth and I hum my pleasure against his lips.

Add smoldering looks and a few teasing kisses to years of suppressed sexual chemistry, and you have a powder keg primed for ignition.

His hands cupping my ass, he lifts me up and sets me on the kitchen counter. My hands free, I explore the width of his chest and shoulders, his skin hot and chest hair bristling under my fingertips. The next thing I know, I lose his mouth, my arms are yanked up over my head, and my Walmart T-shirt is whipped off.

"Tell me to stop," Wapi growls, his fingers struggling with the front closure on my sports bra.

Impatiently, I brush his hands away and take care of the tiny hooks and eyes myself, mumbling, "Like hell I will."

The moment my breasts are freed, his hands are right there, molding and shaping them.

"Fuck, you're so damn beautiful."

In response, I curl my arms around his neck, wrap my legs around his hips, and pull him close so I can feel his skin against mine. Dropping my head back, I catch the heat in his gray-blue eyes staring down at me.

"You're not half bad yourself," I whisper.

Now there's an understatement.

I wasn't a fan of that big bushy beard he came back with last year, but he's since trimmed it down. Now, the contrast of the darker beard against his dirty-blond hair looks fantastic. With those smoldering eyes, that strong nose, and those full lips, he's a stunner.

And right now, he's all mine.

Feeling brazen, I nip at his lush bottom lip and rock my hips against the solid length his jeans barely seem able to contain. I'm pretty sure he's commando underneath, which only makes my nipples pebble harder and slick heat flood my panties.

"Easy, Princess. I wanna take my time, I've got no place to be," he mutters against my mouth as his hands start roaming again.

I shiver at the rasp of his rough hands against my back and roll my hips again.

"I want to feel you inside me."

He curses softly as he shoves his hands in the back of my pants and his face in my neck, sinking his teeth into the tender skin where my neck meets my shoulder.

"You're not making this easy."

"You wouldn't want me easy."

"That's for damn sure," he says, grunting as he digs his fingers into my ass cheeks and lifts me off the counter. "Hold on, baby."

I hook one arm around his neck, tangling the fingers of my other hand into his hair, and pull his head down, as he carries me into the bedroom. My mouth fused to his, I hang on as he lowers me to my feet, but when his hands start pushing my pants down my hips, I lower one of mine to work on the buttons of his jeans.

I'm just able to get the first two buttons of his fly loose, when I'm toppled backward onto the mattress. Wapi looms over me, a wolfish grin on his face as he reaches for my pants, stripping them along with my panties off my legs. I feel the heat of his scrutiny burn my skin as he slowly straightens up, unbuttons the rest of his fly, and drops his jeans to the floor.

There is so much to take in, but my eyes are inevitably drawn to his cock, proudly jutting from a neatly trimmed patch and, frankly, demanding attention. I'm briefly distracted when he bends over to retrieve his wallet from his jeans, producing a strip of condoms he tosses next to me on the bed. Not that I thought he would be, but I'm glad to see he's not planning a one-and-done deal. I don't think once will be enough with this man.

My legs rub together restlessly in anticipation when he puts his knee on the foot of the bed, climbing on. When he wraps his hands around my ankles and spreads my legs apart, he exposes me to his view and goosebumps surface all over my skin. I watch his face as he strokes the tips of his fingers up my leg.

Something has changed. The almost frantic hunger of just moments ago seems to have been replaced by a quiet reverence. An intrinsic need to experience every sight, sound, touch, taste, every sensation completely, and award them the momentousness they deserve, before engraving them to memory.

His touch, which was claiming before, is now more tentative, and for some reason that nearly brings tears to my eyes.

"I'm almost afraid," he confesses in a raw voice, trailing his fingers almost distractedly over the thatch of blond hair at the apex of my legs. "When you've wanted something for so long—dreamt about it…"

I hiss when he brushes the pad of his thumb through the wet slicking my folds.

"…and you finally have it in front of you, you don't want anything to fuck up that moment."

My hips roll involuntarily, and I moan when his touch centers in on my clit.

"That would be impossible," I pant. "Trust me."

His eyes lock on mine as he purposefully lowers his head between my legs, and I hold my breath in anticipation. When the flat of his tongue boldly strokes along my crease, bringing every nerve ending along the way alive, my breath releases in a whoosh.

Here, his touch is not in the least tentative, but confident and sure and before long I'm rocking myself against his face, making sounds I don't even recognize. I'm so close my legs start trembling. Then suddenly, he eases off and starts moving up the bed. He drags his tongue up the center of my body; over my belly, between my breasts, and up my neck until his mouth closes over mine in a deep kiss, and I can taste myself on him.

I open my legs to welcome him between, but instead he wraps me up and rolls to his back with me on top. Scooting up with his back against the headboard, he rearranges me so my knees hit the mattress on either side of his hips, my pussy slick against his hard shaft. My mouth open at the sensation, I throw my head back and rock myself against the ridge, craving the friction.

"Nooo," I complain when he firmly moves me back a few inches. "I was so close."

"You come with me inside you," he manages in a strangled voice, as he quickly rolls on a condom.

First, he moves my hands to hold on to the headboard behind him, before taking a firm grip of my hips. Then, as he latches on to my breast, sucking the tip deep into his mouth, he lowers me onto his cock, filling me completely.

I want to move fast, my body eager to reach that pinnacle, but Wapi forces a different pace, slow and thorough. His reach inside my body so deep it's hard to know where he ends and I begin. We're fused, his cock, mouth, and hands exploring every part of me, while all I can do is hang on for dear life, my fingernails digging grooves into the headboard.

It may have been hours, or taken just minutes, but eventually the tsunami which has been building deep in my belly starts to crest, threatening to wash over me. As the first waves start to pull me under, Wapi abruptly flips us, landing me on my back with my legs up on his shoulders. Then he cranks up the pace, pistoning his hips and pumping inside me hard.

I literally see stars as my body flies apart.

———

Wapi

I take one more look over my shoulder at her sleeping form as I slip out of the room.

When I woke up, she'd been curled around me but now she's starfished on her back, the sheet tangled around her limbs. Completely out of it. She didn't even notice me digging around to find my jeans and socks on the floor.

I still can't believe I spent a lot of last night, and part of earlier this morning, living out every damn fantasy I've been harboring since the first time I set eyes on Lindsey. Reality surpassed every last one of them. The night left me a little raw, but that was to be expected considering my hand has been the only activity my dick has seen in a long fucking time.

I tried once, hooking up with a chick when I was on the road. It was an attempt to get Lindsey out of my head, but it failed miserably. I couldn't even fucking finish and was so embarrassed by the whole thing, I gave up on trying. It's what scared me earlier, the possibility I might not be able to perform. With Lindsey my performance clearly was not a problem.

Ducking into the bathroom I catch a glimpse of my face in the small mirror as I relieve myself. The sappy smile on my face makes me look like a fucking goof, not that I care. There's no one here to give me a hard time about it.

I wash my hands and slip on my jeans and socks, before exiting the bathroom and walking to the front window to peek out. The sky is just starting to lighten up a bit and over by the big barn I can see some activity. A couple of guys look to be unloading horses from the back of a trailer.

That's what woke me earlier, the sound of a heavy diesel engine, probably the heavy-duty truck pulling the horse trailer. My guess is, this is the team coming back from their search for the missing hiker. I shove my feet in my boots and dig through the paper bag to find something I can wear. I pull out a checkered shirt I normally wouldn't be found dead in, but beggars can't be choosers, and maybe it'll make me look less out of place. Next, I fish my new phone from the pocket of my cut, which is hanging on the back of a dining chair, and head outside.

Time to introduce myself to the locals.

Three heads turn when I approach the barn. Luckily, one of them is Dan's. He recognizes me.

"Up early," he observes.

"Truck woke me."

I take in the two other cowboys, both older, one sports a white beard and the taller one looks like he might be Native American. Both eye me with equal scrutiny.

"Not sure who I should be addressing, but I just wanted to say I appreciate the hospitality." I hold out my hand to the taller man first, and without thinking introduce myself, "I'm Wapi."

The guy's eyes narrow. "That supposed to be a fucking joke?"

"No joke. It's the name I was given by the only family I've ever known," I explain. "It's the only name I use, because it means something to me."

I normally don't explain myself or justify my name, but I want to make sure this man understands I'm not mocking him or his heritage. He hums, which I'll take as some form of acknowledgement.

"You just met James," the other guy indicates, offering his hand. "I'm Jonas Harvey. I own High Meadow. Dan tells me you're with his sister."

"I am."

"Is she okay?"

"For now she is."

The man named Jonas tilts his head. "I know you met my wife already, she's up at the house throwing together some breakfast. You're welcome to join us."

I have a feeling the invitation is more than simple hospitality, but I don't mind. I figured eventually they'd want to have an idea of what brought Lindsey and me here, and this gives me an opportunity to see how much or how little they need to know.

"I appreciate it. I won't say no to a coffee."

I walk with him to the house, James and Dan following behind us.

"So does that mean you found the hiker?" I ask to make conversation.

"Not yet. The rest of the guys are still out there, but someone's gotta keep the ranch running."

He guides me inside and down a hallway leading to a large open kitchen and living space at the rear of the house. The woman who introduced herself as Alex last night is by the stove, stirring a large pan with scrambled eggs. This time her hair is loose, hanging in waves down her back. Jonas fits himself behind her, brushes her hair out of the way, and kisses her neck. Then he turns to the far side of the counter where a large thermos and a collection of mugs sit on a tray.

"Black?" he asks me.

"Please."

Alex turns at the sound of my voice, giving me a once-over.

"I see you found a shirt," she comments, adding on a whisper, "Pity."

"I'm right here," Jonas complains, throwing his hands in the air.

"You should take it as a compliment," she states with a smirk. "It means there's nothing wrong with my eyesight and yet I'm still keeping you around."

Then she waves everyone to a harvest table in front of a large glass wall of sliding doors with a view of fields and the mountains beyond.

"Go, sit, and eat something." For me she adds, "Where is your girl?"

"Still sleeping," I respond as I take a seat across from Jonas. "She's had a few rough nights."

"About that," Jonas starts. "Anything we should be aware of? In case trouble finds its way here."

It's a fair question and I feel pretty comfortable giving him an answer.

"The weekend before last, Lindsey was in Denver at a friend's wedding when her asshole ex, who wasn't supposed to be there, showed up. Then that same night at the airport on the way home, a man ran into her, taking her down to the ground. Early the next morning, he was found dead at the bottom of a stairwell only feet from where the collision took place." I take a sip of my coffee while I try to remember the sequence of events accurately. "She talked to local law enforcement and later to a Denver PD detective, who implied the murder was connected to an ongoing larger investigation but couldn't, or wouldn't, specify. Then a couple of nights ago, Lindsey came home from a run to find her ex bleeding out on the living room floor and a strange man coming down her stairs. She beelined it out of there but was chased down and shot at."

"Jesus," Alex mutters behind me. "How did she get away?"

She leans over to set a tray of bacon on the table.

"By crawling into the open luggage hold of a charter

bus. With the help of her father, she managed to get here, making sure her trail ended in Salt Lake City," I explain with no small amount of pride in my voice.

"Smart cookie," she comments.

No doubt about that, she had been thinking on her feet.

"And where were you when this went down?"

The question comes from Dan, who's been quietly listening so far. I don't blame him for the sharp tone, I'm kicking my own ass for not being around.

"I was out of town for the club, trying to locate a missing boy. We found him and were already on our way back, so I didn't find out what was going on until I got to the clubhouse at three or four in the morning. I searched for hours, made myself a pest at the local FBI office by inserting myself into their investigation. Then the moment Lindsey contacted me and told me she was in Montana, I cut off communications with everyone else and hopped on my bike to follow her here."

"Why didn't she find a safe place and simply call the cops?" James wants to know.

It's a question I asked her as well. I'm about to answer him when I notice Jonas suddenly looking over my shoulder.

"Because it's possible the guy shooting at me was FBI."

I turn to see Lindsey standing just inside the kitchen, an older woman with long dark hair right behind her. I immediately get up and walk over to her, but her eyes are fixed behind me. I tilt her chin up, forcing her to look at me.

"Morning." I lightly brush her lips. "I'd hoped you could catch up on some sleep."

"I found her wandering outside and figured you'd be here," the older woman announces, moving through the kitchen like she belongs. "By the way, I'm Ama."

She heads straight for James, whose stoic face cracks with a faint smile. It soon becomes clear those two are a couple.

"FBI?" Dan prompts.

Lindsey turns to answer her brother.

"That's how I heard him identify himself to the bus driver when I was hiding in the cargo hold."

"You sure it was the same guy who shot at you?" he pushes.

I'm about to step in, but once again Lindsey shows she can handle herself.

"Positive," she responds with conviction. "I saw him, that's the reason I hid in the bus."

"All right," Alex intervenes. "Enough talking for now. You two sit down. I didn't haul my ass out of bed to cook breakfast for you all to let it get cold."

We've barely sat down when Ama slides a coffee mug in front of Lindsey, who looks a little shell-shocked.

Jonas grins at her.

"That's Alex, my wife. She's a bit bossy, like Ama. The two of them basically run this place."

"And don't you forget it," Ama cautions.

"I value my life too much," he fires back instantly.

Then he turns a grin on Lindsey.

"I know my place."

I've never met these people before, but even without knowing anything about them I can tell they are as much a family as Arrow's Edge is.

CHAPTER
NINETEEN

LINDSEY

Well, this is a new one for me.

After breakfast, Alex lured me to the stable with the promise of a newly born foal. The little guy is cute, black, with a star-shaped white marking on his forehead. He is bouncing around like one of those baby goats you see on those animal videoclips all the time.

While I'm admiring the little fella named Banner—as in Star-Spangled Banner, Alex tells me—I notice she is putting a saddle on the foal's momma.

"Ever ridden a horse before?" Alex suddenly asks.

"Me? Uh, let me see. The only time I vaguely remember was at a birthday party where we all took turns being led around the backyard on a pony. I was probably six. The only other time I came close was a trail mule."

"So, that would be a no. Good thing Maisy here is as docile as they come."

Banner picks that moment to take a corner of my jacket pocket in his mouth and start chewing.

"Hey, buddy, that's the only jacket I have," I mutter, tugging the fabric out of his mouth.

"He's teething," Alex volunteers.

I look over at her and notice she's leading another, much bigger, horse from its stall, tying it up next to Maisy.

"This is Sarge," she shares, patting the horse's neck. "He's been my trusted companion for twelve years already. Haven't you, boy?"

Then she disappears into the tack room, only to reappear a moment later with another saddle, swinging it effortlessly on the large horse's back. He doesn't even flinch.

I still don't clue in until she hands me Maisy's reins and asks me to follow her and Sarge out of the barn.

"Oh, I don't think…I'm not really dressed—"

"Nonsense," Alex interrupts. "It's only a ten-minute ride out to the field where we're putting Maisy and Banner out to pasture, and Sarge needs his daily exercise, so we're killing two birds with one stone. Like I said, the mare is docile, she rides like a lazy chair. Besides…" She turns and grins at me. "You can't spend time at a ranch and not ride. I figured a woman who runs from bullets, hides in cargo holds, and manages to travel well over a thousand miles under the radar might welcome a fun thrill for a change. Unless, of course, you're scared?"

If that's not a challenge, I don't know what is. Of course, I don't back down from a challenge, running shoes or not.

"Not at all," I bite.

Then I lift my foot to slip the toe of my Lululemon Blissfeel 2 runner in the stirrup Alex is holding firm for me. I grab the horn of the saddle and pull myself up, swinging my other leg over Maisy's back as I've seen done many times watching every episode of all three time periods of *Yellowstone* religiously. Unfortunately, it's only now I notice last night's athletics with Wapi have left me a bit sore.

"Are you okay?" Alex asks with concern when she catches my hiss.

"Just a little stiff."

And definitely tender, but I guess that's to be expected when muscles and tissues that were unused for many years suddenly get a high-intensity workout.

I haven't really had a chance to check in with Wapi since I woke up alone in bed this morning. I'd gone looking for him and bumped into Ama, who was just arriving at the ranch. During breakfast we obviously didn't have a chance to talk and when I left with Alex to go to the barn, Wapi was just heading back to the cabin for a shower.

I did notice he looked pretty good in flannel, turning him into some kind of biker-cowboy hybrid. I could see him on horseback.

"Hold the reins loosely in your hand, and if you want you can hold on to the horn with the other," Alex instructs. "For the most part, Maisy will follow where Sarge leads, and Banner will stick like glue to his mother, so you don't have to worry about him," she adds as she easily mounts her horse.

She looks tiny on the big animal, but appears fully in charge as she decisively steers him toward the back of the corral. As promised, Maisy doesn't need any prompting and follows suit.

For the first few minutes I have a death grip on the saddle horn, until my body adjusts to Maisy's gently rocking gait. Then I start to relax and allow myself to enjoy the unexpected experience.

Talk about being out of my element.

It's not until we crest a hill and Alex points out the view

of the ranch in the valley behind us, and on the other side a group of horses already grazing in the field, that something occurs to me.

"If Maisy and her foal are to stay behind, how am I going to get back to the ranch?"

Alex grins at me over her shoulder as she leads her horse down the hill to the herd below.

"Sarge can handle us both."

Yikes.

Forty-five minutes later we crest the same hill, this time with me in Sarge's saddle and Alex behind me. It's damn high up here.

I take one last glance over my shoulder to where Banner is making new friends with some of the other foals already in the field. We left Maisy's tack hanging on the wooden gate. Alex assured me one of the stable hands would pick it up on a stop to fill up the water trough. Apparently, they have to cart it in by truck at this distance from the ranch.

"Now that's a sight I never thought I'd see," Wapi comments when we arrive at the barn.

He was waiting, watching us approach. To my surprise, he casually grabs hold of the horse's lead—making it look like he knows what he's doing—and holds Sarge steady as Alex dismounts first. She then takes the reins and he moves to my side, reaching to help me off the horse. I groan a bit as he sets me on my feet.

"Bit sore?" he guesses on a whisper, his lips brushing the shell of my ear.

"A tad," I admit.

More than a bit, actually, my legs are trembling with it, but the arm Wapi wraps around my waist keeps me steady. When he steers me toward the cabin, I stop him and turn around to Alex.

"Thank you for the ride. I really enjoyed it."

I actually did, once I gave myself over to the moment. Despite the ache in my nether regions, I feel so invigorated and alive, I can't stop smiling. Mom would probably get a kick out of the fact I rode a horse.

Alex nods with a smile. "There's nothing like a little taste of nature to put things in perspective. Anytime you want a repeat, let me know. Sarge seems to like you."

With that, she turns to lead the horse to the barn, and we resume walking toward the cabin, Wapi's arm still firmly around me. It's the kind of PDA I'm not used to, but I don't hate it. It feels nice.

"So what have you been up to? Other than taking a shower?" I ask him, tilting my head so I can see his face.

"Had a little chat with Jonas, who let me use his secure network to get in touch with Ouray."

I grind to a halt and twist to face him. "You talked to him? Was there any news?"

I don't like the look on his face when he nods affirmatively.

"Wagner is talking."

———

Wapi

"Inside."

I urge Lindsey into the cabin where I feel I can better contain her when she hears, because I'm pretty sure it's going to freak her out.

She walks partway into the living room before swinging

around with her fists on her hips. A battle-ready pose, bracing for whatever is coming her way. This woman is no wilting flower, no matter how much of a princess she sometimes can be.

"What is it?"

I could tell Ouray was pissed when I called and wouldn't share my location. I got it, I was basically saying I didn't trust his loyalty as my brother and my president. Once I was able to explain what kept me from telling him where we are, and that I didn't want to put him in a position where he'd be stuck between loyalty to the brotherhood or to his wife, he simmered down a bit.

He still wasn't happy but was able to give me an update on what was happening there, and it wasn't good.

"Wagner is awake and talking."

"That's what you said, what is it you aren't saying?"

She reads me too easily.

"He claims you invited him over to your place."

"What?" Shock is clear on her face, not that I was buying into that story anyway. "Like hell I did."

"It was his explanation as to how he ended up inside your house. He says you gave him the code for the alarm."

She's shaking her head violently, even as I speak.

"Nuh-uh. Why the hell would I do that? This is crazy."

She grabs at her hair, pulling strands free from the sloppy knot on the top of her head. I take her wrists and carefully pull her hands away.

"How is that even possible?" she continues, her eyes wide as she looks to me for answers. I don't have any to give her. "Wait. Then how did he end up shot and bleeding on my floor?"

This is when I know I'm about to make it worse, and I hate to have to do that. I wrap my arms around her, holding her tight, and take a deep breath in as I fix her with my eyes. She guesses before I even say the words.

"You're kidding, he says I did it, doesn't he?"

When I nod, she struggles to get out of my hold, but I hang on tight.

"Calm down, Princess. We'll get to the bottom of this."

"Calm down?" She barks out a bitter laugh I don't like the sound of. "Wow. This is too much."

She stills and I loosen my hold, which she immediately makes use of by twisting free. Instead of hauling out the door—which I half-expect her to do—she drops down on the threadbare couch and buries her head in her hands. She looks utterly defeated. I'd much rather have her pissed off and ranting than looking like this.

I crouch down in front of her.

"That accusation won't stand, Lindsey. You and I both know you had nothing to do with this. Hell, there are witnesses who saw the guy chasing you. Shooting at you."

"Yeah, but what about the rest? The police? The FBI? Jesus, is everyone after me?"

I shake my head. "From what I understand they just want to talk to you."

She snorts disbelievingly, "Sure they do, and the next thing you know I'll be in jail or dead because whoever was shooting at me gets a second chance. He finally found it, didn't he? Galen," she clarifies. "The ultimate revenge. This is what he does; he always finds new ways to torture me. He can't exert physical control anymore so he tries to rattle me, keep me off-balance by manipulating situations so I looked like a crazy person. I've always known there would be payback at some point for escaping him, but even I couldn't have imagined him resorting to this level of vindictiveness."

A renewed sense of hatred for that dirtbag has my blood boiling, but as much as I'd like to exert my own form of revenge on him, I have a job here. A far more important one.

"Look, whatever game that fuck is playing, he won't get away with it," I promise her. "But I think it is important you at least talk to Luna. Not in person," I quickly add when I see she's about to object. "But from here. The same way I talked to Ouray, over the ranch's secure network. You might be able to clear all of this up without the need to reveal our location. The sooner you can get law enforcement to take the focus off you and concentrate on chasing down the real bad guys here, the better it is."

She abruptly surges to her feet, almost knocking me on my ass, and starts pacing the room.

"All I *fucking* did was go to a wedding to do a friend a favor, and *this* is how the universe decides to repay me? With all eyes on me for something I had nothing to do with? Well, *fuck* that! I'm the least violent person there is!" she rants, impatiently pulling her arms out of her sleeves.

I'm relieved to see her anger back, but the next moment I have to duck as her jacket comes sailing over my head, landing on the coffee table behind me.

"Shit. I'm so sorry," she immediately apologizes, looking remorseful. "I didn't mean to hit you."

I get to my feet and snatch the jacket off the table.

"You missed me, but good try," I tease her with a wink, hoping to lighten things up a bit.

Hanging the jacket on the back of a dining chair, I notice one of the pockets is damp and seems to be damaged.

"Did you get caught on something?" I ask her, pointing out a small hole showing a corner of some kind of plastic sticking out.

"Dammit, Banner chewed on it." When she catches my look, she clarifies, "A baby horse."

She lifts the bottom of the jacket to investigate it closer, poking at the piece of plastic, mumbling, "I didn't know that was in there."

Then she unzips the pocket, sticks her hand in, and pulls free what looks like a memory card.

"Weird. That's not mine."

CHAPTER
TWENTY

WAPI

"Thank you."

I glance over at her, but she seems to be avoiding my eyes. I squeeze her hand in mine to get her to look at me.

"For what?"

We're taking a walk toward the river, which is supposed to border the meadows behind the ranch house. The trail starts right by the cabins and meanders in and out of the woods. It was something to do to kill time. There'd been another way to distract Lindsey that had come to mind, but I'm not sure that suggestion would've gone over well. She's about to jump out of her skin, waiting for a Zoom call with the FBI office in Durango.

"Oh, I don't know. For being honest—even though you probably figured I'd lose my shit—for being patient with me while I did just that, for not breaking my trust, and for driving across however many states to find me."

I tug her hand, stepping off the trail before turning her with her back against the trunk of a tree. I lean into her, bracing my forearm against the trunk above her head. I want to make sure I have her full attention before I answer her.

"Princess, I'll always be honest with you, I'll do my damnedest to always be patient with you, I will honor your trust, and I thought you'd have figured out by now I will follow you to the edge of nowhere."

"I'm starting to get the gist," she mumbles, her eyes welling up.

I shake my head. "None of that," I scold her, brushing a stray tear off her cheek with the pad of my thumb. "Kiss me instead."

She cups my face in her hands and does exactly that.

"Mmm," I hum against her mouth, when the burner phone starts buzzing in my pocket. "Phone."

I'd left my number back at the ranch, just in case, but the number on the screen belongs to Lindsey's father.

"David."

Lindsey's eyebrows shoot up to her hairline, and I put the call on speaker.

"Hey, Dad."

"Hey, darlin'. Two things," her father starts. "The FBI was just at my door. It didn't take them long to find me. They wanted to know if I'd heard from you. If I had any idea where they might find you. I told them I had no idea, and never really gave them an answer to the first question, I just shared I wasn't really that good at maintaining a relationship. It's not a lie, and if they took it to mean we haven't been in touch, that's their problem."

"They didn't ask to see your phone?" I wonder out loud.

"They did, and I asked them for a warrant, which they didn't have."

"Good. That at least buys us a little time," I point out. "Because they might be back."

"Right, which is why I decided to go on an impromptu road trip to Spokane. I have a friend there I haven't seen in a while."

I catch Lindsey rolling her eyes, as she mouths, *"Girlfriend."*

"I can hang out there for a couple of days, maybe a week," he suggests.

"Sounds like a plan," I approve. "You mentioned two things, what was the second?"

"I spoke to your mother again last night," he addresses his daughter.

I don't think I'll ever be his favorite person. That's fine by me, as long as I'm Lindsey's favorite person.

"Is she okay?" she asks right away.

"She's fine, but brace yourself, darlin'...she heard through the grapevine they found cameras in your house."

"The fuck?" I bark, a red haze suddenly blinding me. "They were watching her?"

"Hey, you wanna take that down a notch?" David snaps back. "You're not helping matters."

His words have me glance over at Lindsey, whose shocked, ghostly white face is like a cold bucket of water on my hot head.

"You okay?"

Probably a stupid question to ask a woman who just found out her privacy had been invaded in the worst possible way.

She turns her wide eyes on me and slowly shakes her head.

"I'm so far from okay, it's not even funny." Then she goes on to ask her father, "Where were they?"

"Now, sweetheart, I'm not sure—"

"Dad? Where. Were. They?"

I take a step closer to her, but she lifts her hands defensively and steps out of my reach.

"Dad?"

"Living room, bedroom, bathroom," he lists grudgingly.

I fight to control my temper before I plow my fist into that damn tree. Sadly, I'm not fast enough to control Lindsey, who lets out a yell and plants a hard right hook in the unforgiving bark of the trunk.

"Jesus, Linds." I reach for the hand she's now clutching against her chest.

"What's happening?" David's tinny voice demands to know.

"Galen," Lindsey hisses.

"Sounds more like the work of organized criminals than a spurned ex," I suggest.

Someone would have to find a way into her house without tripping the alarm, and have the knowledge to install those cameras in a way that went unnoticed.

Her father throws in his two cents.

"As much as I'd like to blame that motherfucker, this reeks of a professional, sweetheart."

Lindsey determinedly shakes her head, repeating, "It was Galen. He called the night before, warned me he was watching me. It was him, I'm not sure how he got in the house, but this is what he does; he hides cameras to watch me when he can't be around. It's his way of controlling me."

"No way that fucker is controlling you," I bite off, hating the man even more than I already did.

"No?" she asks in a bitter tone. "Do I need to remind you what we were doing in my lounge chair just a few nights before I came home to find him *in* my house, bleeding? He watched us, in my chair, in my living room. He watched us, got pissed, and decided to pay me a visit."

That makes me even angrier. The idea of him being witness to my first highly anticipated taste of her sours a memory I would've otherwise treasured.

"Well, ahem," Lindsey's father clears his throat, evidently uncomfortable with the direction of the conversation. "I think that's my cue to sign off. I'm sorry to spoil your day like that, sweetheart, but it sounds like maybe you should get in touch with law enforcement."

"That's exactly what I intend to do," his daughter announces, as she steps around me and starts walking.

By the time I end the call with David and catch up with her, she's halfway back to the ranch, her chin held high and her step determined.

———

Lindsey

I can feel the barely contained fury coming off Wapi in waves.

I'm angry too, but I guess after finding out about the cameras, it wasn't as much of a shock to me to discover Galen had been staying at an Airbnb, three doors down across the road from me. Not only did he have cameras in my house, he had eyes on me outside.

Luna was able to confirm it had been Galen. They found a laptop at his rental place with the video feed from those cameras being recorded. According to her, those files are being looked at as we speak which, I guess, is in part why Wapi is pacing the office at the ranch house with his hands in fists clenched by his side.

Whoever is checking the video feed from the living room in particular, is going to get an eyeful when they come across what should've been a very special, private moment.

It's not that it doesn't upset me, because it does, but at least I know watching that feed might help them identify who else was in my house. I'm more upset about Galen stealing even more from me than he had already taken.

"Who is looking at that computer?" Wapi wants to know.

"We're doing our best to keep it here," Luna explains. "Jasper is looking at it and Gomez is working hard to make sure it stays here. But it's complicated. We have several agencies wanting to lay claim on that computer because of what the contents might reveal. We have come to a tentative agreement Jasper will isolate material pertinent to the ongoing investigation, and only that will be turned over."

I drop my head in my hands. I don't think I'll ever be able to look Special Agent Greene in the eyes again. A familiar hand lands between my shoulders and begins a slow rub, before giving my neck a squeeze.

"Tell Luna about the memory card," he prompts.

I don't ever put memory cards in my pockets, not since I once took a hair-raising trip to the bottom of the Grand Canyon on the back of a mule, braving sheer cliffs and stifling heat to snap picture after gorgeous picture of the stunning vista I was assured I wouldn't be able to get any other way. I was so wrung out and rattled, I tucked my full card in my pocket, and accidentally ran the card through the laundry cycle when I forgot to take it out of my jeans. I literally cried, still unable to walk from the ordeal three days later when I pulled my jeans from the dryer and found the card ruined.

So it threw me a little when I found that card in my pocket earlier.

"What card?" Luna's voice demands sharply.

"It's an SD card," I explain. "I found it in my jacket pocket earlier. I'm pretty sure it's not mine and we tried to access the files on it, but it looked to be encrypted. I'm not in the habit of encrypting my files."

"If it's not yours, then how did it get in your pocket?"

I'd been thinking about that too, and unless someone got in my house, went into the closet, and tucked it in my pocket, there's only one way I can think of.

"Last time I wore it was when I was coming home from Denver," I share.

"When you collided with Douglas Spurnell," Luna finished.

"Was that the man's name? Spurnell?"

That's the first time I hear it. From what little news I've seen I don't think it was made public. Suddenly I wonder if he had a family, maybe he still had parents. The man who seemed rather abstract before, all of a sudden becomes real.

"Yeah," Luna responds. "He was a CI."

"CI?" I echo.

"Confidential informant. He was reporting to the FBI."

"I thought he was an accountant?" Wapi asks for clarification.

"For the project management company responsible for the ongoing Denver Airport expansion project, yes. But being an accountant and a CI are not necessarily mutually exclusive," she elaborates.

Expansion project. I remember reading something about

that. I definitely saw the evidence when I was at the airport. There was a lot of new construction going on, getting in and out of the airport had been a nightmare, with large portions of the existing infrastructure being torn up, I guess to make room for bigger and better.

A massive project with the hefty price tag of over a billion dollars, if I remember correctly. That's the kind of money people die for. Or kill for. If Spurnell was the accountant for the project management company, what information might he have had access to that would be of interest to the FBI?

"I would imagine an accountant working on a big project like that could be a fount of information," I volunteer.

Wapi glances at me while I wait for Luna's response. When it comes, I know I'm probably in the ballpark.

"You'd think. But I'm afraid I can't discuss details of the ongoing investigation at this time."

She gives me the "party line," which I take to mean I'm on the right track. She also quickly jumps topic.

"That SD card. I'd like to think it might be the target on your back."

Right, the card.

"In that case, I'd love to be rid of it, but I don't see how to get it to you without letting on where I am."

"Let me think on that. There may be a way to not only get the card to the right people, but to do it in a way that protects the information, while also taking the heat off you, so you can get back to your life."

Even just a couple of days ago I would've said, hell yes, but now I'm not so sure I want to get back to my life, at least not to the way it was. This outdoorsy lifestyle is growing on me. As much as I seem out of my element and not in control of my situation, I feel alive with a vibrancy I don't think I've felt since I was a teenager and the world was my oyster.

My life in Durango, my job, it's all pretty humdrum. So much so, a country rodeo a town over is the highlight of my year. It's sad, and I sometimes forget there is so much more to see and experience in this world. I may not get out much now, but I'd like to change that.

I listen to Wapi sign off with Luna, as she promises to get in touch via email before ending the call. I'm not sure what the next step is going to be, but for once, I'm in no hurry to find out.

When Wapi holds out his hand, I don't hesitate taking it. We step out of the High Meadow office and right in the path of Ama, who also looks to be on her way out the door.

"I'm heading to the store to pick a few things up for dinner. Do you guys have anything in particular you'd like?"

"Well…" I start, as we follow her out onto the porch, but Wapi quickly takes over.

"Appreciate the thought, but I think we're heading out for a bit this afternoon."

"Fair enough."

I wait for Ama to get in her SUV before turning to Wapi. "We are?"

He shrugs, with one of those half-smiles nearly hidden behind his beard.

"You looked like a natural on the back of that horse, and you definitely knew what you were doing bouncing on my dick early this morning, so I'd love to find out how you feel on the back of my bike going for a ride in the mountains. We can pick up some food to take with us. Dine *al fresco*. What do you say?"

I blush a little at the reminder of my dawn-inspired initiative this morning, wanting to do a little exploring of my own that ended up with Wapi's hands holding on to the headboard while I had my way with him.

Wapi misinterprets my slight pause and inadvertently reveals his own insecurity. "No one's looking here. I promise you'll be safe with me."

"I know I am," I assure him, slipping my arm around his waist as we make our way back to the cabin. "With you is the only place I *feel* safe."

CHAPTER
TWENTY-ONE

WAPI

Damn, I missed this.

Except this is better, with Lindsey's arms around me and her body pressed up against my back.

There isn't a helmet law in Montana—at least not for those over eighteen years of age—but I made Lindsey wear my half helmet. First chance we get, I'm gonna get her a proper one with full protection.

Luckily, Montana is a fairly thinly populated state and traffic doesn't get too crazy, especially here in the northern mountains. Also, I'm not a maniac on my bike, I'm a careful driver, especially with my precious cargo.

We stopped in Libby, a small town about ten or so minutes north of High Meadow, and were able to pick up a few things to eat and drink. From there I plan to take her up to Kootenai Falls. There's a suspension bridge we can walk across and a trail on the other side of the river we can take. Plenty of spots along the river for us to sit down and have a bite.

Then after, I was hoping to catch the sunset somewhere. Ama was very helpful with that and suggested I head up to Leigh Lake, near Snowshoe Peak. She said the forest service road there was decent and should be drivable on the bike, and that the views up there are stunning. Added bonus is that it's secluded, far from the civilized world and therefore perfect for my plans, which are not necessarily suited for public display.

"Ohh…this is so pretty," Lindsey observes when we reach the riverside from the parking lot at the trailhead.

I hum my agreement. It is pretty. I remember stopping here on my way back to Colorado. I'd been in Alaska for an extended period of time and was doing a bit of sightseeing on my way home. I recall having stopped in Banff, Alberta, Canada for a couple of days, when I got a call from Paco. He was the only brother I'd kept in touch with during that time. He mentioned Nosh, the club's founding father and its former president, was not doing well. So instead of sticking around in the Canadian Rockies for a while as I'd hoped to do, I ended up dropping south, and following the Kootenai River across the border back into Montana.

Now that's a drive I'd love to repeat when I'm not in a hurry, and preferably with Lindsey on the back of my bike. In fact, I'd love to take her to see Banff, which has to be one of the coolest mountain towns I've encountered, and if possible, take her all the way north to Alaska to show her my little homestead. Not more than a cabin without running water—other than the river outside—or many other amenities for that matter, on a piece of desolate, but beautiful country.

A few weeks ago, I wouldn't have been able to even imagine her out there with me, roughing it, but I have to admit, Lindsey has shown more adaptability and grit than I would've given her credit for.

I swing the tote bag with groceries over my shoulder and grab Lindsey's hand with my free one, lacing our fingers as I pull her toward the suspension bridge.

"This was one of the few stops I made on my way home last year."

She lifts her eyes to me in immediate understanding. "When Nosh took a turn?"

"Yeah. I had a hard time coming to terms with the prospect of losing him. He wasn't an easy man by any stretch of the word, but he made me feel I belonged. To him, to the club. I'd never had that before, so for me that was a big deal."

"I'm guessing it felt like you were losing a parent."

"Yeah, pretty much. Ironically, that whole road trip of mine had been about proving to myself I could be on my own, that I could sustain myself without needing to belong. One phone call made me come to the realization I already belonged whether I needed to, or even wanted to, or not."

On the north side of the bridge, I pull her off the trail and through the trees, to the large rocks on the edge of the river.

"I was sitting right there when that bit of truth hit me. That there was more in Durango pulling me back than there had been driving me away."

She pulls her hand out of mine and clambers onto the rock, finding one she can sit on. Then she takes off her shoes and socks and sticks her feet in the rushing water. I kick off my own boots and socks, roll up my jeans, and sit down next to her, dipping my feet in as well.

"Holy shit," I curse. "That's fucking cold."

Shouldn't be a surprise, the Kootenai River doesn't really ever get warm, not even in the heat of summer.

"Was that me?" Lindsey asks, her eyes focused on the river.

"Was what you?"

"One of the things that drove you away from Durango?"

"No. What drove me to hightail it out of town was all me. But you *were* one of the main things that pulled me back."

She looks confused and a little flustered.

"Really? You could've fooled me."

I grin and brush the back of my fingers over her cheek.

"Wasn't you I was trying to fool, I was fooling myself, thinking I could keep my distance."

She barely has a chance to huff out, "Oh," before I cover her mouth with mine, kissing her deeply. I smile against her lips at her instant response to me, with one hand hooking behind my neck and the other grabbing on to my shirt.

I pour everything into that kiss and by the time I break away, her eyes look a little glazed over. But when they finally focus on me, she flashes a grin.

"Yeah, you definitely suck at keeping your distance," she teases.

"Are you complaining?"

"Me?" She lifts her hands defensively. "I wouldn't dream of it. I rather enjoy being irresistible."

"To me," I add. "You enjoy being irresistible to me."

She leans in and lifts her hand to my face, brushing her fingers through my facial hair. Then she tugs on my beard, forcing me to tilt my head down for her to brush my lips with hers, and with a vexing little smile, she mocks me.

"Of course, dear."

Lindsey

"That was really good."

I lick the last fleck of wasabi off my finger.

I was surprised to see a Japanese eatery in town and even more so that Wapi directed us there. It was different, the name Kaiju Bar and Grill didn't scream Japanese to me, nor did the mostly bar and grill style decor, but the place had great choices on their menu. Some traditional, some fusion, and sushi of every kind.

Wapi seemed to know his sushi and I gladly left ordering to him. It's funny how I am now learning how liberating it can be—and frankly, quite enjoyable—to let go of control. I guess the essence is in the "letting go," suggesting a voluntary release. Very different from having control manipulated and forcefully taken away from you.

In any event, letting someone else drive the car every so often has only expanded my views and enhanced my experiences.

"It was," he rumbles, popping the last bite of his roll in his mouth. "Definitely a place to remember next time we're in town."

I turn to him. "Next time?"

It wasn't really that which caught my attention, but rather the use of the term, "we."

"Your brother lives here. I can see us spending more time here in the future."

There it is again, another inclusive term. I don't get back

to it, but use the drive to the next stop Wapi planned to mull it over in my head, noting absentmindedly how much I enjoy being on the back of his bike.

The ride is beautiful, especially once he turns us away from the main highway south of town and we find ourselves on a dirt road heading up the mountain. Wapi explains it's a forest service road and should bring us to our destination.

On some turns, where the ground drops away on one side of us, I cling to Wapi like my life depends on it, which it technically does. However, the views into the valley below are stunning and make the occasionally white-knuckle ride worth it.

Once again, I wish I had my camera on me, but for lack of better, I end up snapping a few shots on my pay-as-you-go phone. The quality will suck, but at least I'll have something to remember this outing with. The only reason I don't call it a date is because the timing seems a little odd for a date, in the middle of trying to hide from people who mean me harm.

When Wapi pulls up to the edge of a pristine mountain lake with water so turquoise it looks like a painting, I hop off the back of the bike the moment it rolls to a stop.

"Stop bringing me places I need my camera for!" I exclaim unreasonably as I swing around at him. "This is breathtaking."

He pulls me in his arms and smiles against my lips.

"I will bring you back here. In fact, next time we'll bring a tent and set up camp here."

"Camp?" I echo, slightly mortified.

I mean, yes, it's beautiful, and I could look at it all day long, but sleeping out here? On the ground? Without a bathroom? That might be taking it a little too far.

"I'll show you how comfortable it can be," Wapi offers, opening one of his saddle bags to pull out a rolled-up mat. From the other one he pulls a sleeping bag and a couple of Turkish towels.

"Where did you get all that?" I want to know.

"I always carry the mat and sleeping bag, they've come in handy at times, but the towels I borrowed from Ama.

In no time he has the self-inflating mat laid out, the sleeping bag zipped open, and the towels spread out on top. Then he starts taking off his boots and stripping down.

"Not that I'm complaining," I make clear. "But clue me in?"

The moon is starting to rise, still a bit pale against the dusky sky. It'll be beautiful reflected off the still surface of the lake when it is fully dark.

"Strip, and I'll tell you."

"I'm not going to strip here, where anyone could walk up on us," I protest.

Wapi just raises his eyebrows as he drops his jeans to his ankles with a flourish. He really is beautiful; even mostly flaccid his cock still impresses, and the bulk he added to his body the years he was away, as well as his handsome looks, make for an appealing total package.

A very appealing package that is becoming even more so the longer I stare.

"Linds, stop ogling me and get naked. We're going in."

To my shock he walks right into what must be freezing lake waters.

"Oh my God. How are you not freezing?"

"Ama says except for a twenty-foot pit at the center, this lake is otherwise shallow, only about six feet deep so with the solar radiation at this elevation, it heats up quickly. It's nice," he adds.

I only manage to hold out for about two seconds before I cave, stripping down as fast as I can. I don't have to look to know Wapi follows my every move. When I'm naked as the day I was born, shivering a little against the cooling air, he rises out of the water, his arms stretched out for me.

I don't walk, I run and jump in his arms, which close on me instantly. With my legs wrapped around his hips, he holds me suspended. I brace my hands on his shoulders and smile down in his face.

"Hey."

"Hey, yourself," he returns.

His eyes are dark with passion as he slides his hands under my ass, his fingers exploring my slit.

"I wanna fuck you like this."

"Are you asking? Because I'm pretty much a sure bet at this point," I return, my breath hitching as he brushes my clit with a fingertip.

"Didn't bring any condoms."

"Do we need them?" I ask. "I'm on the Depo shot."

I started getting the shot about five years ago when I discovered Galen messing with my pill pack. No way was I going to get tricked into having a child with the man.

Wapi's face lights up in a way that sends a tingle down my spine. He likes the idea of nothing between us.

"I'm clean," he shares.

"Me too."

I bite my lip and sigh when I feel his digit work inside me.

"Fuck, yeah…" he groans, his blunt head probing my opening.

Only for a moment, because the next moment he surges up in me.

"Oh fuck, yeah."

———

"Open your eyes, baby."

I'm cuddled against his warm skin, my body relaxed and limp after he not only fed me, but fucked me *al fresco* as well. The days have been nice and warm, but at night—especially here in the mountains—it can get chilly. Wapi is like a stove though, and wrapped around him I almost doze off.

"Princess, look at the stars."

"You already made me see stars. Twice," I remind him.

I can feel the chuckle rumble in his chest.

"Open them," he insists. "I promise you it's worth it."

I peel back one, and then the second eyelid, squinting up at the night sky.

Oh wow. He's right. It *is* worth it.

Sitting up, I grab for my shirt and shrug it over my head.

"I didn't mean for you to get dressed," he grumbles, making me smile.

If anything, Wapi is certainly good for my self-esteem.

"It's beautiful," I sigh, taking in the countless stars dotting the sky.

So many there is no way to ever count them.

"Sure is," he confirms, but when I throw him a quick glance, I catch him looking at me instead of the stars. "One of these days I want to take you up to my cabin in Alaska," he continues. "On clear nights, from September to about April, you can catch the northern lights up there. You would love it."

"I would love that," I concede. "And I hope I'll have my camera with me then, although it might be hard to beat this."

I wrap my arms around my pulled-up knees and tilt my head back to look up at the skies. Then I feel Wapi slide in behind me, stretching his long legs on either side of me, as he wraps his arms around my entire body.

Looking up, with my head resting on his shoulder, I can see sections of the Milky Way, occasionally catching a glimpse of a steadily moving satellite, or the tail of a shooting star. A moment of peaceful magic in the crazy chaos my life has become.

Wapi starts speaking softly in my ear, as if he's able to hear my thoughts. "If ever you need a moment to ground yourself, I'll take you up on Baldy Mountain, near Durango. It's the same sky, and I have a spot up there I'll share with you. I sometimes spend the night there when I need to think. It keeps me anchored."

I grab onto his arms, and pull them tighter around me.

"I'd like that too."

I'm not sure how long we sit there, but at some point Wapi indicates it's getting a little chilly, and maybe we should make our way back down the mountain. As comfortable as I was snuggling on that mat in his arms, I prefer a bed to sleep in. So I quickly put on the rest of my clothes, while he does the same.

When Wapi starts rolling up his sleeping mat, an alert sounds on his phone. He checks the notification and glances over at me.

"What is it?"

"Email from Luna. She wants us to know if we can meet her in Denver at the FBI main office the day after tomorrow."

"Denver? That's not a lot of notice. Are we flying?"

"No," he responds right away. "Too public, too easy. We'll be coming in on our terms and on my bike."

"In two days? How long a drive is it anyway?"

"Seventeen hours in perfect conditions."

As much as I like riding on the back of his bike, seventeen hours of it does not sound like my idea of fun.

"Ouch."

He grins. "No shit. I'll send her a message back. We'll be there in four days. Three days driving, one day to get a lay of the land. I'll tell her Friday afternoon."

I'll be sad to leave the ranch. The place and the people have been wonderful, but to be honest, I can't wait for this mess to be over. Maybe after, like Wapi suggested, I can come back to visit with Dan, and perhaps get to know him better if I stay a little longer.

That is, if they'll have me.

CHAPTER
TWENTY-TWO

LINDSEY

"You are welcome back any time."

I'm surprised when Alex pulls me in for a hug.

She and I are still standing on the porch of the big house saying our goodbyes. Wapi, Jonas, and Dan—who'd come back from the search last night—are congregated around Wapi's Harley.

"You know, if you didn't already have a great guy, I would've liked to have introduced you to my son, Jackson," Alex volunteers. "I think you might've hit it off." She winks at me. "Although, both he and Jonas might disown me if they found out I'm vetting potential daughter-in-law material."

I smile back. "Well, for the record, I'm flattered, and thank you. I look forward to meeting your son and the rest of the team next time I visit. Hopefully under less stressful circumstances."

Alex stays on the porch when I go down to join the

guys. Jonas claps me on the shoulder and wishes us safe travels before joining his wife at the railing.

"Ready?" Wapi asks.

I nod and turn to Dan.

"Thank you for being cool and giving me a safe place to stay. I wish we'd had a chance to get to know each other a bit better."

He grins at me. "Me too, but now that the cat is out of the bag, I'm sure there'll be plenty of opportunity."

Then he too pulls me into a quick, slightly awkward, hug before taking a step back with his arms crossed over his chest, as Wapi fits me with his helmet.

"We're stopping at the Harley store in Kalispell," he announces. "Getting you your own."

We don't have a lot to lug with us, just a clean change of clothes—we were able to wash our own laundry at the ranch yesterday and will send back the borrowed clothes later—a couple of toiletries, and some food and water Ama had packed up for us. Between us we should have enough cash to last us for gas, food, a couple of motel rooms, and any eventualities that pop up along the way.

The memory card is safely tucked into the inside pocket of Wapi's leather vest, by his insistence. As if by taking responsibility over the card, he could take the target off my back. It seemed important to him, so I gave him that. In all honesty, it's a bit of a relief.

Wapi swings his leg over his bike and waits for me to climb up behind him before starting the engine. I turn around and wave, as he pulls away from High Meadow. I feel like I started a new chapter here and expanded my horizons.

I come away with new friends, a surprise brother, a meaningful and much anticipated relationship, and a brand-new sense of self. It feels like I am starting to find my own rhythm in this world, instead of dancing to someone else's music.

Pressing myself a little closer to Wapi's back, I open my eyes and enjoy the ride.

Our first stop will be Kalispell, because Wapi insists I need a few things from the bike store for the long road trip, but as it turns out, I'll also be able to give my dad a quick hug. When Dan got in touch with him last night to fill him in on what was happening, he hadn't left for Spokane yet. His plan had been to leave first thing in the morning, but now he's scheduled to meet us at Glacier Harley-Davidson before heading out.

Dan brought up the idea I use Dad's phone to make a quick call to my mother, which I thought was very considerate. He pointed out if anyone was monitoring either of my parents' phones, a phone call from one to the other wasn't likely to raise any flags.

Meeting Dad at the Harley store will keep the trip interruption to a minimum, since Wapi is hoping to make it as close to the Idaho border as we can get before stopping for the night. Ours is not going to be the most direct way to Denver, but we agreed traveling a less predictable route is probably the safer option.

The hour and a half it takes us to get to Kalispell goes quickly, and before you know it we're pulling into the Glacier Harley-Davidson parking lot. It's a pretty nondescript, one-story building with a patio with picnic tables I could've easily mistaken for maybe a diner or something, if not for the massive Harley-Davidson sign in front.

I recognize Dad's pickup one row over from where Wapi parked his bike alongside a few other motorcycles. No sign of Dad though, just a few bikers sitting at a picnic table having a smoke and eyeing us with suspicion. Probably a territorial thing, since Wapi is wearing his Arrow's Edge MC cut.

Wapi hooks the helmet on a handlebar, grabs my hand, and with a chin lift for our audience on the patio, leads me into the store.

"Anything I can do for you, sugar?"

A gum-snapping, buxom brunette, with hard eyes in a pretty face, addresses Wapi. I'm clearly being ignored, which is fine. She probably doesn't care for the way I look, which is nothing like someone who belongs on the back of a handsome bad boy's bike. Not that I care, because as hard as she's trying to draw his attention, his hand is holding on to mine, and I can feel his annoyance climb.

"A helmet, some proper boots, and rain gear for my old lady."

He almost snarls the words and I give his hand a warning squeeze.

"Easy, tiger," I mumble against his shoulder.

The woman finally glances at me, obviously taking stock, but her voice is not unfriendly when she asks, "What are you? Size ten? Twelve?"

"Twelve is probably a safer bet," I concede.

"And your shoes, a nine?"

"Yes. You're good," I add.

She nods and moves from behind the counter to a rack along the rear wall of the surprisingly roomy store. We start to follow her when a fitting room on the other side of the counter opens and my father walks out, decked out in leather. I have to shove my face into Wapi's shoulder to stifle my bark of laughter.

I love my father, I do, but he looks ridiculous. First the whole cowboy getup, and now with the biker leathers I'm sure meeting Wapi inspired him to try on. I'm about to say something when I catch a hint of vulnerability on his face as he looks at me, and I promptly swallow my snide comment.

Even with Dad's short stature, I grew up seeing him as larger than life. He was always a bit loud, plenty boisterous, and generally demanded attention, although he received plenty of it in his heyday. I never really considered my father might not be quite as confident once stripped of his NASCAR career and all that came with it. In that world, everyone identified him with what he did. He may well have a hard time being just a man and is looking to belong. Hence the Stetson almost as big as he is, and these shiny new leathers that make him look like a kid dressed up for Halloween.

I'm suddenly a little concerned what is going to come out of Wapi's mouth when he addresses my father, but once again he surprises me.

"I didn't know you were interested in motorcycles," he shares without a trace of humor in his voice at my father's appearance. I could kiss him for that.

Dad shrugs. "Thought about it."

"Well, I suppose for you riding a motorcycle might be a nice hobby, but I'm sure it won't give quite the same thrill as driving a race car at breakneck speeds. Not that I'd know, I've never driven one and would probably be too much of a chickenshit to even try anyway."

Okay, it's official; I love this man. With each word I can see my father's chest puffing out a little more. For a young man in his prime, like Wapi, to admit that—whether true or not—I'm sure makes my father feel ten feet tall.

I grin as I walk over to Dad, giving him a hug. "Looks sharp, Dad. Are you really thinking about it?"

He glances over at Wapi before looking back at me. "Nah, I think I'll stick to cars. That's more my speed."

———

Wapi

The relief on Lindsey's face is palpable when her father brushes her cheek with a kiss.

"Hang tight for a second, I'm just going to change out of this."

Lindsey nods. "Sure. I have to try on some stuff myself."

David disappears back into the changing room, as his daughter lifts up on her toes and presses her lips against mine.

"Thank you."

"Sure thing," I mumble back.

Twenty minutes later, we're sitting outside at one of the picnic tables, eating a couple of pizza slices David picked us up from a place down the road. Lindsey's new rain gear is packed away on my bike, her new helmet with sun visor is hanging next to mine on the handlebars, and her sneakers are tucked into the saddlebags, because she's wearing her new, sturdy, biker boots.

An early lunch, and then we're back on the road, hopefully making it to Dillon, Montana, before it gets too dark out. It'll be a four-and-a-half-hour drive, but there are a few overnight options in Dillon and a couple of restaurants we could hit up for dinner.

But first we need to get in touch with Mel. It's actually Lindsey's father who makes the call, putting the phone on speaker and setting it in the middle of the table so we all can hear.

"What do you want, David?" Mel's voice comes through sharp.

"Hello to you too, Melanie. Are you alone?"

"No, Paco is here. Why do you care if I'm alone?"

"Hey, Mom," Lindsey jumps in.

All you can hear on the other side is a whoosh—like the release of a breath—and then a muffled, "It's Linds."

"Mom?" Lindsey repeats.

"Hey, girl," Paco answers instead. "Your mom needs a moment."

Mel is tough as nails but a softie at heart. Lindsey herself is not much different, she seems affected as well. Like mother like daughter.

"So does Linds," I speak up when I catch her grabbing one of the napkins off the table to blow her nose. "Which gives me a chance to ask you a favor. I assume you heard we're supposed to meet Luna in Denver?"

"Yes."

"Well, I wouldn't mind having a brother at my back for that."

"I'm there," Paco fires back right away.

"Actually, I'm not so sure that's a good idea. Someone may be keeping an eye on you, as Lindsey's stepfather, but I don't think anyone would be monitoring Honon. We've gotta get on the road here shortly, but if you wouldn't mind getting hold of him, see what he has going on the rest of this week? I hope to make it to Rock Springs, Wyoming, tomorrow night, because on Thursday I want to get into Fort Collins at a decent hour. I need some time to plan."

"Leave it with me. Any idea where you're gonna be staying in Fort Collins?"

"Not yet. I'll let him know when I get close. And Paco? Keep this between us."

He grunts his agreement when Mel interrupts, snapping with her full bristles up.

"If you guys are done chitchatting, do you think I can talk to my daughter now?"

"Geeze, Mom, chill. I'm right here," Lindsey instantly responds.

"I will chill when I have you in front of me so I can see for myself you're okay."

Lindsey softens her voice, "I'm all right, Momma. I'm safe, Wapi's not letting me out of his sight."

"Good, he'd better not. I expect you home in one piece," Mel grumbles.

"I should be there by the weekend," Lindsey promises, before she adds, "Oh, and Mom? When I get there, I have some exciting news to share with you."

"Oh, fuck…you're not pregnant, are you?"

"Jesus, Mel," Paco mutters in the background.

I feel David's glare burn a hole in my head, but my eyes are fixed on Lindsey, who looks mortified.

"Ma! How do you even come up with stuff like that? And worse…say it out loud," she lays into her mother. "Besides, what if I was pregnant? Nice way to spoil what should be happy news."

"Well, if you're not pregnant, what *is* the news?"

Lindsey sighs, closing her eyes as she shakes her head. "I'll tell you all about it in a few days, Mom."

"Not if we don't get going soon," I interject, worried this back-and-forth could go on for days.

My comment may have prompted the goodbyes, but it still takes another ten minutes for Lindsey to end the call and say goodbye to her father, who is driving off now.

"Come here." I reach for Lindsey, who is struggling to close the strap on her new helmet. "So…I'm curious too. If not pregnant, what news were you planning to share?" I clip the buckle under her chin. "Us?"

"My brother," she shares, stepping back as she adjusts the helmet on her head.

I get on the bike and wait for Lindsey to get on and wrap her arms around me from behind.

Then she adds, with her lips brushing my ear, "I'm pretty sure she's already figured out there's an us. Hence the pregnancy question."

That makes sense.

I start the engine and check the fuel gauge before pulling onto the road, heading south.

The four and a half hours it was supposed to take to get to Dillon, Montana, turned into almost seven. We got stuck behind a tractor trailer rollover on the I-90 about twenty-five miles outside of Butte. The Canadian truck's load of beer from a brewery in British Columbia spilled all over the eastbound lanes, ground traffic to a standstill. It lasted a good hour and a half before they had the one lane open and we were able to crawl toward our cutoff to the I-15 South.

A lot of those almost seven hours, the conversation between Lindsey and her mother about pregnancy continued to play through my mind, until an image of Linds, round with my baby, popped in my head and I almost ran my bike off the damn road.

By the time I finally pull my bike in front of room seventeen of the Beaverhead Lodge in Dillon, Montana, I'm starving, grungy, and exhausted. Lindsey looks like she's not faring much better. She carries the bag of McDonald's we picked up on the way into town and unlocks the door. I quickly grab our things and follow her inside.

"You go first," I tell her, after we've scarfed down our food.

When she ducks into the small, but thankfully clean bathroom, I flip on the TV to watch some news and lean back against the headboard.

I can hear her in the shower. It's damned tempting to strip down and join her, but if I'm already sore and exhausted, I imagine it would go double for Lindsey. She's not used to long rides on the bike and we have another at least seven-hour ride tomorrow, provided we don't hit any delays on the road. What we both need is a shower and sleep.

When I walk into the room after my shower, Lindsey is already curled up in one of the beds and looks asleep. For a moment I'm undecided, not sure whether she's expecting me to get into the second bed, or crawl in with her.

"Are you coming in or what?" she mumbles, making the decision for me.

I slip in bed and curl my body around hers. For a moment, I close my eyes and enjoy the feel of her skin against mine, her scent in my nose.

"Do you want kids?"

Don't know how that slipped, but now that it's out there I'm curious what Lindsey's response will be.

Except none is forthcoming. She's already asleep.

CHAPTER
TWENTY-THREE

WAPI

It's still early, judging by the watery light I can see coming in through the threadbare curtains.

I stretch carefully, trying not to wake Lindsey who, once again, crashed hard last night when we checked into this sub-par motel. It's far from the only place in town, but it was the first one we encountered driving into Rock Springs.

Yesterday was another challenging ride. Not due to an accident, but summer construction on just about every damn road through Idaho and parts of Wyoming. It's not exactly fun driving over rough surfaces on a motorcycle for long stretches at a time. Even less so, when doing it in the kind of weather we encountered for most of the day.

A major system went through the region, creating strong winds, rain, and cooler temperatures than is normal for this time of year. Under any other circumstances I would've holed up until it passed, or aimed my bike in a different direction, but unfortunately those weren't options. As a result, when we finally hit Rock Springs around dinner-time, both of us were drenched to the bone and done. The routine was the same, eat, shower, and sleep.

My stomach growls. We had a pizza delivered to the room last night, but I guess my body needs food again, even though I'm already getting sick and tired of fast food. Beside me Lindsey stirs.

"Is it time to get up?" she mumbles sleepily, as she turns and drapes an arm over my noisy stomach.

A quick glance at my phone shows it's only six thirty. We have four hours on the interstate today and clear skies predicted, so we should be fine if we get on the road by nine. That leaves two-and-a-half hours for breakfast and other stuff. Not necessarily in that order. We'll start with the other stuff first.

"No need to rush out of bed, Princess."

I roll us so Lindsey is on her back and I'm on my side with full access to her body. Just the way I like it.

"Mmm," she purrs with a satisfied little smile, stretching her arms over her head. "I thought you were hungry?"

Who am I to resist the generous offer of her gorgeous tits arching up to me? I drop my head and close my mouth over the closest nipple, my hand reaching for her other breast. I love her soft moans and the way her body responds to my touch.

"Hungry for you," I mumble my response against her skin as I switch breasts, giving them equal attention.

I hiss when her small hand closes around the raging hard-on I'm sporting.

"Not gonna last if you do that," I warn her.

"I'm good with hard and fast," she fires back without hesitation.

How the hell am I supposed to resist that?

Forty-five minutes later and freshly showered—again—I pull the door shut behind us. We'll find a place for breakfast in town before we hit the road again. As much as I enjoy having Lindsey on my bike, this particular trip is one I don't mind coming to an end.

"What'll it be?" the grumpy waitress asks, tossing two menus on the table.

"Morning to you too. Coffee, to start. Please," I pointedly add.

She throws me a dirty look and turns her back.

"Something tells me she didn't get the same wake-up call I did this morning," Lindsey observes with a grin on her face.

A grin I return, because that was pretty spectacular. A good start to the day I'm determined not to have spoiled by a waitress with a pissy attitude. Not even when, moments later, she slams two mugs of coffee down, sloshing hot liquid over the table.

"Sorry," she mumbles, not sounding sorry at all.

I'm not quite sure what her beef is but she clearly has one. At this point I wouldn't put it past her to spit in any breakfast we order, which would be a shame, because it smells damn good in here. Luckily, the diner has an open kitchen and I can pretty much see the food being prepared.

"Tracy, can you come here for a sec?"

An older guy with a hairnet covering his head and wearing a white apron steps out of the kitchen and gestures for our waitress to approach him. I can't hear what's being said, but two minutes later she rips off her apron, tosses it on the counter, and storms out of the diner.

She's barely gone when another waitress stops by our table.

"I'm so sorry for the delay, we appear to be a little understaffed this morning. My name is Liz, I'll be your waitress this morning. Have you had a chance to decide yet?"

Both of us order straightforward bacon and eggs, which are delivered to our table less than ten minutes later. By the cook himself.

"Breakfast is on me," he announces unexpectedly. "I apologize for my sister. Bad breakup. Her ex is a biker, rides with a local club, and he's done her dirty. Guess she saw your cut and decided to take it out on you. Don't want that to reflect bad on us. We've always welcomed bikers."

"Not to worry," I assure him. "We all have bad days, and I'm sorry she was treated poorly."

"Appreciate it," he shares, and with a nod for Lindsey, he heads back to the kitchen.

"Wow, a side of drama with breakfast," she comments, digging into the scrambled eggs she ordered. Swallowing a bite, she studies me with a slight tilt to her head. "You handled that very graciously."

"I'm determined not to let anything mess with the good mood you put me in this morning," I confess.

I can tell she likes that.

So three or so hours later, when an asshole in a Beemer merges onto the I-80 East, forcing me out of the righthand lane and sandwiching me between him and the truck passing me on the left, I keep a cool head.

However, when I catch blue flashing lights in my mirrors, I'm afraid my good mood has run its course.

———

Lindsey

"Were we speeding?" I ask, when he kills the engine.

Wapi shakes his head as he takes off his helmet. I take mine off as well, chancing a glance over my shoulder where the state patrol cruiser is parked on the pavement behind us. I catch sight of the officer getting out of his vehicle, and I can already tell by the way he hitches up his pants, straightens his shades, and strokes a hand down the front of his uniform before placing it on top of his service weapon by his hip, he's not planning to let us get away with anything.

Not that I know what the hell he pulled us over for in the first place.

"Can I see your license and registration?"

"Sure," Wapi answers. "I'll have to get off, it's in my seat."

"Go ahead," the officer responds.

I get off first and step out of the way so Wapi can dismount. I watch him flip open the seat and pull out what I assume is the bike's registration. He fishes his license from his wallet, and hands both to the officer.

"Was there any particular reason you pulled us over?" he asks the officer. "I'm pretty sure I wasn't speeding."

"Caught you lane-splitting back there. That's illegal in the state of Wyoming." The officer turns to me. "Could I see some ID for you as well, miss?"

I'm about to launch an objection when I notice a shift in Wapi's stance, and I don't like the vibe I'm getting when I see his hands curl into fists by his side. I quickly pull my driver's license from my pocket and hand it over.

The officer nods, turns on his heel, and takes our paper-work back to the cruiser.

Taking a step closer, I reach out for Wapi's hand, closing both of mine around the tight fist and peeling his fingers away from his palm. When I press my own palm against his and entwine our fingers, I can feel some of the sudden tension leave him.

"That's a bullshit call," he mutters.

"What is lane-splitting?" I want to know, stepping in front of him so his focus is on me.

"If I were to pass a car without changing lanes, or slip between two cars, that would be considered lane-splitting," he explains.

"He's talking about that thing back there with the asshole in the BMW? But you didn't do that, *he* pushed *you* out of the lane."

"I know. I'm the one sitting on the bike though," he states bitterly.

I never realized how often these guys have to fight stereotypes and preconceived notions, even when they do nothing wrong. It's no wonder these men don't trust easily, when they in turn aren't shown any.

As much as I feel the state trooper is in the wrong, I'm not going to voice my displeasure, because I'm afraid if I do, Wapi won't be able to hold on to the thin veil of control.

Now, that could lead to some real trouble.

Wapi sits down sideways on his bike and pulls me between his legs.

"Why does he need my license?" I wonder out loud.

"Probably just throwing shit at the wall to see what'll stick," he grumbles.

The trooper makes us wait for close to ten minutes

before he returns and hands me my license back. Then he passes Wapi his paperwork plus a ticket.

"For?" he asks.

"Lane-splitting. You can pay online within ten days; the web address is on the back. You'll find information there too on how to fight the ticket, should you choose to do so."

I know it takes a lot out of Wapi to keep quiet, but we discussed not prolonging this any more than is necessary while we were waiting, no matter what happened.

So he accepts his ticket without a word, and quietly tucks it in his pocket as the officer returns to his vehicle. We watch as he pulls away from the shoulder and continues on his way. Then Wapi turns to me, putting his hands on my shoulders as he leans down to bring us at eye level.

"I'm guessing another hour or so to get to Fort Collins, but I'd like to make a stop in Laramie, which is just up ahead. I need to give Honon a call, see where he's at, and we also need to figure out where we're going to stay."

"Okay."

The realization we're this close to the Colorado border rattles me a little. I wonder if my growing nerves are showing on my face, because he squeezes my shoulders, smiles reassuringly, and drops a kiss on my lips.

Coming into Laramie, we pull into a Petro Travel Center where Wapi gasses up and I head inside the small restaurant attached to the gas station to grab a few sandwiches and some coffee. When I meet Wapi outside, he points us to a small empty picnic area at the back of the property.

I force myself to eat while he calls Honon. I listen with half an ear and only catch bits and pieces, but enough to know he's already arrived in Fort Collins. I was feeling great after the start we had this morning, but with the passing of time and distance, I no longer feel so hot.

"He already scoped out places for us to stay. Apparently, he picked the Fort Collins Inn because it is in an industrial area of town. It has parking behind the building and out of sight of the road, with only a single entry point."

I don't want to ask why those things are important because I'm pretty sure the answer would confirm what I already know. Closer to Denver means closer to danger. I hope to God this is all going to work out.

Wapi gestures at the remaining half of my sandwich. "Is that all you're going to eat?"

"Yeah, I'm still full from breakfast."

For a moment it looks like he's going to call me on my lie, but then he picks it up and downs it in two big bites, while I finish the dregs of my coffee. He takes my empty cup, tosses it along with the rest of the garbage in the trash can, and grabs my hand to pull me to my feet.

"Hang in there, Linds," he urges, bruising my lips with a short, hard kiss. "It'll be all over soon."

Damn, I hope so.

Half an hour later we pass a welcome sign to "Colorful Colorado."

Just south of Laramie we took the exit onto HWY 289 which runs straight to Fort Collins. There is far less traffic here than was on the interstate, but this isn't a four-lane highway. I do my best to focus on the landscape, which is mostly flat here with the occasional cluster of trees when we pass over a river or creek, but my mind keeps zoning out.

So much so, I don't even register the large black SUV parked on a trail that runs along the creek up ahead.

At least not until I catch a flash, and then another.

The sound comes after, as Wapi's bike starts to wobble

and veers across to the other side of the road, into oncoming traffic.

Then I hear him yell, "Head down, Linds!" and I know we're in a heap of trouble.

CHAPTER
TWENTY-FOUR

WAPI

Fuck.

It's a goddamn miracle we haven't crashed yet.

I'm too scared to lift my hand off the handlebars to make sure Lindsey is okay behind me. I'm doing seventy miles on the shoulder of a fifty-five-mile-an-hour highway going against oncoming traffic. It was the only way to get some cover, since there is nothing on this stretch of highway to hide behind. Flat, with fields and grassland forever.

A quick check in my mirrors tells me the black Expedition that came flying onto the road back there is still hot on our tail. So far, we've lucked out with a steady stream of vehicles going northbound, but there's bound to be a lull in traffic at some point, leaving us open for them to take potshots at.

I need a fucking plan.

The good news is we're not that far outside of Fort Collins, which means help isn't that far away.

"Lindsey! Get my phone from my pocket. Redial the last number and tell Honon we're coming in hot on the 287."

I don't get verbal confirmation but I know she heard me when I feel her shaky hand try to work its way into my pocket. A moment later I hear her voice.

"We're being shot at… 287. He wants me to tell you we're coming in hot… I don't know, I don't think far… They're in a black SUV."

"Expedition!" I yell.

"Did you hear that?… Expedition, yes. We're on the opposite shoulder…"

I notice up ahead a tractor trailer ends the flow of traffic heading my way, the road is empty beyond. I slow down immediately, hoping to keep vehicles between us and the shooter as long as possible. My eyes are peeled for a turnoff or an intersection to give me some options, but there's nothing.

The only thing I've been able to spot is a dirt road running from farm to farm, meandering parallel to the highway. Unfortunately, it's impossible to see how deep the ditch is on the edge of the shoulder because of the tall grass. Last thing I want to do is crash.

Seconds later I no longer have the luxury of waiting. As soon as the big rig passes me, I hear the snap of gunfire and catch a glimpse of the SUV veering across the center line in my mirror.

I manage to yell, "Hold on," to Lindsey before I jerk the bike sharply to the left and brace for impact. To my relief, there's only a slight slope and no deep ditch. Still, the bike bounces through the brush and I'm struggling to maintain control. This bike wasn't made for off-roading.

At some point I think Lindsey may have screamed, but her body is still plastered against my back. I'm sending up a silent prayer she's not hurt, but right now the only thing in my power is to get out of range of the bullets and find shelter.

The instant my wheels hit the fine gravel of the dirt road, I can feel them spinning, the bike sliding sideways. I manage to straighten her out, just as I hear Lindsey behind me.

"Oh my God, look up ahead!"

When I glance up, I immediately see what she's referring to, and my heart sinks like a stone. *Fuck*. I was so busy staying upright, I forgot to keep an eye on the SUV, which at some point must have pulled ahead of us. The Expedition is parked on the shoulder a few hundred feet ahead. Shielded from passing traffic by the parked vehicle, I see a man lifting a rifle to his shoulder as he takes aim.

Without a second thought, I steer the bike toward the shallow ditch separating the dirt road from a cornfield. The bike goes down hard and this time I can't keep it upright. As I hit the compact dirt, I hear a heavy grunt behind me. Immediately I roll over and do my best to cover Lindsey's prone body with my own.

"Stay down," I urge her, and am relieved when I get a whispered response.

"Okay."

I lift my head and try to get a look at the shooter but the sharp crack of a rifle shot has me duck back down. Still out there, and still shooting. The good news is, if we can't see him, he likely won't be able to see us either. But that means he probably will come looking for us.

I've lost all concept of time, so I have no idea how long before backup gets here, but in the meantime, I don't plan on being a sitting duck.

"Don't move," I caution Lindsey, before rolling off her and crawling over to my bike.

I need to get to my saddlebag and the Glock with spare ammo I keep in there. I should have thirty-four rounds in total; seventeen loaded and another seventeen in the extra magazine. Not enough for a shootout, but I should be able to keep the shooter at bay until backup arrives.

Hopefully.

I must've tweaked my shoulder when I hit the ground, because when I try to reach in the saddlebag my right arm is too heavy to lift, so I switch to my left hand to retrieve the gun and ammo.

"*Jesus*," Lindsey hisses behind me. "Wapi, you're bleeding. You've been hit."

"I'm fine," I respond automatically.

So that's what that warm, heavy feeling is. My right arm is useless—dead weight—I can't even wrap my hand around my weapon, so I'm forced to hold it in my left hand. I probably couldn't shoot an elephant at twenty feet, but flying bullets—regardless their direction—demand attention.

"Give it to me."

Lindsey indicates the gun.

"Have you fired a gun before?"

She narrows her eyes on me. "It's been a while. But I'm not injured and can aim and shoot."

She seems determined and we don't have the luxury of time to debate, so I hand the Glock to her.

Still, I'd like to find another way to maximize our chances, since we continue to be in a pretty precarious situation with the shooter on higher ground, and this ditch our only cover. However, we're limited in our movements and it's difficult from our vantage point to assess our surroundings.

I'm still contemplating options when I notice Lindsey slowly start to raise her head.

"Linds…" I hiss in warning, but she cuts me off with a chop of her left hand.

The next moment she ducks down again, turning to look at me with eyes wide.

"He's coming."

———

Lindsey

I may have overstated when I told Wapi I can aim and shoot, or at least misled him somewhat.

Technically, yes, I'm able to aim, I'm able to shoot, but what I failed to mention is that I can't seem to be able to hit anything. Then again, he won't be able to either.

Noticing the blood on his back and shoulder had been a shock, but knowing he was injured did kick me into action. The gun feels heavy, and a little awkward in my hand, but it also makes me feel less helpless.

I was able to get a glimpse of the shooter coming down the embankment, which means it won't be as easy for him to see us. If we're going to move, we need to do it now. The ditch stretches as far as I can see to the right, but to the left of us there's an access point for the farmer to get onto the field. An embedded culvert provides a channel for water to travel, and perhaps a place to hide for us.

"Can you crawl?" I whisper.

Wapi glances in the direction I'm pointing. The pipe looks to be about two feet in diameter which I shouldn't have a problem fitting into, but it might be tight for him.

Instead of answering, he starts to move in that direction, and I follow, trying to make as little noise as possible, while keeping an eye on the ledge above. That guy as much as peeks over the edge, I'll start shooting.

"You first," he mutters when we reach the culvert.

Like hell. I'm the one with the gun, so I'll be going last. I shake my head and motion for him to continue. The fact he doesn't argue tells me his injury impacts him more than he's willing to let on.

I hear his soft grunt as he crawls into the pipe, feet first. As soon as he disappears from sight, I reverse and move in backward, like he did. That way I can keep an eye on what's behind us. I crawl back far enough so I'm just hidden in the shadows where the sun can't quite reach me, and do my best to ignore the slimy residue at the bottom of the pipe.

"Lindsey?"

Even whispered, Wapi's voice carries in the narrow confines of the culvert.

"Right here."

"Good call."

The compliment makes me feel ridiculously good. But I don't have a chance to bask in it because up ahead, right above where Wapi's bike is still lying on its side in the ditch, I catch sight of the shooter peering down over the edge.

I never got a really good look at the man who was chasing me in Durango, but this guy could well be the same person. I get as low to the ground as possible, stretching my arm and pointing Wapi's gun at the man when he starts to turn in this direction.

No matter how hard I'm trying to keep my hand still, it's shaking so hard I accidentally bang the grip of the gun against the bottom of the pipe. The clang is loud to my ears, and it's clear the shooter heard it too, drawing his focus to the culvert.

Time passes in slow motion, and I watch him start moving closer as he swings the rifle around. Then he lifts it to his shoulder. During my brief hesitation, he manages to get one shot off, but I don't wait to see where it hits, I start firing blindly.

I don't know how many shots I fired off, but my ears are ringing when all of a sudden, I feel myself being yanked deeper into the culvert. I just get a last glimpse of the shooter as he appears to go down.

Did I hit him?

Then suddenly a lot is happening at once. There's yelling and people running into view. More of them?

Panicked, I shove my face in the muck and cover my head with my arms. It's not until I feel Wapi's hand patting my leg and his voice penetrates the continued ringing in my ear, that I realize I'm still clutching the gun in my hands.

"Pass it to me, Princess," Wapi whispers. "The gun. Quickly."

I don't understand, but I do as he asks and reach my hand with the gun back. The moment I feel him take it from me, he yells out.

"Honon! In here! In the culvert!"

Lifting up my head, I see not only Honon but Trunk—another of Wapi's brothers—rushing toward us through the ditch.

"*Fuck*. You hurt anywhere?" Trunk asks me, the two of them crouching down by the opening.

"No, but Wapi was shot."

The words have barely left my mouth when I'm grabbed under my arms and feel myself hauled out of the pipe. Honon helps me to my feet and cups my face.

"Sure you're good?"

I nod, distracted by the activity near Wapi's bike, where I saw the shooter go down. I'm surprised to recognize a few more of Wapi's brothers, as well as a few people who look like law enforcement.

"Is that FBI?" I ask him.

Honon looks over his shoulder at the group.

"Yeah. The good guys."

"Need a hand, brother," Trunk rumbles behind me.

I swing around as Honon goes down on his knees beside him, both reaching into the culvert. Wapi is on his back, the gun lying on his belly and his arms crossed over his chest—the left cradling the right one—as they pull him out carefully. His face is chalk white, but his eyes are sharp as they seek me out immediately.

"He needs an ambulance," I point out.

"Trunk can check me out," Wapi suggests. "He's a doctor."

"Bit of a stretch," Trunk observes. "I fix heads, not holes. And, brother, that hole needs some attention."

"We've got a couple of ambulances en route." This from agent Jasper Greene who comes walking up.

The first thought through my mind is, did he already go over the video from my living room? I feel my face flush and hope they can't see through the guck I'm covered in.

"Help me to my feet," Wapi asks, and Trunk supports him so he can get his legs under him.

He hands off the gun to the agent. "I returned fire," he claims, before moving immediately to my side, wrapping his good arm around me. "I guess I hit him."

"Looks like it. You disabled him but he's still breathing."

If not for Wapi's arm holding me up, I might've hit the ground. On some level I knew I must've hit the man, but I hadn't allowed myself to think about it yet. Now it's confirmed, and real, and it makes me sick to my stomach.

Wapi must feel the trembling in my body.

"Boys, we need to sit down somewhere."

The guys start helping us out of the ditch, when I look toward the highway and see a bunch of bikes and a few random vehicles parked on the shoulder. Including the black SUV.

"Did you get the other guy?" I ask.

"There was more than one?" Greene snaps.

"One driving, one shooting."

"She's right," Wapi agrees. "Shooter was in the back seat. I caught a flash from the rear window."

"There was no one else," the agent shares.

"How did you guys get here anyway?" Wapi wants to know.

Honon darts Greene a funny look.

"Yeah, about that…"

Honon is interrupted by the sound of approaching sirens as we watch two ambulances pull onto the shoulder.

Not that much later Wapi is getting strapped to a gurney, something he's not happy about, but that's too bad. Luckily, his brothers agree with me.

"Have you seen him before?" Greene asks me when EMTs roll the second gurney with the unconscious shooter to the other ambulance.

The man has dark hair, graying at the temples, a nose

that looks to have been broken a few times, and a square chin.

"Yeah, I'm pretty sure he's the same guy who was shooting at me in Durango."

"That's the only other time?"

"Yeah. Why? Who is he?"

"Joseph Chino. We've had him on a watch list for a while. He's an enforcer for the Zeola family."

"As in Aldo Zeola?"

I've heard that man's name before in the news. He was on trial for murder several years ago, but was acquitted. There was a lot of speculation at the time there was something fishy with that trial, but those stories petered out.

"Same family. Own several construction companies, you've probably heard of A to Z Contracting?"

I can see the signs in my mind. They're all over the Denver airport. General contractors for the billion-dollar expansion project Luna had referred to. I'm starting to fit some of the pieces together.

"Excuse me, ma'am?" One of the EMTs leans out the back of Wapi's ambulance. "Your boyfriend says he's not going anywhere without you."

"Get your butt in here, Princess!"

"Hold your horses," I yell back, lifting my foot on the step.

Agent Greene covers his smirk with a hand.

"You never answered Wapi…earlier," I point out. "How *did* you know where to find us?"

"Luna," he answers. "She suspected something was up when several brothers suddenly decided to go on a road trip and had us followed."

I know he read the expression of concern on my face when he hastens to add, "Discreetly."

TWENTY-FIVE

LINDSEY

"I thought you might like to know; Wagner came clean."

We're in a room at the Fort Collins Inn in Agent Jasper Greene's protective custody. We, being Greene, who took a seat in the desk chair, Wapi, who's propped up on one of the beds, and I'm sitting on the other.

I have no idea where the others went, they were gone when we left the hospital.

Wapi was lucky that bullet didn't do more damage. They flushed out the wound, packed it, and planned to put him on IV antibiotics for twenty-four hours, but of course that stubborn man refused to stay in the hospital. In the end, they sent him packing with wound care instructions, some painkillers, and a seven-day course of antibiotics.

The shooter was apparently in much worse condition and had to be transported by AirLife to the UC Health Trauma Center in Denver. I've been sitting here, silently hoping and praying he doesn't die, only listening with half an ear, but I pay attention when I hear Galen's name.

"He did?"

Greene nods. "After we confronted him with what we found on his computer, he did. Not just the contents of the video feeds, but we also know how he managed to bypass security at your house in the first place."

"How?"

That's one of the things that has continued to bug me. No alarms were ever tripped.

"Your laptop, how long have you had it?" he answers my question with a question.

I don't even have to think about it, I remember clearly.

"My twenty-sixth birthday, five-and-a-half years ago."

It was a brand-new MacBook Pro and the last present Galen bought me. The last time he tried to bribe me. Two months later, I was on my way to Durango.

"He gave it to you," Greene concludes correctly. When I nod, he continues, "I'm afraid the computer wasn't the only thing he gave you. Let me guess, it was out of the box when you got it?"

That rat bastard. He said he wanted to make sure it was ready for use and had transferred all my files over already.

"Spyware? Seriously?" Wapi comments.

"A backdoor, actually. He's had complete access to your files and programs, so was able to access your security system remotely."

"I never even considered that," I admit, feeling rather sick.

"When he was confronted with that evidence, it all came out. His obsession with you, his anger when he found out you were seeing someone, and his determination to get you back."

Wapi—who was reclining against the headboard—tries to sit up, cursing when he hurts himself.

"By installing fucking cameras?"

Greene shrugs. "He spent enough time watching how-to YouTube videos."

That sounds like him.

"By chance, was one of those cameras installed over my dresser?"

It would make sense; the dresser is straight across from my bed. I thought it was weird there was zero dust on the top and smelled of orange. The made bed, the nightlight, and even the furniture oil on the steps. Galen was always obsessively tidy.

Greene looks puzzled. "Yes. One there, and we found one in the light fixture in your walk-in closet."

Yes, it all makes sense now.

"Whoever shot him should've finished him off," Wapi growls. "Or someone should finish the job."

The agent grins. "I'll pretend I didn't hear that."

"By the way, how did he get shot?" I'm curious.

"That was Joseph Chino. The security feed shows Wagner coming in—he must've waited for you to leave—rummaging through your stuff. Next you can see him turn around like he's startled, before he abruptly drops to the ground. A moment later Joseph Chino comes into view, brandishing a gun and casually stepping over his victim. My guess is, Chino was surveilling your house when he saw Wagner go in and, capitalizing on the easy access, followed him, shot him on the spot, and clearly started looking for something."

"The SD card," Wapi contributes.

"That's what we figure," Greene responds.

I glance over at him. He looks right back at me and I don't need the words to know what he's asking. Nothing

I'd like more than to be rid of that damn thing. Be done with all of this.

Then I turn my head and find Wapi's eyes on me too. He nods, and I reach for the leather cut he tossed on the foot end, slipping my hand into the inside pocket.

"If I give you this, will that be the end of it? I mean, you have the guy who was after me."

I drop the SD card in the agent's outstretched hand.

"I'd love to say yes, but I wouldn't jump the gun. We still haven't been able to locate the driver of the SUV, we don't know what we're going to find on this card, and I'm pretty sure Chino was just a hired hand, which means whoever is pulling the strings may still consider you a threat."

He stands up and tucks the card in his pocket.

"I've gotta get to work on this, but Agent Barnes is through that connecting door, and your club brothers have the rest of the units in this wing. For the time being, I suggest staying in the room. At least until I've had a chance to talk to Luna. She's flying in tomorrow morning."

He walks to the connecting door, unlocks it, and knocks, before turning back to us.

"For an extra layer of protection, I suggest you leave the main door locked at all times, and use the connecting door for visitors to get in and out."

When he disappears to the other room, I let myself fall back on the bed with a deep sigh.

"Is it me, or should we have stayed at High Meadow?"

"Yeah," he mumbles his agreement.

Then I hear the bedsprings creak, and him groan. I twist my head to catch him getting to his feet.

"Where are you going?"

"Shower."

I shoot up from the bed and catch up with him at the door to the bathroom.

"You can't have a shower for three days," I remind him. That apparently annoys him, but I don't care. "Doctor's orders."

"I reek. I'm filthy."

"I can run a bath for you," I suggest, but I can tell from his expression what he thinks of that idea.

"I don't take baths."

"What if I tell you I'll wash your back?"

That puts a glimmer in his eyes. "Just my back?"

"Your back, your front." I run a finger down the middle of his chest. "Hey, I'll even wash your hair."

"I have a better idea," he mumbles, hooking me by the neck of my shirt to pull me closer. "You get in the tub with me."

I lean back and poke my head inside the bathroom. Thank God it's a full-sized tub and as luck will have it, outrigged with jets.

"I think we can make that work."

————

Wapi

My shoulder hurts like a sonofabitch, but I don't want to move and risk waking Lindsey.

Both of us fell asleep after an unexpectedly enjoyable bath. I wasn't exactly an active participant, but Lindsey seemed to enjoy looking after me, and funny enough, I enjoyed letting her. After, she lay down beside me on the bed, curled up against my good side, and we were both out in minutes.

But now my left arm is numb, I need to piss, my right shoulder is on fire, my stomach is growling because we haven't eaten anything, and it's dark outside but I have no fucking clue what time it is. Did I mention I need to piss?

I'm still trying to figure out how to untangle myself from Lindsey, when a knock on the door connecting us to the next unit startles her awake.

"Are you guys decent?" Honon's voice filters through the door.

The question has Lindsey, who is as naked as I am, scrambling off the bed.

"Give us a sec," I call out, giving her a chance to pull on a pair of leggings and a T-shirt.

I personally don't give a flying fuck if my brothers see me in the buff—it wouldn't be the first time—but my bladder has me swing my legs out of bed.

Making sure Lindsey is covered up—I wouldn't want them getting an eyeful of her in all her glory—I duck into the bathroom, calling out.

"Come on in!"

I can't hear what is going on in the other room while I take care of business and wash my hand, but when I walk out of the bathroom—still buck naked—there's a damn crowd in the room.

"Shee-it, brother," Trunk complains, clapping a hand over his eyes. "Killing my appetite here."

Each of my brothers can be overwhelming, let alone a roomful of them. I'm surprised to find Lindsey snickering at Trunk's antics, as she hands me my jeans.

I put out a call for one brother, and not only Honon

showed up, but Trunk, Mika, Yuma, and Tse did as well. It means a lot.

I busy myself trying to get my damn jeans on with one hand before I blurt out something sappy none of these bastards will let me live down.

"Need a hand?" Lindsey whispers, when she catches me struggling with the buttons of my fly.

"Not sure that's a good idea, Princess," I warn her.

"Awww, look at them…you're so cute together," Honon mocks with a big, fat grin on his face.

"It's about fuckin' time," Yuma grumbles. "Was getting tired of seeing a grown man constantly look like someone kicked his damn puppy."

I don't bother reacting to the ribbing, I know from experience it'll make it worse. For the brothers, this is a love language.

"Can we fucking eat already?" Tse bitches.

I'd noticed the smell of food, but missed the stack of pizza boxes Trunk's large frame was blocking. Apparently, they also brought a twelve-pack of beer, which Mika starts distributing.

"Is that a good mix with your pain meds?" Yuma asks me when I accept a beer.

He's sipping from a bottle of water himself, since he doesn't drink at all anymore. He's been sober for years.

"What pain meds?" I lob back, taking a deep swig.

"He hasn't taken any since we left the hospital," Lindsey spills, giving me a stern look as she piles pillows against the headboard and motions for me to sit down.

I don't argue and get back in bed. It's not that I'm trying to be a stubborn ass, I just don't like the way painkillers affect me. Same reason I don't do drugs—and never have— I don't enjoy feeling out of it.

"Where is Barnes?" I ask, changing the subject.

"He had to take a call," Trunk volunteers, sliding an open pizza box on the bed beside me.

Only half a pie is left ten minutes later, when the agent shows up. To my surprise, Luna walks in right behind him.

———

"…evidence of tender fraud on the airport expansion project. Pictures, documents, recordings—you name it—it was in those files. Not that any of it was a big surprise, when A to Z Contracting was awarded that one-point-two-billion-dollar contract back in February, suspicions were raised immediately. It wasn't the first time A to Z won a substantial contract on a city funded project," Luna explains.

Luna and Dylan Barnes are the only two left, aside from Lindsey and myself. As soon as the pizza and beer were done, my brothers disappeared to their respective rooms. Luna waited until they were gone before she started to fill us in on what Jasper was able to pull off the SD card.

"At the time, a task force was pulled together representing a variety of agencies, some of which had already been keeping a close eye on the Zeola family. The suspicion from the start was the involvement of one or more city employees feeding Zeola information, or manipulating the outcome of the bids, but they were never able to find hard evidence. One of the FBI agents on the task force was able to forge a connection with Douglas Spurnell, who was the expansion's on-site accountant for A to Z. It's common for projects this big to require a full on-site office. As you know, Spurnell turned informant."

She winces in disgust as she takes a sip from the coffee

she brewed in the small, dinky coffee maker that came with the room.

"I should get one of the guys to pick up a Keurig somewhere. This stuff is vile," she shares, before getting back to her story.

"The day you encountered Spurnell at the airport," she directs at Lindsey. "He had contacted his FBI handler, claiming he had evidence and would leave it in a designated place. That was the washroom across from B16, the gate where you were waiting for your flight to Durango," Luna clarifies. "Something clearly spooked him because he planted it on you rather than leave it taped to the bottom of the toilet tank in the second stall."

"And then he was killed," Lindsey observes.

"Yes. In the task force meeting the FBI agent attended that afternoon, he mentioned he was expecting evidence to be dropped off at the assigned location."

"There's a leak on the task force," I observe out loud.

Luna aims her nod at me. "That is the suspicion, which is where we come in. Our director, James Aiken, asked us to look into the leak as a separate investigation. That's why we have to be careful what we share and with whom. The evidence recovered may show us who with the city is connected to the Zeola family and A to Z in particular, but it doesn't indicate where the leak is."

"Do you think it's someone from the FBI?" Lindsey asks.

"You mean because Chino pretended to be an agent?" Luna shrugs. "It's possible, but the reality is it could be anyone present at that task force meeting. We have local law enforcement and several federal agencies represented, plus support personnel. Quite a number of people we'll need to look into."

That touches on something I've been wondering about.

"How did Chino know what road we'd be coming down? How would he have known what direction we were even coming from?" I question, before suggesting, "The only plausible explanation I can think of, is that state trooper pulling us over on the I-80. He ran both our licenses. Someone could've flagged Lindsey's name."

"We'll be looking into that," Luna assures me as she gets to her feet and starts pacing. "Unfortunately, the nature of organized crime is insidious, with a tendency to seep into all levels of society through corruption, bribery, intimidation, force. Law enforcement, sadly, is not immune to that."

It should be, but I keep that thought to myself.

"What about us?" Lindsey asks. "Are we supposed to stay here indefinitely?"

Luna shakes her head. "No. There's a task force meeting scheduled tomorrow morning I'll be attending. I was thinking that would be a good time to have Jasper drive you two back to Durango. Dylan can take your bike and ride back with the others."

I'm not a fan of anyone else's ass on my bike, but I guess his had already been there, since he rode it from the side of the road to the motel earlier. The old me would've probably protested, and insisted I ride my bike myself, but priorities have changed.

It's not long after Luna leaves, we're in bed, some stupid show on the oversized TV to help us wind down, when Lindsey suddenly sits up, turning to face me.

"Where am I going to stay?" she blurts out. "I'm not sure I can stay at my house after what happened, and I'm definitely not going to stay with Mom and Paco, because what if this isn't over yet? I don't want to draw any attention to them. Or Mason, *Jesus*. The thought of anything happening to him. I just—"

She's rambling and sounds increasingly panicked.

"Hey," I interrupt, recognizing a bit of a delayed reaction to everything that happened today.

Part of me was expecting it. I hook my hand behind her neck and pull her toward me, touching my forehead to hers.

"You'll stay with me. At the clubhouse. You'll be safe, and there's no rush for you to make any decisions."

CHAPTER
TWENTY-SIX

LINDSEY

I look up when Wapi walks into the bedroom.

"Shall I turn a light on, or do you want to continue sitting in the dark?" he asks.

It doesn't take a genius to figure out he's annoyed, and I don't blame him either. I'm annoyed with myself, but I can't seem to pull myself out of this funk.

We got to the clubhouse early Friday night. It had been another long-ass day on the road, and I was so tired, I was barely aware of my surroundings and crashed face-first in the large king-sized bed Wapi showed me to.

Saturday, when Wapi got out of bed, I rolled over and went back to sleep. I slept most of that day, the only people I saw were my mom, who wanted to check in on me, and Wapi, who occasionally popped in to see if I needed anything. Yesterday passed much the same, with me lying in bed, dozing, watching a bit of TV, and generally avoiding any interaction.

I'd had every intention of getting up and out this morning, but in the end, I couldn't bring myself to face the world.

Today it's mostly shame keeping me in here. I'm embarrassed because I should be the one taking care of Wapi, instead of the other way around. After all, he's the one who was injured, but I've done nothing while letting him fuss over me.

I don't know what's wrong with me.

"Whatever you want," I answer, my voice cracking as a sudden flood of tears takes me by surprise.

"Ah fuck, Linds…"

He sits down on the edge of the mattress and pulls me up and onto his lap, where I proceed to lose it. I can't contain it.

"Easy, baby," he whispers, rocking me. "You're okay, I've got you. It's okay, let it out."

I couldn't hold back if I tried. It feels like the seams holding me together rip open, one by one, and my sanity is leaking into the mattress. My body shakes violently; an avalanche of emotions putting so much pressure on my chest, for a brief moment I wonder if I'm having a heart attack.

I hurt; my stomach, my chest, my head.

Through it all, Wapi rocks me, holding me tight as he murmurs softly, although I no longer hear the words for the ringing in my ears.

I've lost time, missing chunks when I slowly become aware of a dripping sound. I'm warm and wet, cocooned in strong arms as I feel water raining down on me. When I open my eyes, I recognize the bathroom. I'm sitting on the floor of the shower, surrounded by Wapi's strong body; his arms trapping mine against my body, his legs scissoring mine, still being rocked.

My throat is raw and my eyes feel like I have glass stuck under my eyelids.

Then I become aware of Wapi's voice, chanting something so softly I have a hard time making out the words.

"…*love you…love you…love you…*"

"I have towels."

I turn my head to see Lisa come in with a stack of towels.

"Hey, sweetheart. How about I turn that shower off now, okay?"

She reaches over my head and turns off the flow of water.

"Can I help you up?" she asks, reaching out her hand.

I try to lift my arm, but it's still pinned under Wapi's.

"You can let her go now, brother," she tells him, tapping his forearm.

He groans when his tight hold on me loosens and I can grab on to Lisa's hand. I'm a mess, and I don't even care a woman I don't know that well is wrapping me in towels and rubbing me dry. I'm depleted.

But when I turn and see Wapi still sitting on the shower floor, his head leaning back against the tile wall, his left hand covering his right shoulder.

"Oh no," I croak, noticing a hint of pink on the white T-shirt plastered to his body.

I drop the towel Lisa had me wrapped in and drop to my knees next to him.

"It's fine," he claims.

"Bullshit," Lisa interjects, "But he wasn't gonna let go of you. He probably just pulled a stitch. We'll fix him up." She looks from me to Wapi and back. "You guys okay now? You can take it from here?"

Surprisingly, I hear myself answer, "We've got this."

By the time Lisa closes the door behind her to give us some privacy, Wapi is already on his feet.

"Let's get those clothes off you," I suggest.

He doesn't say anything, but is watching me closely as I help him strip off his soaking T-shirt. His jeans and socks are next. Then I hand him a towel, noting his bandages are wet as well, but it looks like any bleeding is minimal. We can check for any damage after we get some dry clothes on.

Not a word is spoken in the bathroom while we dry off, and the silence follows us into the bedroom. I pull clean clothes from the duffel bag with my stuff Mom dropped off and get dressed. I haven't even bothered unpacking it. Wapi does the same, but I stop him when he tries to put on a clean shirt.

"We should really look at your wound first," I suggest, ducking back into the bathroom to grab the supplies I need.

When I walk back into the bedroom, Wapi is sitting on the edge of the bed.

"Lindsey…"

At the sound of his voice, I know I can't avoid his eyes any longer and look up.

"Yeah?"

"You scared me."

"I'm sorry…" I shake my head and lower my eyes. "I'm not sure what happened. I scared myself too."

"I'm not an expert—that's Trunk's specialty—but I'm guessing maybe there's only so much trauma a person can try to bury."

"Trauma?"

He pulls me to stand between his legs, looking up at me with a whirl of emotions in those beautiful eyes.

"Princess, it's been a lot. You spent years in an abusive relationship, then four years ago, when you were just getting your feet under you, you were kidnapped and tortured. Once again you got up, brushed yourself off, and toughed it out. You and your mom are no different in that respect."

"No use in crying over spilt milk," I echo one of my mother's favorite sayings when I was growing up.

Wapi shakes his head. "Baby, in the past week or so your house has been violated, you've been chased, shot at, forced into hiding, discovered a brother you knew nothing about, rode across the country on the back of a bike, got chased and shot at again, had to fire a gun to stay alive, and through it all, you simply absorbed the next impact and kept on trucking. That's trauma upon trauma, Linds. That's a lot to process by yourself," he suggests.

When he lists it like that it does seem like a lot, but I don't really know what else to do than shove it down. I panic when I feel tears welling again and I blink furiously to keep them at bay.

Wapi gives me a gentle shake. "No, let those tears come, they're cleansing."

When I shoot him an incredulous look, he chuckles.

"Believe me, I know. I know the damage unprocessed and suppressed trauma can do, and I've learned tears can set healing in motion. What do you think I was doing those three years in seclusion?"

"Crying?"

He smiles up at me. "Yes, at times."

"I'm not used to it," I admit.

"I know."

"It's uncomfortable."

He takes my hand and presses a kiss to my palm.

"It gets better."

This man…how did I get so lucky?

I've never felt so seen, so heard, so cared for. And if what I heard Wapi mumble on repeat in the shower is true, I should add loved to that list.

But before I can broach that subject, a knock sounds at the door and Lisa's voice calls out.

"You two decent yet?"

———

Wapi

"Looks like Joseph Chino is going to live."

I glance over at Lindsey, who is sitting across from me on the couch in Ouray's office. Her relief is visible on her face.

"Oh, thank God," she mumbles.

"Are you shitting me?" Mel explodes beside her, looking at her daughter in disbelief. "He deserved to be finished off. He shot at you, he's a killer. A piss-poor one, since he couldn't even properly finish off that son of a bitch, Galen, but he tried to kill you! More than once."

Paco chuckles, shaking his head, and Ouray snorts, but, as much as I get where Mel is coming from, I don't really find it funny. I know how Lindsey struggled with the possibility she may have taken a life. Even if that life belonged to a known mob enforcer.

I'm about to jump to her defense but don't need to, Lindsey's taking care of it.

"Right," she snaps at her mother. "And then the FBI would lose a potentially important witness, who likely has information that could bring down a major mob family, and if that wasn't enough, I would've had to carry the knowledge I killed a man with me for the rest of my life."

As rebuttal, her comments are about as effective as could be, silencing the chuckles and putting a damper on Mel's outburst.

"She's right," Luna speaks out in support. "He could have information to help us put a nail in Aldo Zeola's coffin, but almost more importantly, he can tell us who the leak is."

"Do you think he will?" I ask.

I can't imagine he'd be so ready to impart with that information, seeing as that would make him a target himself.

"Maybe with the right incentive. We'll have to see; he's only now starting to show signs of waking up, and it may be several days yet before we'll actually be able to talk to him."

"So we're no further along?" Lindsey observes.

"I wouldn't say that," Luna responds. "There's some progress. We discovered that black SUV was registered to a subsidiary company of A to Z Contracting, which enforces the case against Aldo Zeola. As we speak, the task force is getting warrants together for Zeola's arrest, and the arrest of several other major players, including high-ranking city employees with Denver's Department of Aviation, as well as the Department of Transportation and Infrastructure. I suspect there will be more to follow. There are some pieces yet missing, but it's coming together."

"Do you figure it's safe for Lindsey to be out and about yet?" I want to know.

"Once arrests have been made in the next twenty-four to forty-eight hours, I don't see why things couldn't return to normal." She turns to Lindsey. "By then it should be clear we have the information on that SD card and you shouldn't pose a threat to them any longer."

"Okay, that's good. It's about time I got back to the office."

I have my own ideas about that, but I opt not to get into that right now, in front of everyone.

"Oh," Luna continues. "That reminds me, we recovered your camera equipment from the back of that SUV."

"I didn't even know it was missing," Lindsey volunteers.

"Yeah, your laptop too, we found that as well. Jasper can make sure to get rid of whatever program Wagner installed on there."

I catch the grimace on Lindsey's face.

"No need," I jump in. "We're buying a new laptop."

Like hell she's going to be using a computer that fuckwit bought her.

I fully expect Lindsey to protest, so it surprises me when she stays quiet. But her eyes study me intently.

———

"How are you?"

I lean against one of the posts holding up the porch roof outside the clubhouse, watching Ouray flip burgers on the massive grill.

"Well enough to flip goddamn burgers," he grumbles.

He's still pissed because Lisa handed me the tray of meat and asked me to grill, when it's traditionally been Ouray's job. Symbolic for him, cooking the meat for his family. So I understood when he snatched the tray from my hands and stormed outside, but I followed him anyway.

I don't bother responding and wait him out. My patience pays off a few minutes later.

"Like fucking shit, if you must know. I'm tired, brother. Feel goddamn useless. Got a beautiful, hot-blooded woman in my bed and my fucking dick doesn't work." He glances at me from the corner of his eyes. "Side effect, I'm told. They say function—at least some—might return but it could take a fucking year."

"That sucks," I commiserate.

What the hell else is there to say? He doesn't want to hear there are other ways for him to satisfy his wife. He probably knows that better than I do.

I get it. For any guy, but maybe even more so for guys like us, being unable to perform is a big fucking deal.

"Yeah," he agrees. "It really does." Then he continues, "Anyway, I'm trying to convince my wife to take an early retirement, as soon as this damn treatment is done I want to do some traveling. Maybe a road trip, like the one you took and head north. Get some quality time in with my woman any way I can."

"If you do, it'll be the trip of a lifetime. I have a homestead in Alaska you're welcome to use. It isn't much; it's a single room, with an outhouse and no running water, but it has a wood stove that'll keep it as warm as you want it, enough of a woodpile to last a month or two, if need be, and views that cannot be beat."

"'Preciate it. We never had that meeting last Friday, but since everyone is here for the cookout, I'd like to talk to the brothers tonight. Let them get used to the idea I'm planning to put your name forward when I hand in my gavel in a few weeks."

A few weeks.

Holy shit.

———

I'm still reeling hours later, lying in bed, waiting for Lindsey to be done in the bathroom.

The club meeting in Ouray's office next door was a bit of a revelation. I mean, I have no doubt my brothers have my back—last week's events are clear evidence of that—but what blew me away was they didn't seem surprised at all. Not even a little. I seem to be the only one who didn't see this coming.

"Who was that little boy? The one you were talking to at dinner?" Lindsey asks when she walks out of the bathroom and climbs into bed.

"That's Zach."

I'm ashamed to say with everything that happened this past week, I'd almost forgotten about him. I'd made that boy some promises and the way he looked at me, he didn't believe for one second I'd follow through on those. So, I set out to prove him wrong.

"The boy I was looking for in Alamosa," I clarify as I snuggle Lindsey against my side. "I'd promised him I'd made sure he could visit his grandma."

She tilts her head up and flashes me a smile. "That's sweet of you."

"Yeah, well...I kinda volunteered us to take him to Alamosa to see her next weekend."

"Another road trip?" she says with some trepidation, pushing herself up so she can look down at me.

I tug on a strand of her hair. "We'll take a truck. It's a pretty drive."

"Oh, all right."

Leaning down she drops a sweet kiss on my mouth

before she lays her head down on my shoulder again, tucking in close.

A few minutes go by and I wonder if she's already fallen asleep.

"Wapi?"

"Hmm."

"This afternoon, when we were in the shower…did you—"

"Yes, I did," I interrupt, knowing exactly what she's asking me. "You heard me right."

I roll her on her back and brush a strand of hair from her face. Her eyes shimmer in the sparse light filtering in from outside.

It's like looking straight into her soul.

Which makes it easy to speak my heart.

"Love you, Lindsey Zimmerman."

CHAPTER
TWENTY-SEVEN

LINDSEY

"What do you think?"

Mom leans over my shoulder to see the screen.

"Wow. Yeah, I like it. How many bedrooms?"

"This layout has three bedrooms, three bathrooms but hang on..." I click on another tab. "This is the four-bedroom layout. The main bedroom and en suite are the same, but the secondary rooms are a little smaller and share a bathroom between them."

"Do you need four bedrooms?"

"I have no idea."

I don't, because I haven't even really talked to Wapi about this.

As he promised, he came back to the clubhouse one day last week with the latest model MacBook Pro. I could've bought one myself, and I might've insisted on that, if I wasn't convinced his gesture was important to him. More important than it was for me to insist on paying my own way.

So, I thanked him in a way there would be no doubt about my gratitude, and proceeded to spend the next few days surfing the net. When I came across the first real estate ad, I was sucked down a rabbit hole.

One that landed me on the Greatland Log Homes website, which is where I found my dream home. They provide the plans and have the option of a full package with pre-cut logs, and all you need is a piece of land.

I can't see myself moving back to the house Mom and I shared. It would be impossible not to feel the violation every time I walked in, even though there are no longer cameras in the house. So, I need to find a new place to live. As much as I appreciate being able to stay at the clubhouse, this isn't a permanent solution, at least not for me. I love Lisa, but the clubhouse is her domain, and having lived there for over a week made it clear I prefer a space of my own.

"What does Wapi think?"

Trust Mom to narrow in on my biggest issue.

I haven't talked to Wapi. I have no idea what he wants or how he envisions a future. Any future. My issue is, it feels a little soon to be discussing things like living arrangements when we've only actually been together for less than a month.

Sure, I'll acknowledge we've been heading to this place for a much, much longer time, but it still feels impulsive. Yet, something tells me Wapi would be on board with whatever I decide, as long as it includes him.

Or maybe I'm afraid when we start talking about the number of bedrooms, the subject of kids will come up, and I'm not sure I want to hear how he feels about children. He seemed a bit shaken that time Mom mistakenly guessed I was pregnant, giving me the impression he might not be in the market for any. Then again, when I've seen him interact with Zach or Mason, or any of the other kids in the club-house, he's really good with them. Seems to enjoy them.

Oh, hell, I don't know. Maybe I can stop obsessing once I get my period, but it is a few days late, which could be stress. I don't get much of a period on the Depo shot, but I've always stayed like clockwork.

"I'm not sure, Mom. I have to sit down with him, but he's had enough on his plate recently, taking over for Ouray. He's kinda stressed, so this may not be a good time. I'm just looking at options for now."

"Dear child of mine, I don't care how stressed a man is, I can guarantee he won't be happy if he finds out you're keeping stuff from him."

"I'm not keeping anything from him and besides, there's nothing wrong with gathering information before I bother him."

It sounds lame, even to me, but from the way Mom is looking at me I swear she knows something. The woman is like a human bloodhound.

"Hey, aren't you supposed to be in court this after-noon?" I promptly change the subject.

"Don't think I don't know what you're doing," she says, wagging her finger threateningly. "But yes, it's the Dawson case. The judge wants to meet with all three attorneys in chambers before the trial resumes tomorrow."

"Why the meeting in chambers?"

"Presumably to share the findings from the physical and psychological assessment he ordered done on Samantha. Which tells me the information likely confirms what we were concerned about, which is bound to generate an explosive reveal. I'm pretty sure he's giving us a heads-up so we can prepare our clients."

"Poor girl."

It's disturbing how often child abuse—in its many forms —takes place under the radar in households that look picture-perfect from the outside. Too often, as I've learned working in this office. It's the kind of thing that slowly wears on your soul.

I don't know how my mother still does it day in, day out; dealing with the disappointment, pain, and devastation of families. I wouldn't doubt that's a large part of what has been taking a toll on her health. Luckily, she can now go home to Paco and Mason, to give her some balance. That wasn't always the case.

It's funny, this is my first day back in the office and I don't really want to be here. Don't get me wrong, I love working with my mother and we make a good team, but something has shifted in the past few weeks. I used to enjoy implementing order where Mom has a tendency to create chaos, like she did on the top of the filing cabinet and the conference table. Both are piled high, and before my hands would've been itching to sort through it all, but today that holds no appeal and I've been putting it off.

I'd rather be tinkering with my pictures—I just finished putting together a package for Thildy and Ben—or snapping photos with my camera, which I've been doing a lot of, both in and outside of the clubhouse. It had been a compromise I made with Wapi. I had been eager to get back to the office, but he suggested I take a bit of time to catch my breath. So, despite the all-clear coming from Luna last Wednesday, I postponed going back to work until today.

"All right, I'm off then," Mom announces, the leather satchel she uses as her file bag tossed over her shoulder. "Before I forget," she continues "Gina Dunlop. She's a new divorce client. Can you prep her an information package?

She's stopping in tomorrow morning; it was the only time she could. No kids, but she'll need a sample financial statement, and have her fill out a case information sheet when she gets here. Sounds like a pretty straightforward case."

"I'll get it ready. Are you heading straight home after?" I ask her.

"Was planning to. Don't you stay too late."

"Wapi is picking me up at four."

"Good. Lock the doors behind me."

Damn Wapi. This morning when he dropped me off, he made sure to say that loud enough so my mom could hear him.

"Yes, Mother," I sneer.

"Don't be difficult, Linds. Can't blame people who love you for worrying. Hell, I had to stop Paco from coming in with me. He was prepared to sit in the waiting area all day. We've been a bit shaken by all this too, and have felt pretty helpless, so have some patience with us."

Mom still knows how to put me in my place.

Duly chastised, I follow her to the back door where I give her a quick and rare hug. We're not usually this demonstrative.

———

Wapi

She doesn't look nearly as happy as she did this morning when I dropped her off.

I could see her through the window and clearly startled

her when I knocked. She's already slinging her bag over her shoulder as she rushes for the door.

"Hey," I greet her as she slips outside, immediately closing and locking the office behind her.

"Hi," I get back distractedly, as she tries to squeeze past me when I block her path.

"You in a rush?"

"What?" Her eyes meet mine and slowly her expression changes. "Oh, sorry. No, I'm not. Not really."

Then she puts her hands on my chest and lifts up on her toes for a kiss.

"Bad day?"

She shakes her head. "Not really," she says again.

Something is clearly going on with her, but I'm not about to pry it out of her while standing on the sidewalk. Instead, I take her hand and lead her to my bike. I was thinking about hitting up the food trucks at 11th Street Station.

"Let's pick up some food in town and find a quiet spot by the river. How's that sound?"

She shoots me a half smile.

"Yeah, I'd like that. I have some things I'd like to talk to you about."

That sounds a little ominous. I wonder if I should be worried, after all, she never did tell me she loved me back. Despite not getting the words, I was pretty sure she did, but it could be I have some more work to do.

I have been a bit preoccupied with the new changes at the club, which feel like a pretty heavy load on my shoulders. Ouray leaves some pretty big shoes to fill. I thought I had a grasp on the scope of his responsibilities, but I've been getting a crash course and it's been pretty overwhelming. As a result, I perhaps haven't paid Lindsey the attention I should have.

The 11th Street Station is crazy busy tonight and we end up ordering a Mesa Verde pizza from The Box. Taking the pie and a couple of ice teas to nearby Iris Park, we find a picnic table in the shade of the trees along the Animas River.

The rush of the river drowns out most of the traffic noise. This place is like a little oasis in the middle of the downtown bustle, which is more than usual during the summer months with the influx of tourists in town.

We eat in silence for a few minutes, although Lindsey seems to be restlessly picking at her slice.

"Get it off your chest," I tell her. "Whatever it is that has you in knots, rip it off like a Band-Aid so we can deal with it."

She puffs out a breath and rolls her eyes. A hint of the prickly Lindsey I know.

"Fine."

She puts down her slice and takes a drink from her tea. I wait patiently.

"I don't like my job."

When it looks like no more is forthcoming, I probe. Given she was so eager to get back to it, this is a surprise.

"Any particular reason? Did something happen today?"

"No." She shakes her head and aims her gaze at the rushing water. "Not today, but I think maybe it has in the past few weeks. All I know is I loved my job before…" She waves her hands around. "All this, but now I don't. I have no good reason, and I'm conflicted because I work for my mother. She offered me this job when I was in a really bad place, and it almost feels like a betrayal to her."

I reach across the table and take her hand in mine, rubbing my thumb over her knuckles.

"First of all, I thought we agreed what you went through is not something that can easily be brushed off or shoved aside, and with that in mind, it isn't really surprising that you may see the world, and your place in it, a little different now than before. But secondly, I don't for a minute believe your mother would feel in any way betrayed if you stopped working for her. In fact, I suspect if she found out you weren't happy in your job anymore and didn't share that with her, she'd be pretty pissed."

She shrugs, and I watch her closely as she seems to consider my thoughts. Whatever is going on in her mind is reflected on her face.

"But she's going to ask what it is I plan to do instead, and I don't really have an answer."

"So?"

"It doesn't make sense to give up my job without having some kind of idea of what I want."

"Okay, fair enough," I concede, even though I don't necessarily see an issue. I know her well enough to realize it may be one to her. "Although you seemed pretty happy last week lugging around your camera and shooting pictures. That could be a direction to look in."

"No…" She chuckles at the notion. "You're right, I love it, but that's a hobby, not a job."

I pause for a moment before I share my thoughts on that.

"Only because *you* made it a hobby instead of a career. You could change that if you wanted to."

"Yeah, but I don't even know if that could earn me a living," she voices her doubts.

"Nope. And you never will, unless you give it a try," I point out.

"My life already feels upheaved, if that is even a word," she counters.

"Right, so what could be a more perfect time to try a new direction?"

"What if it fails?"

I lift her hand and kiss the inside of her wrist.

"I don't think you will, but if you do, you find something else you love."

"You make it sound so easy."

"It could be," I suggest. "I've got your back, no matter what."

"Yeah, about that…" She pauses, a little too long for my liking, and for a second my stomach does a little flip. "I have to confess something; as grateful as I am for the club's hospitality, I can't stay there."

"You want to go back to your place?"

She keeps her head bowed and her eyes fixed on our entwined fingers.

"Not really. I've been thinking about putting it on the market." She peeks up at me through her eyelashes. "Find something else, maybe build something. There's this house—"

"Do it," I encourage her. I agree, staying at the club isn't ideal for us. We need a space of our own. "Sell your house, pick a place—although I like the idea of building—but it'll have to be in Durango because I can't be too far from the clubhouse. I have a decent chunk of change put aside, so that won't be an issue, although I have a feeling you're going to want to contribute somehow." The semi-annoyed expression on her face reveals a lot. "And I'm open to talk about that," I offer magnanimously.

"Well, isn't that kind of you," she sneers sarcastically, a tad worked up. "It's a good thing I love you and know you mean well, but I'm not looking for a sugar daddy, I want a partner in every sense of the word."

"You love me," I repeat, a grin almost splitting my face in half.

The instant blush on her cheeks is cute, as is the way she tries to hide her own smile.

"Yeah, well…what can I say? You kinda grew on me."

"That's a relief, because for a moment there I thought you wanting to talk to me meant you were about to try and give me the boot."

"Try?"

I lean over the table and tag her behind the neck, pressing a hard, claiming kiss to those pretty lips of hers.

"You don't honestly think I'd walk away from you, do you?"

As happy as she looked just a moment ago, her expression drops in an instant.

"Don't say that, you might still."

"Nothing would change my mind," I enforce.

"What if I told you I didn't get my period."

It takes me a moment to process her words and still it doesn't quite compute.

"What are you saying?"

She looks straight at me, those big blue eyes filling with tears I hate to see on her.

"I might be pregnant."

CHAPTER
TWENTY-EIGHT

WAPI

Fuck yeah.

Fuck. Yeah.

I feel her walls clamping down, locking me inside her, and I can't hold back the eruption that has been building since she told me I might become a father. I may have already planted a baby inside her, but if it turns out I haven't, now that the possibility has been put on the table, I'm determined to make that a reality.

I wasn't sure if she wanted kids and, apparently, she had the same question about me, but we both skirted around the topic. Communication is an acquired skill, and we're obviously still learning. Although our bodies don't appear to have any trouble connecting.

For a moment I allow myself to collapse on her, fully spent, but quickly remember to roll to her side so I don't crush her. Or the possible baby.

"Are you smiling?" she asks, probably feeling my mouth against her skin.

"I might be."

"A little smug, are we?" she teases.

"Didn't I give you two orgasms already?" I lift my head to glance at the alarm clock on the nightstand. "And it's not even seven thirty."

I also gave her one last night. Only one though, since I'd been too eager to get inside her when we got back to the clubhouse, and while we were looking at a website for this fantastic log home she wanted to get my opinion on, she fell asleep before I could have seconds. So, I made sure to wake her up early this morning.

Mentioning the time was a mistake, because she suddenly scrambles away from me and hops out of bed.

"Where are you going?" I call after her as she darts into the bathroom.

"Work. I need to be in early and make sure Mom has everything she needs for court today."

I hear the sound of the toilet flushing and next of the shower turning on. I'm tempted to jump in there with her, but I'll give her her space if she needs to get ready. Instead, I head across the hallway and into what has always been my room, and the small bathroom attached. This past week Lindsey and I have been staying in what used to be Ouray's private suite which—since he met and married Luna, and built a house across the road—has since been used for guests.

By the time I head back across the hallway to grab my phone and wallet from the nightstand, Lindsey's already out of the bathroom and putting in her earrings. She smiles at me, but it doesn't quite meet her eyes.

"What's wrong?"

She crinkles her nose and tilts her head. "You know you're way too observant, right?"

"Talk to me."

"It's nothing. I'm just a little nervous about going to the house to meet with a real estate agent. That is, if I can find one who has time to come out."

We talked about calling an agent last night, she wanted to unload the house as fast as possible to know exactly where she stood, and that made sense to me. Even though I am fully capable of carrying any financial load, but seeing as we may need to figure out our shit sooner than later, it's not a bad idea to get started on the process.

"See if they can meet around lunchtime. I have a few errands I have to run this morning in town so I can stop by when I'm done, go with you. In fact, that can save us some time this morning. Instead of taking you to pick up your car at the house, I'll drop you off at the office, and come get you to meet the realtor at the house. You can grab your car when we're there."

"If you're sure," she asks.

I can see the relief in her eyes at my suggestion, so I'm gonna make it work, even if it potentially means cutting my meeting with George Macias short.

He's the Oxbow Motel's owner who has continued to give us trouble, despite the damn gate I had put up on our parking lot. In talking with some of the trades he has working on the renovations, I've discovered he has been late in paying them.

With a little digging I found out Macias is in a deep well of financial trouble. Trouble the club is happy to help him with, by way of a buy-in or a buyout. It'll be up to him whether he wants to maintain a—minor—stake in the motel or would prefer to wash his hands of it altogether.

Either way is fine by us, since the motel would be another good source of revenue for the club. Paco and Kaga helped work out the financials, and we were able to present the plan to the other brothers at the club meeting last Friday. It was the first one I wielded the gavel at, which was a bit surreal.

"Of course," I assure her, grabbing for her hand. "We have a little extra time, let's see what Lisa has going for breakfast."

In the hallway, I catch Mika coming out of his room.

"You go ahead," I tell Lindsey. "I'll be a minute."

As she continues to the kitchen, I turn to Mika.

"Do me a favor; if you have a chance today, can you get the information off the for-sale sign on the property half a mile north of Yuma's place? It's been for sale for a while. See what you can find out."

Yuma and Lissie's place is actually the next property over from the compound. There aren't very many properties along that road and the one I'm thinking about has a house on it I don't think anyone has lived in for decades. It's hard to tell from the road, because it's pretty overgrown, and that building would probably have to come down, but it's minutes from the clubhouse, which counts for a lot.

I'm thinking it might make a perfect location for that dream house Lindsey has her heart set on.

———

Lindsey

"Did you talk to him?"

The first thing out of Mom's mouth. She does not beat around the bush.

"I did. I showed him the website last night and he loves the house."

I can't stop from grinning. Mom shakes her head at me but the corner of her mouth twitches.

"Of course he does. And I already know Paco is going to want to have a hand in building it."

"I'm okay with that, but we're not nearly ready for that yet. It still needs a piece of land."

"Ah, I'm pretty sure that'll get taken care of soon enough." She stuffs a yellow pad in her bag and tosses in a couple of pens from her drawer. "Did you get the copy of that report the court clerk sent last night printed out?"

"Yes, I put it in the folder. I had a peek at it. That's pretty damning."

"Oh yeah. One of the reasons the judge wanted to talk to counsel was to discuss the possibility of Chris Menzies being placed into custody right there in the courtroom today, depending on what happens when he calls the psychologist to testify."

The report concludes Samantha's stepfather has been sexually abusing the girl, and it makes me sick to my stomach.

"I should get going. I'm meeting Brian for coffee before court resumes at nine thirty, and I need that time to prepare him."

She stuffs the file in her bag and slings it over her shoulder.

"Oh, I was gonna ask you." I stop her. "I need the name of a realtor. Do you know anyone?"

She jerks a thumb in the direction of her office.

"Check the old Rolodex on the credenza in my office. John…Morrison, Morris…Norris, that's it. Anyway, you'll find him under R for real estate. He helped me get the house when I first bought it, but I'm pretty sure he's still in business."

That was as organized as Mom got before I started working for her. A Rolodex. She even wrote notes on those little cards and stuck them on there if she didn't want to forget anything.

"Okay, thanks, Mom. I'm gonna see if he has time to meet me at the house at lunch."

"You're going to the house alone?" she asks, opening the back door.

"Wapi is coming."

She gives me a thumbs-up and heads out, I close and lock up behind her.

A few minutes later I sit down at my desk, Mom's Rolodex in front of me, and the card with Mom's nearly illegible scribble in my hand. John Norris was not only still in business, but he remembers the house, and can meet us there at twelve fifteen.

I shoot off a quick text to Wapi.

Success. Meeting at 12:15. Pick up at noon?

His response comes two minutes later. A thumbs-up.

Feeling a lot better, I head for the kitchen, put on a kettle of water for some tea, and tackle the first pile of paperwork on the conference table. I'm not sure when I'll talk to Mom about my job here, but I can at least make a start on getting things in order.

With the idea of leaving a clean slate behind for my

mother, or whoever will be my replacement, I'm actually enjoying sorting through all of it. I'm not sure what Mom was doing with all these files—some of them date back to before I came here and are no longer active—so the ones not active, I alphabetize in an empty file drawer. That way, if she pulled them for a reason, they're all together, but if they need to go back into the general files, it'll be easy enough to move them to the appropriate spot in the drawers above.

I get lost in the work and have no idea of time, when there's a knock at the front door. It takes me a second to remember Mom's new client was supposed to pick up her information package today. Gina Dunlop.

I get a glimpse of a curvy figure in a cream-colored pantsuit with carefully-coiffed, blond hair. She has her back to the door and swings around when she hears me flip the deadbolt.

"Gina Dunlop?"

"That's me," she says with a reserved little smile.

Very carefully made up—her suit obviously high quality, and her jewelry expensive, but tastefully understated—she looks the part of a forty-something, wealthy socialite. When you go visit a country club you're bound to bump into a few women looking much the same. She looks almost familiar.

I gesture for her to come in and offer her a visitor's chair, while I round my desk to take a seat.

"I'm Lindsey, I'm Mel's assistant. She asked me to prepare some paperwork for you."

"Right. Is it ready?"

"I have it right here." I hand her the manila envelope I slid the package into, as well as the clipboard with the case information sheet. "I need you to fill out that form. We need the information to draft the proper documents to file with the court."

When she takes the envelope and clipboard, I notice her hands look much older than I would have expected based on first impression. It makes me take a closer look at her face, which I now see is heavily caked.

"Yeah, sure. Uhh…" She gets to her feet, setting the stuff I just handed her down on her seat, as she looks around the office. "Is there a washroom I could use?"

"Yes, of course."

I show her to the powder room in the back hallway, pulling Mom's office door shut on the way. I haven't had a chance to tackle her office yet and it's a mess too.

As I head back to my desk, I start thinking there's something about this Dunlop woman that seems a bit off. I'm not sure why, but there's something about the careful way she walks on the three-inch heels she's wearing, like she's not accustomed to them.

But it's not until I watch her walk into the front office space, her eyes locked on me, it hits me, but before I can ask her, she makes an announcement.

"I'm afraid I'm unwell," she shares. "I think I'm going to have to take those forms home and work on them there."

She bends down and grabs the envelope but leaves the document on the clipboard.

"I'm sorry to hear that."

She hums and walks to the door.

"Umm, Gina? Have we met before?" I ask.

I'd only seen her for a few moments outside the bathrooms at the Denver airport and things were a bit chaotic, plus I'd just been knocked to the ground. I wonder what the odds are for her to walk into my mother's Durango law office.

The moment I hear the lock snap shut; I curl my fingers around the first thing they encounter.

The woman turns slowly but instead of looking at me, she seems to be looking past me.

"Told you she'd recognize me."

I snap my head around to find an older Black man walking into the front office from the back hallway. He is dressed in a UPS uniform, but I'm pretty sure he's not a delivery man.

"You were at the airport."

I turn around and my eyes catch on something outside the window, but I don't allow anything to show on my face, and quickly focus my attention back on the woman.

Her smile is almost apologetic. "You know, I told LaVine you looked like a smart cookie. He wanted to leave you be, didn't want to rock the boat after poor Papi was arrested. I told him, a girl smart enough to outwit us every step—a girl who managed to escape not only my righthand man, Chino, but a decorated detective as well—will be able to put two and two together when she sees my face on TV or in the newspapers." She tilts her head to one side as she produces a gun from her pocket. "Am I right?"

I'm still reeling from the avalanche of information coming at me, and I'm frantically trying to process what she just shared with me. The Papi she talks about must be her father, Aldo Zeola, and by the sound of it the guy chasing me was employed by *her*, not her father.

I glance at the man I now know is Detective LaVine of the Denver PD. He's holding a gun too, but it's aimed at the ground.

"I'm afraid I'm going to have to ask you to accompany us," the woman announces. "I want you to know I don't derive any pleasure in doing this, but I've spent too many years staying in the shadows, doing my father's work while his health and mind declined. This is supposed to be my time, and I can't allow a small error in judgment to stop me from getting what is my due."

There's no way I'm leaving here with them. There absolutely is no way I will put my mother, Wapi, or myself through that hell again. If I'm going to die, they'll have to kill me right here.

She motions with her weapon, but I ignore her.

"Come on, Ms. Zimmerman. It'll only be a short drive."

CHAPTER
TWENTY-NINE

WAPI

She looks right at me, but doesn't react.

I know something is wrong right away. Even before we became an item, she would have a reaction whenever she saw me, good or bad. But she looks at me like I'm not even there.

So I take note of the blond-haired woman I'm able to see with her back to the door, and the faint outline of a larger individual—probably a man—standing closer to the back hallway, before slowly backing away. Then I call Paco as I run around the building to check the back door.

"Surveillance in and around Mel's office, tell me it's still active," I snap the moment he answers the phone.

"The fuck is going on?"

"Answer the question," I pant, coming around the corner of the building.

A UPS truck is parked right up against the back of the building, blocking the back door from view. This is not good.

"I'm pulling it up now… Oh Jesus, *fuck*," he follows it up with. "Blond bitch with a gun on Linds. Oh dammit, there's a Black dude behind her he's carrying also, but his gun is down."

"Paco, listen to me. I need you to be my eyes inside. I'm gonna try getting in the back but I need to know if they know I'm coming."

"You're fucking nuts. The guy may have his back turned but the bitch can see you."

"Not at that angle. She can't see down the hallway, and by the time she can, I hope to be in control of the situation."

I'm not quite sure how, but I'm sure as fuck not going to sit around with my thumb up my ass until the cavalry gets here. I dig my earbuds from my pocket and pray they still have a charge left. I haven't used them in weeks.

I blow out a breath of relief when I hear the canned voice announce "power on" and tuck my phone in my pocket so I have my hands free. Then I pick up a discarded piece of cardboard I spot on the ground.

"Lemme put you on speaker," Paco announces. "Ouray just walked in; he's calling in help."

Slipping between the UPS truck and the back door, I press my back against the brick, pull the gun I've started carrying since I got shot, and take off the safety.

"About to open the door, tell me if they hear."

"Be fucking careful," I hear Ouray grumble. "Cops are on the way."

The steel door is pretty heavy and works on one of those hydraulic doorstops. The key is opening it slowly and closing it carefully. I wrap my hand around the handle and pull.

"Going in," I whisper.

"You're good," Paco rumbles back. "But both guns are pointed at our girl now. Get her out."

Unfortunately, I can't just barge in, I have to wait to let the door ease closed behind me. Right before it shuts, I slip the piece of cardboard I hung on to between the door latch and the strike plate, to prevent noise.

"We need to get a move on," I hear a man's voice say down the hall.

A woman responds, *"You heard him, Ms. Zimmerman. Get a move on."*

My heart seizes in my chest when I hear Lindsey speak next.

"You'll have to physically drag me out of here or shoot me on the spot. I will not go voluntarily."

Jesus, Princess. Balls of steel, standing firm with two guns in her face.

Time for me to get moving.

I press my back against the wall to my right and ease down the hallway. I stop when I see the back of a guy wearing a UPS uniform. Beyond him, I can see a glimpse of Lindsey, standing behind her desk, glaring at someone in front of her.

I wish I could warn her, that she'd glance my way, even for a second, but against two guns, surprise is the only advantage I have. I'm going to need to prioritize my targets because I can only tackle one at a time. Who is the bigger threat to Lindsey, UPS guy or the blonde?

"Cops are on scene. The blonde's peeking out the window," Paco's voice crackles in my ears.

That's my go-ahead.

But just as I lift my gun to press the barrel to the base of the guy's skull, I catch sight of Lindsey hauling back her arm, looking ready to pelt something at the window.

The man in front of me freezes when he feels the steel touch his skin but before he can react, I growl, "Drop the fucking gun," just as a loud crash and the sound of shattering glass drowns out everything else.

Then behind me the door is yanked open and a loud voice calls out, "Police, drop your weapons!"

———

Lindsey

"Linds, are you hurt?"

I poke my head out from under my desk, where I ducked after I threw Mom's Rolodex at the window as hard as I could.

Wapi's touch is gentle as he brushes a few shards of glass out of my hair.

"You're bleeding."

My hand automatically goes to my head, but he stops me.

"Don't touch, you have some glass in your face."

Better glass in my face than a bullet.

It was a split-second decision. When I saw a glimpse of Wapi outside earlier, I hoped he would come around the back. I felt I'd have a decent chance with the woman if Wapi would be able to take care of LaVine.

But then Gina's attention was drawn by the cop walking up to the front door, and I feared she'd shoot at him, so I reacted.

It worked out in the end, since both Gina—or whatever

her real name is—and LaVine are currently in handcuffs, by the looks of it.

"Hold on to me," Wapi orders when I try to get to my feet.

I'm grateful for his steady hand, because mine is shaking. In fact, I'm shaking all over, so he eases me back down to sit.

"Adrenaline," he mumbles as he clamps two firm hands around my left bicep. "Just stay where you are. Medics will be here shortly."

"If you give me a second, I can walk," I tell him.

"I don't think that's a good idea."

I look down at where his hands are still tightly wrapped around my arm, and am surprised to see blood dripping down. Immediately I become aware of a deep, throbbing pain.

"Oh."

A bit startled, I search for Wapi's eyes, finding them steady and warm on me.

"Yeah," he mumbles. "That's not just a scratch, so let's just stay here like this until the medics come, okay?"

"Okay."

I nod my head but the movement makes me dizzy, so I lean forward until my forehead rests against Wapi's chest.

"Is she all right?" I hear a voice I recognize as Bill Evans ask.

"I don't know her name but she said Zeola was her *papi*," I start rambling with an urge to tell the detective what I know. "She's the woman who stopped to check on me outside the bathrooms at the airport. She wanted to kill me because I could recognize her. Also, LaVine works for her, but I don't think he wanted me dead. I think there's more, but I can't remember now."

"You did well, Lindsey, hang in there. The EMTs are just pulling up."

"Good," I mumble, before suddenly the lights go out.

———

Wapi

"You broke my Rolodex."

I can't believe that's the first thing out of Mel's mouth when Lindsey's eyes flutter open, but the blatant emotion in the woman's voice and the tears brimming on her eyelids tell a different story than the words suggest.

Lindsey, barely awake from the anesthesia, impressively fires back.

"It met a hero's end."

I can't hold back the chuckle, which instantly dries up when she turns her beautiful eyes on me.

"Wapi…"

"Hey, Princess." I take her hand and press her palm against my cheek. "How are you feeling?"

"Loopy. I'm not sure I like it."

"Aftereffect of the medications. It'll wear off," I assure her. "The good news is, you're gonna be fine."

"Because you held me together. Again," she adds, and her smile is sweet, but her eyes are getting visibly heavy. "Mom?"

"Right here, sweetheart," Mel answers.

"I'll buy you a new Rolodex," Lindsey mumbles.

"I don't think they sell them anymore."

Lindsey rolls her head so she can see her mother. "I know an antique shop or two, or there's always eBay."

Jesus, these two.

"Actually," Mel returns. "I don't think I need one anymore."

"Ha…are you finally embracing technology?" her daughter mocks.

"No. But I think the demise of my Rolodex may be a sign I should start considering a life beyond work."

Lindsey's head surges off the pillow, only to drop right back down.

"Ouch, that hurt. You mean retiring?"

Mel grimaces and shrugs her shoulders. "That makes me sound so old, but yeah, it's been on my mind."

"That would be perfect," Lindsey responds with a beaming smile, before turning to me. "Isn't that perfect?"

I answer with a nod, grinning. She's funny when she's drugged. It's like watching one of those videos of kids post wisdom-tooth surgery.

Then she flips back to Mel.

"I'm gonna retire too."

"You?"

"Hmm," she hums, her eyes finally closing all the way. "Hate my job," she mutters. "But I love you, Mom."

"What was that all about?" Mel wants to know from me.

"Probably wouldn't hurt to talk to Linds when she's not drugged to the gills, but she basically told me the same thing last night. A lot of stuff has happened to her she's still trying to process."

"And she talked to you about this?"

"She did last night."

Among some other things, but there's a time and place for everything.

"She loves you, you know?"

"I know. And I love her."

Mel presses her lips together and nods.

"That's good then." Then she abruptly changes gears. "You should eat something while she's sleeping. You're not gonna do her any damn good if you can't take care of yourself. Mika should be here with that pizza by now."

I nod at Mel and drop a kiss to Lindsey's lips before I leave the room to go in search of Mika.

Linds fell asleep hard, the aftereffects of the surgery, the meds, and probably the remnants of shock, so I expect she'll be out for a while.

A large chunk of the heavy glass from the front window at the office had done some damage to her right arm. It was a good-sized laceration that went deep enough to cut the brachial artery, which is what caused the excessive bleeding.

I about had a heart attack when she slumped against me, passed out, and squeezed even harder on her arm. The moment EMTs arrived, they replaced my hands with a pressure cuff to stop the bleeding, and loaded her immediately onto the gurney.

My complete focus was on her as I hopped into the back of the ambulance, ignoring everyone else. With Lindsey unconscious, I ended up providing them with what information I could, which wasn't really a whole lot, except perhaps for the caution that she might well be pregnant.

When we got to the hospital, it didn't take them long to whisk her to the OR to repair the damage to her arm, and I was relegated to a waiting room, where I was soon joined by Mel and Paco, who had swung by court to pick her up.

Her surgery went well, and was relatively fast, and we were assured she'd be fine. Since they'd had to give her some blood and she'd suffered from shock when she was brought in, they wanted to keep her overnight.

It's been a long afternoon, and this morning's breakfast sandwich in Lisa's kitchen at the clubhouse has long run out, so I'm going in search of Mika who, according to Mel, was instructed to pick me up a pizza.

Apparently, Paco went to the clubhouse to check on Mason and Mika is supposed to take Mel after I've had a chance to eat. Initially, Mel announced she'd be staying the night with her daughter, but I made it clear that was my place. Mel fucking scares me, but I would've gone to battle for that privilege. I ended up not needing to because Paco backed me up and Mel conceded.

"Hey, how is she doing?" Mika asks, handing me a bottle of iced tea when I join him in the waiting room.

"A little loopy from the meds and sleeping now, but she should be fine."

The first slice of pizza goes down in two bites, and I grab for a second piece.

"Before all this shit happened, I did get a chance to dig up that information you were looking for," Mika announces, earning my blank stare.

I don't have a clue what he's referring to.

"Refresh my memory," I tell him with my mouth full with half a slice.

"The property on County Road 205," he clarifies. "It's still for sale, but the house has been condemned. I drove out there, climbed the gate, and took a few pictures. The land's nice, views are good, but if you're thinking of a place to live, you'll probably have to start from scratch."

I swallow my bite and grin at him. "That's the plan, brother. Send me what you've got."

Maybe later, when Mel has gone home and Lindsey wakes up, I can see what she thinks.

I've just polished off three-quarters of the pizza and most of my tea, when Mel barges in. She points a finger at me.

"You're up. The doctor's on his way to see her and Lindsey wants you, so get your ass in there. I'm heading home."

I reach her room at about the same time the doctor does.

"Husband?" he asks when he sees me grab her hand.

"Sure," I respond as Lindsey snickers.

"As you probably already know, we were able to repair the damage to your arm and you should have a full recovery. Because of the extent of the damage though, I suggest you limit the use of that arm, maybe use a sling so you're not tempted, and I'll assess at your follow-up appointment in a week or two. I'll pop in tomorrow morning to make sure your night was okay and then we'll let you go home. Sound good?"

He nods at us and starts to walk toward the door, when Lindsey calls after him.

"Excuse me, uh…did they do my bloodwork?"

He stops and flips through the papers on his clipboard.

"Yeah, they came back fine. Was there anything…" His voice drifts off as he appears to read something, and then his stern face cracks a smile. "Oh, I see." He looks up at Lindsey first and then me. "Congratulations."

I don't even see or hear him leave the room. There's a persistent buzzing in my ears and it feels like I can't quite catch my breath, as I hang on to the side railing of Lindsey's bed to keep me upright. Her face, wide-eyed and slack-mouthed, almost looks like it's underwater.

"Did he just…?" I manage, my voice no more than a croak.

"Breathe, honey," she urges. "We've got this."

A baby. *Fuck yeah.*

We've got this.

CHAPTER
THIRTY

LINDSEY

"Mom is making her samosas."

I lean closer to the mirror to check another pimple on my chin that popped up this morning.

What is with that? My teenage years were pretty blessed with only an occasional little bump, and now I'm in my thirties I get hit with an almost daily new addition of a miniature Mount Vesuvius on my face? I know it's hormones, but isn't it enough my ass is already too fat to fit into my favorite jeans?

"Ohh, that sounds good."

As long as the spices don't give me heartburn. This pregnancy is not for the weak of heart.

"Is there anything I can bring?" I offer Anika.

Her phone call caught me coming out of the shower with an invitation to her housewarming party. I'm so happy for my friend, whose business is thriving, which allowed her to buy her own home.

I'm even happier, because the house she ended up

buying was first Mom's and then mine. Selling the place was a little bittersweet, because I enjoyed living there, both together with my mom and later by myself. Unfortunately, it had too many shadows for me.

I won't ever be able to forget seeing Galen in that pool of blood on the floor, or imagine cameras recording my every move. I don't want to spend my days looking over my shoulder when I should be looking ahead. But I'm thrilled my friend voiced interest in buying it and was ready to put her own stamp on the place.

"No, just yourselves," Anika replies. "I can't wait for you to see it. The guys did such a great job."

The guys being her brother, Bodhi, who is a firefighter in town, and some of the members on his crew. They've apparently been making a few upgrades in the past three weeks since the sale closed.

"And I'm excited to see it. So…Saturday at what? Four-ish?"

"That sounds perfect. I'll see you then."

We end the call and I resume getting ready so I can go and give a certain someone hell for making me sleep late.

I don't think of Galen much anymore, not with everything I have in my life to look forward to, but while I blow-dry my hair, my thoughts go back to the last time I saw him. That was at his arraignment, right after he was released from the hospital. Wapi didn't want me to go, but I felt the need to be there. I wanted him to know I am not cowering in a corner, and he does not hold any power over me.

Of course, Wapi came and so did four of his brothers. Wapi explained later it was a show of force intended to encourage Galen to permanently forget about me. It surprised me when he entered a plea of guilty to the charges against him. Wapi was convinced it was their intimidation tactics, and I wasn't going to argue with him.

I'm learning there are many reasons why it is important for Wapi to feel like he has to place himself between me and any perceived threat. More important than it is for me to prove I can look after myself.

There's not a doubt in my mind, if and when the time comes I'm called as a witness in the trial against Gina Dunlop, Wapi will be there as well.

Yes, that was the woman's real name. She apparently is married to an actuary by the name of Gary Dunlop and at face value led a moderately boring, mundane, middle-class housewife's existence. Behind the scenes, however, she was discovered as leading the criminal, family dynasty her father and grandfather built here in the Denver area.

In the world of organized crime, a man still yields more respect than a woman, so her father had remained the face of the family, but no longer had the stomach for the work it took to keep the family on top. His daughter apparently did and, by all accounts, was not afraid to get her own hands dirty to demand respect, like she did when she discovered one of the company's accountants was about to funnel information to the FBI.

Of course, that information had come from a member of the task force—Denver PD Detective LaVine himself—who'd been recruited by Gina herself when she discovered he had a drug problem. He was blackmailed and, once found out, did not hesitate to sing like a canary.

Gina Zeola/Dunlop's trial is highly anticipated, and her arrest—as well as the arrests of the Denver city employees involved—put not only the expansion project at the airport, but several other construction projects in the city, on its ass.

The scandal is big and featured all over local and

national media outlets, to the point where I've stopped watching or reading the news. I don't have the mental or emotional bandwidth to get smacked in the face with it day in, and day out. I have enough going on in my own life that requires my attention.

Like the stunt my man pulled this morning, I'm sure convincing himself he was doing it for my benefit.

Something I'm about to set him straight on.

———

I stand there for a moment, taking in the view, which is pretty damn fantastic.

Wapi, without his shirt, his jeans hanging low on his hips, sweating as he swings a huge mallet.

I drop the cooler bag and lift my camera to snap a few pictures. Heck, I could easily turn this into a calendar, like they do with firefighters. Since it's hotter than Hades out today, none of the guys appear to be wearing a shirt.

Not counting my stepfather, of course—because, ewww —the other three are nothing to sneeze at either. Different shapes and sizes, but all lookers in their own right.

"Hey! When you're done ogling my brothers…" Wapi calls out, stalking toward me.

I grin at him, tucking my camera away and offering my cheek for a kiss. That's not what Wapi has in mind as he wraps me in his arms and dives in for a thorough kiss.

"You're all sweaty," I complain when he lets me up for air.

"I thought you liked me that way," he brings up.

"In bed, yes. When every time my body shivers from the aftermath of a mind-blowing orgasm, I can feel your cock still inside me, *that's* when I like you sweaty."

"Jesus, Linds, you've got my fucking dick poking out of my waistband, and my shirt is way the hell over there."

I press a kiss on his sweaty chest and twist out of his hold.

"I've got something for that."

Bending down I flip the lid on the cooler and grab an ice-cold bottle of water, holding it against the bulge in his jeans.

"*Fuck*, you're cruel, woman."

I jerk my chin up at him.

"That's what you get when you fail to wake me up as promised so I could come help."

He gets this "aww-shucks" look on his face he some-times gets when he thinks something I say is cute. I'm not cute, I'm also not helpless, and not an invalid, but try and convince this handsome lug nut of that.

I told him I wanted to be there to help tear the old house down. I don't know much about construction, but I defi-nitely know how to break stuff. I've seen it on those home improvement shows and it looks like fun.

More importantly, this was a milestone moment for our future I wanted to be present for.

"Princess, I couldn't wake you, you're sleeping for two. And besides, I'm not so sure demolition is on the approved list of activities for pregnant women."

"Say it louder and everyone will know," I hiss at him. "Mom will kill me."

We decided to wait to tell her, or anyone else, until after we get our first ultrasound, which is this afternoon. I'm twelve weeks along, which means they should be able to determine the baby's sex. I want to know what we're having. At first, Wapi wanted it to be a surprise but he wasn't too hard to convince. Now he's excited, and so was I, until he pissed me off.

"I wanted to be here, Wapi," I complain.

He shrugs. "Why? It was just going to be a big mess, I figured you'd probably rather catch up on some sleep. Dust and dirt flying, stuff falling. I didn't want you to get hurt."

Dammit. He makes it so hard to stay mad at him.

"Maybe so, but this is our land, our house, our future, and it's important to me to be present every step of the way."

He drops his head and clasps his hand on the back of his neck.

"Fuck, Linds. I'm sorry."

He tilts his head sideways and peeks at me. "Wanna see what we've done so far?"

I can't help but laugh at that. The fucking house is now nothing but a pile of rubble the guys are piling in the massive containers we had delivered to the property yesterday.

"I can see that from here, honey," I respond with a hint of sarcasm.

"Right. I did find something I thought you might like though."

He grabs my hand and drags me toward a pile of junk at the rear of what was the house.

"Cold drinks in the cooler!" I yell at the guys in passing.

"Here it is."

It takes me a moment to recognize the rusty old claw-foot tub underneath what looks like a pile of old window coverings. I crouch down and run my fingers over the delicately shaped feet. It feels like the rust is only surface, which is a good thing. I've seen these refinished and made to look gorgeous on TV.

"I can refinish it. Tse says those things are hot commodities," Wapi shares.

"They are. It's beautiful. It'll look awesome in the new home."

He pulls me back up on my feet and folds my arm behind me, holding me close.

"So am I forgiven? A little?"

I hold up my thumb and index finger a fraction apart.

He kisses me hard in response.

"What time do we leave for the thing?"

"Twelve forty-five, but please make sure you give yourself time to shower first. Otherwise, I'm going by myself."

"Like hell you are," he grumbles behind me.

———

"Shouldn't that be me?"

I hand the T-shirt with "#1 Babysitter = Grandma" printed on the chest to the salesgirl and turn to Wapi.

"No. You're not a babysitter, you're her father."

I made Wapi stop at this store where they do custom prints on all kinds of shirts. I want to give it to Mom by way of announcement.

We just found out we're having a little girl.

The OB/GYN said she looked to be closer to thirteen weeks than twelve, but the whole way they calculate age is confusing to me. Apparently, when a baby is forty weeks on the due date, they're in effect closer to thirty-eight weeks, because they calculate from the first day of the last period, not from the date of conception.

All that said, our due date is the twenty-fifth of March. I swear Wapi was walking on clouds when we came out of the hospital.

"I was thinking," he says, helping me into the passenger side of my own RAV.

It's a thing now, where he has to drive when he's in the car with me. Mom tells me to pick my battles, which is probably good advice.

"About what?" I ask when he gets behind the wheel.

"We haven't really talked about names. Have you thought about it?"

He starts the engine and eases away from the curb.

"I have," I confess.

I've actually spent quite a bit of time thinking about it. Wapi's legal name is Jordan Danvers, although he never uses it. But now that he's having a family of his own, he'll have to use his legal name more often. I would want our baby to have the last name Danvers. Not because I'm always a proponent of children carrying their father's name, but because this baby will be the only blood relative Wapi has.

"What are they?"

"I liked Ryder, for a boy. I also had Emmett, Liam, Boris."

"I like Ryder. We can keep that one in our back pocket for the next one."

I bust out laughing. "Please, can we deal with this one first before we discuss any more kids?"

He glances over with a smug smile and a sparkle in his eyes.

"Sure thing, but you know, with the prowess of my little swimmers, it's inevitable we're going to have a houseful."

"Or…" I point out. "You can have the swimming pool shut down permanently."

He looks at me with a pained expression, cupping his junk with his free hand.

"Damn. That's harsh. Fine, what about girls' names?"

I lean my head back and stare out the window, catching glimpses of the Animas River as we come up to the bridge.

"Emily, Tara, and Ember."

I catch his quick smile from the corner of my eye.

"I think I like Tara out of those," he shares.

"Yeah, I do too," I admit. "But the name I'd really like for a girl is Cherry."

All of a sudden he veers my SUV across the road and into Santa Rita Park, heading toward the boat launch.

"Cherry?" he repeats as he jams the RAV in park and stares out the window at the rushing, white waters of the Animas.

The same waters that hid his sister's body for over twenty years, before giving her up.

"If that's okay with you?"

I startle when he slams the heels of his hands on the steering wheel.

"*Fuck.*"

I watch him and wait, as a single tear rolls down his face. Then he abruptly turns to me, taking my face in his hands.

"You want to give our daughter my sister's name?"

I nod, my own emotions making it hard to speak.

"Yeah…I love you."

The kiss he gives me is sweet, but the words he follows it up with take my breath away.

"You make my heart whole."

EPILOGUE

WAPI

I had no idea.

I love everything about her; her skin, which is softer than anything else I've ever touched, the way she holds on to me with a strength that's surprising, and those blue eyes that look at me as if she can see right through to my soul.

The world could literally be on fire right now and I still wouldn't be able to let go of her.

"Quit hogging her," Mel grumbles.

"Leave him alone, Mom," Lindsey says from the bed. "You'll get your chance."

Did I mention my wife is a fucking rock star?

Less than an hour ago, she pushed this tiny human being from her body in a freaking blow-up kiddie pool in the middle of what is now my office at the Arrow's Edge MC clubhouse. The clubhouse, because Lindsey insisted on a home birth attended by a midwife. This little one is three weeks early, and therefore the paint fumes haven't cleared and all the drywall dust hasn't settled yet in our new house.

Linds was amazing though, calm for the most part, she snarled at me only a few times during the last little bit. Seven hours from the moment she woke me up to tell me stuff was happening. It felt like a whirlwind though, calling the midwife and then Mel, who called Anika. All three showed up within minutes of each other. Mel and the midwife setting up the tub, while Lindsey squeezed the crap out of my hand with every contraction, which were coming fast and furious.

Damn, the woman even bought me a pair of swimming trunks she made me wear so I could get in the tub behind her. I told her I didn't see why I had to wear something when she went in naked, which was the first time she snarled at me. I understood then that any opinion I might have would not be welcome, so I kept my trap shut.

A wise decision—if I say so myself—since my woman proved far superior to me over the hours that followed. I already knew she's smarter, but she's also more courageous, more fearless, more powerful, and so much stronger. I am in absolute awe of her.

Seeing our daughter latch on to her mother's breast, while I'm still holding both of them in my arms...*man*...I lost it.

Best moment of my life, bar none.

I can't wait to share her with my brothers.

Walking over to the bed, I bend down to kiss Lindsey, our daughter cradled between us.

"Love you," I mumble against her lips. "I'm gonna take her for a minute, okay?"

She nods. She already knows I want to do this.

Then I head into the hallway.

"Hey!" I hear Mel yell behind me. "Where are you taking my granddaughter?"

"To introduce her to her uncles," I toss over my shoulder. "Don't worry though, after me you'll be the first one to hold her."

The moment I walk into the clubhouse with her—my mother-in-law hot on my heels—my brothers are there with smiles and congratulations.

"I'd like to introduce you to Cherry Melanie Letitia Danvers."

Named for my sister, Lindsey's mother, and the woman who took me in and raised me—Momma.

Ouray steps up and claps me on the shoulder.

"That's a fine name," he recognizes. "And I'm glad to note she has her mother's looks. Now I brought over a good bottle of scotch, Paco's got the firepit going outside, tell me you've got some decent cigars."

I grin. "Cubans, freshly smuggled."

Ouray rubs his hands together. "Excellent, just don't tell Luna."

I turn around and find Mel standing there, Paco's arm around her. I can tell she's emotional and trying to hide it.

"Ready, Granny?"

"Watch yourself," she warns me.

But her smile stretches ear to ear when I kiss my daughter's downy head and hand her over to the next set of loving arms.

My little girl is lucky, she doesn't just have parents and grandparents ready to give her the world, but she has an entire family who will make sure she knows she is loved and protected for life.

Of course, she may not enjoy it so much when she's fifteen and wants to go to the movies with a boy.

Leaving my daughter in her grandmother's care, I go fetch the box of cigars, and head outside, joining my brothers by the fire.

ALSO BY FREYA BARKER

High Mountain Trackers:

HIGH MEADOW

HIGH STAKES

HIGH GROUND

HIGH IMPACT

Arrow's Edge MC Series:

EDGE OF REASON

EDGE OF DARKNESS

EDGE OF TOMORROW

EDGE OF FEAR

EDGE OF REALITY

EDGE OF TRUST

EDGE OF NOWHERE

GEM Series:

OPAL

PEARL

ONYX

PASS Series:

HIT & RUN

LIFE & LIMB

LOCK & LOAD

LOST & FOUND

On Call Series:

BURNING FOR AUTUMN

COVERING OLLIE

TRACKING TAHLULA

ABSOLVING BLUE

REVEALING ANNIE

DISSECTING MEREDITH

WATCHING TRIN

IGNITING VIC

Rock Point Series:

KEEPING 6

CABIN 12

HWY 550

10-CODE

Northern Lights Collection:

A CHANGE OF TIDE

A CHANGE OF VIEW

A CHANGE OF PACE

SnapShot Series:

SHUTTER SPEED

FREEZE FRAME

IDEAL IMAGE

Portland, ME, Series:

FROM DUST

CRUEL WATER

THROUGH FIRE

STILL AIR

LuLLaY (a Christmas novella)

Cedar Tree Series:

SLIM TO NONE

HUNDRED TO ONE

AGAINST ME

CLEAN LINES

UPPER HAND

LIKE ARROWS

HEAD START

Standalones:

WHEN HOPE ENDS

VICTIM OF CIRCUMSTANCE

BONUS KISSES

SECONDS

SNOWBOUND

ABOUT THE AUTHOR

USA Today bestselling author Freya Barker loves writing about ordinary people with extraordinary stories.

Driven to make her books about 'real' people; she creates characters who are perhaps less than perfect, each struggling to find their own slice of happy, but just as deserving of romance, thrills and chills in their lives.

Recipient of the ReadFREE.ly 2019 Best Book We've Read All Year Award for "Covering Ollie, the 2015 RomCon "Reader's Choice" Award for Best First Book, "Slim To None", Finalist for the 2017 Kindle Book Award with "From Dust", and Finalist for the 2020 Kindle Book Award with "When Hope Ends", Freya spins story after story with an endless supply of bruised and dented characters, vying for attention!

www.freyabarker.com

Milton Keynes UK
Ingram Content Group UK Ltd.
UKHW010725050224
437294UK00019B/875